We Dream of Africa

We Dream of Africa

A NOVEL

Mimi Washington

Risen Literary Press
Temecula, California

WE DREAM OF AFRICA
Published by: Risen Literary Press

Yvonne Rose/Quality Press, Production Coordinator
Jenny Wannier, Inc., Interior Formatting

Risen Literary Press Books are available at special discounts for bulk purchases, sales promotions, fund raising or educational purposes.

© Copyright 2017 by Mimi Washington
ISBN: 0980131014
ISBN #: 9780980131017
Library of Congress Control Number: 2016931453
Firebrand Publishing, Temecula, CA

Dedication

I dedicate this book to my daughter Kiah Firebrand

Dream Baby Dream
Live Baby Live
Love Baby Love
God blessed me with you.
I am more than honored
To be your Mom
Continue to Dream
And Live Your African Dreams

Acknowledgments

EVERY ARTIST OWES much to those who teach and nurture her. I thank my teachers who believed in me, Mrs. Stevenson from Quaker Valley, and Sonia Sanchez and Jackie Mungai from Temple University.

I thank all of you who read the book at any point and a special shout out to Benita Stalling, Joyce Easton and the rest of the ladies in Circle of Friends Book Club: Jonetta Carter, Anne Triche-Steen, Lillie Montanez, Mildred Boykins, Clare Stafford, Pam Jones, Barbara Davis, Shirley Talley, Armanda Allen-Mitchell, Jenice Haskins, and Hazel Lambert. They read the book in its infancy when it was a hot mess. Thanks to Cherrill Simmons, Pastor LaMonte Lawson, and Patricia Whitehead who were there from the beginning in Kenya when I started writing the book and championed my efforts.

Thanks to Michelle Daughtery whom I met at the UCLA Writers' Program who workshopped this book with me, as well as Mark Haskell Smith my instructor from the program. A special shout out to Mike Foley, my instructor at UC Riverside and the first editor of my book. Karen Carter, my best friend and visual artist who had to hear about this book for years, and encouraged me to stop talking and write. Carol Taylor, editor extraordinaire, who made sense of these words. Yvonne and Tony Rose who I met at the Book Expo in New York years ago, who encouraged me to keep writing.

To my daughter to whom I dedicate this book, I hit the daughter lottery with you. We look forward to your book, "Turns Out My Momma was Not Crazy After All (well maybe a little)." What a delight and joy you are in my life. Thanks for sharing me with this book, my other baby. Finally, to my mom Thelma Rose

Washington, who passed away while I was in the process of making this dream come true, there are no words sufficient to express my love and gratitude for all you have done and sacrificed for me. Love, love, love you.

Contents

African Soil

SOLDIERS IN JEEPS, with machine guns strapped across their chests, were shooting rounds into the air. Nicole Jefferson counted twenty vehicles. They surrounded the Pan Am plane she was sitting in. Dressed in fatigues, some soldiers looked as young as nine or ten. Blood stained their uniforms. The boy soldiers laughed and pointed at the passengers on the plane and shot off more rounds. The smoke from the gunfire disappeared into the air. Nicole wished she could also disappear. She felt hot and her heart beat as quickly as the gunfire.

Instead of a homecoming to her roots, the violence she had run away from in America was waiting to greet her on African soil. Tears flowed down her cheeks as she rested her forehead against the airplane window. This was not the Africa she'd dreamt about. The one she heard about while sitting on her mother's lap. Ellafare Crawford Jefferson, had told her daughter stories of the great African societies and a communal way of life and Nicole had dreamt of one day experiencing it. She'd even gotten a master's degree in African Studies at Cal State Long Beach. That Africa was her dream.

Her seat mate, Rebecca Downs, slipped her hand over Nicole's. She then closed her eyes and bowed her head. They started to pray. After a few moments, Nicole looked out her window. She wanted to see what was happening. She had to see. During stateside Peace Corps training, their instructor said code red training was mandatory for all volunteers; but with a country like Liberia, West Africa, which had a stable economy and the same President for the past three decades, a coup was unlikely. They must have forgotten to tell the boy soldiers and their leaders this bit of information.

Nicole looked into the eyes of one of the rebels. He was just a boy, barely ten. His eyes were red and glassy. She held his gaze for what seemed like hours. Tears trickled down her cheeks. She saw tears on his cheek too. He lifted the machine gun, and pointed it at her. He looked like Thaddeus, or one of the other young men she mentored back in Long Beach. Before he was killed, Thaddeus was one of the hundreds of young men who joined the Crips or Bloods, or some other street gang because they wanted to belong to something. They wanted security and safety. At home their mothers and fathers worked all day, or tried to finish their education. They hadn't given up. The parents who had given up slept all day, or the mothers tricked all night for drugs. Some just disappeared into the concrete jungle.

Nicole held the boy soldier's gaze as he walked closer to the plane. He stopped and looked up. Minutes passed. He wiped his tears and smiled at her, cocked the machine gun, held it up to his chest, turned, and then he fired on his fellow soldiers. Nicole wanted to look away, or close her eyes, but she couldn't. The young boy's bullets hit another boy soldier in the face. She watched wide eyed in horror as blood spurted from his ear. A second later he fell to the ground dead. Smoke, shouts and a storm of bullets played out on the airfield right in front of her. Nicole's eyes rolled back in her head and she lost consciousness.

Code Red

"VOLUNTEERS, BE STILL and quiet. Your life will depend on you following these orders," the pilot said over the intercom.

The stateside medevac trainer told them code red training focused on emergency evacuation procedures once in the host country. Nicole woke to Rebecca shaking her. When she regained consciousness, she looked out of the window to see a convoy of GM Monster trucks with American soldiers. The plane door opened and Executive Officer, Trent Dubose of the US Marines strode onto the plane.

"Good afternoon Peace Corps Volunteers (PCVs), or I should say trainees." EXO Dubose greeted them. "You landed smack dab in a code red. I know y'all trained for this on the remote chance it might happen, but I'm sure none of you imagined that on your first day in Liberia, you'd land right in the middle of a coup attempt." He spoke softly to not frighten the already scared PCVs. "On behalf of US Ambassador, Thomas Watkins, I assure you my men and I will protect you. What I ask is that you follow directions, remember your stateside evacuation training, and oh yeah," he paused and rubbed his mustache, three times, "try to stay calm."

He looked at the volunteers then continued, "Joint military forces from Liberia and the US have secured this area, but we still need to move quickly. The trucks outside will take you to the US Embassy where the Ambassador will brief you and the other Americans in Liberia."

We're safe Nicole thought. She squeezed Rebecca's hand, closed her eyes and pictured her brothers, her mother, and her family. She thought about Thaddeus' reaction when he received his acceptance letter to Xavier University, and the little girl who was killed at the Move compound. I'm still standing, she thought, still standing for them.

Some of the trainees started to cry. Even Andrew MacArthur, a former star quarterback in college, who stood 6 feet 3 and rocked muscles that bulged through his sweater, wiped away a few tears. Randy Jones, from South Dakota grabbed the plastic bag in the pocket of the seat in front of him and heaved into it. Nicole and Rebecca stood and hugged each other. The volunteers unbuckled their seat belts, and gathered their carry-on luggage. When Dubose left the plane, several marines came aboard. Some stood with their guns across their chests. Many of the marines looked just like the Liberian rebels. African American soldiers on African soil. They even held their guns the same way.

"The American soldiers hold their guns just like the Liberian rebels," Nicole said.

"Rebels. Why do you call them rebels? Maybe they think of themselves as soldiers too, or freedom fighters," Rebecca said.

Nicole ran Rebecca's words through her mind. Soldiers. Rebels. Freedom fighters.

Rebecca went into the aisle to get her luggage from the overhead rack. Nicole sat back in her seat to allow the marines to help the volunteers. Someone in row J had fainted. Two soldiers carried him off on a gurney.

The volunteers deplaned by rows into the waiting trucks. After three months of stateside training in Bethesda, Maryland, the seventy-six new PCVs formed a tight group. They had been told, over and over again, that most volunteers return home because they couldn't adapt to a foreign environment. The stateside Cross-Cultural Trainer told them the word for it was medevacking, but all it meant is that many of the volunteers had come from small cities where they rarely encountered anyone who did not look, talk, or think like them.

They were sent home because their minds couldn't wrap around living in an environment so different from their own. Transitioning into a foreign country caused many of them to mentally break down, because they felt like outsiders. The trainer encouraged them to make friends with other volunteers while still in Bethesda. She explained that a support system already established stateside would help them counter feeling alienated in Africa.

"Someone you can talk to and who's in your same situation has proven time and time again to be the number one factor in volunteers completing their assignments. One of the reasons we start training in the US is to help facilitate these relationships. So make friends, people, make friends," she advised.

Nicole took in a deep breath and exhaled slowly. This is just another trial, she thought. Like when her Grandma Kaitlan and her third husband Lemuel fought or when Thaddeus was killed by the police.

The truth stabbed Nicole like a knife. She was sitting on a plane in the middle of a coup. She came to Africa to find her roots, her heritage, for a sense of belonging, not the same violence she had run away from in America.

Nicole pulled her luggage from the overhead rack and walked down the steps, off the plane, past the tarmac, and onto African soil. She moved off to the side to allow the others to pass on their way to the waiting trucks. She then knelt down to touch the blood-stained ground, bent forward and kissed it. She took a handful of dirt in her hands and rubbed it across her forehead and tear-stained cheeks. She pulled from her bag the jar of dirt from the Move compound and Thaddeus' gravesite and poured a little of it on the ground. She said a silent prayer, then scooped up some of the African soil into the jar and stuffed it back inside of her bag.

Marvin Taylor passed by her on his way to the trucks. He and the other African American volunteers forgot their pact to kiss the ground of their ancestors when they reached African soil. They forgot amidst the gunfire, shouts and little boys whose eyes were bloodshot and yellow. Like jawbreakers. Their eyes looked like jawbreakers. She licked her lips where some of the dirt had fallen. The African soil tasted like burnt grits with ginger. Nicole looked around the airstrip. She could see the terminal a few hundred feet away. American soldiers surrounded the building. They stood straight, machine guns hoisted on their shoulders with the barrels pointing up in the air. Nothing surrounded the airstrip as far as Nicole could see, only dirt and grass.

If she hadn't seen the Liberian soldiers hanging out windows, and on the windowsills of jeeps, she could be in Texas for all she knew. But the African air smelled different. Like ginger and how she imagined sunshine smelled, citrusy— like lemons and oranges. Rebecca walked up and knelt down beside her. She wiped some of the dirt off Nicole's face.

"Leave it," Nicole said. "I've been waiting to kiss this ground since I was in elementary school."

Rebecca touched Nicole's shoulder. "I understand. My head is also spinning. So many emotions all at once. I keep thinking of why I came here to Africa. I thought about Anthony, the black guy I asked to the prom in high school. I need to tell you the whole story, but not now. Right now we need to get going. Dubose is looking at us. We have to get into one of the trucks."

Rebecca looked over at Dubose. A marine was holding a clipboard with papers for the EXO to sign. Nicole didn't stand up. She stayed on her knees on the soil she had dreamt about most of her life. Dubose made a beeline for the two women.

Nicole tried to stand up when she saw the EXO approaching them, her legs wobbled under her. Rebecca bent down to help her up, but Nicole's weight was too much for Rebecca's frail frame. Another soldier stopped Dubose, and handed him a walkie-talkie. Dubose listened to it, while still looking at Nicole. Nicole looked at him, as he looked at her. If not for his slight southern drawl and his marine uniform, he could pass for one of the Liberians. He looked like a Fulani tribesman with his copper coloring and high cheekbones.

"I'll get Andrew to help you up," Rebecca said.

While Rebecca walked to the truck where Andrew stood waiting for them, Dubose handed the walkie-talkie back to the soldier, and walked over to Nicole.

"Do you need help getting to the truck?" he asked. "We need to get out of this area before the rebels come back. They're dangerous. Some of them are so hyped up on drugs, liquor and years of hate."

Dubose offered Nicole his hand. She took it and thought it felt too soft to belong to a soldier. He couldn't be much older than her twenty-one years, not one wrinkle graced his smooth-shaven skin. But his close-cut hair had gray at the temples. Dubose helped her up. It had to be prematurely gray, she thought. His eyes looked young. She felt the humidity enter her lungs as she inhaled the thick African heat. She swayed, and fell against his chest.

He caught her and wrapped his arms around her, but then he quickly pushed her away from him and onto her feet. He stepped back and held her by her shoulders. She felt moisture on her cheeks. He pulled a handkerchief out of his pocket and handed it to her.

"You favor my daughter. She wears her hair like yours. All those little blond and red twists all over her head, just like yours."

"You favor a Fulani."

"I know. From the first day I set foot on this continent, people have mistaken me for a Fula man."

"Is Liberia your first assignment?"

"No, I started out in the neighboring country of Sierra Leone. I graduated from The Citadel. After graduation I wanted to serve in Africa. Seems so long ago."

"The blonde and red twists are a result of my Irish and Native American grandmother. What about your daughter?" Nicole asked.

"Well, I believe hers are a result of Dark and Lovely."

The two smiled at each other for the first time. It hadn't been a day for smiles but it felt good. A soldier walked over to them. Dubose handed Nicole off to him to be escorted to the truck. Nicole turned to look at Dubose. She didn't wipe the tear from her cheek. Andrew opened the door to the last truck to let Nicole slide past him to a middle seat. She glanced over at Rebecca who was sleeping with her head against the window. The trucks moved out in single file. The air conditioning was welcomed after the sticky heat. Nicole held Dubose's handkerchief up to her face. His scent filled her nose. He smelled like Africa, like ginger and sunshine.

West Africa, 1980

NICOLE SAT IN the back of the truck between Andrew and Rebecca. Clusters of stars linked together looked like giant sparklers filling the sky. She thought of her mother, Ellafare, who always told her to follow her dreams while she was still young and full of superwoman possibilities. She could hear her voice as if she was sitting in the truck beside her.

"Nikki. I know you worry about me, you're my baby. The last child, but you need to live your life. Your brothers and sisters are living theirs. You keep accomplishing your goals. First Philly, for college, then Long Beach to work and grad school, now Africa. I also dream of Africa. We all dream African dreams. Dreams bigger than us, dreams that help us face the daily grind of life. I married your father, met him at nine, and married him at fifteen. I thought he was my dream. Right now, you may not understand what I'm saying to you. But it's settled, they chose you out of thousands of applicants. They recognized what you could contribute. You go ahead and join the Peace Corps so you can go to Africa. You can go for both of us."

She also thought about Mrs. Goldsmith, one of her grade school teachers, and her back to Africa announcement-the impetus that ignited Nicole to search for identity.

"All Negros will be shipped back to Africa. What a glorious day. That communist, rabble-rousing, Martin Luther King was put out of his misery last night." Mrs. Goldsmith announced the day after he was assassinated.

Although the class was in alphabetical order, and the Js sat in the second row, Mrs. Goldsmith placed Nicole in the back of the room with the XYZs. All her classmates turned to look at her. Nicole did not blink an eye, or allow a muscle in her face to move. She sat frozen. She remembered the fights between her grandmother and Lemuel. Although she felt a river break open inside of her and rush to her eyes, she did not shed a tear. If she could survive those fights that often escalated into Lemuel pushing or kicking her grandmother she could survive Mrs. Goldsmith's hateful words.

As Nicole sat there holding back her anger and pain some of her classmates started to cry. Most of the students had known each other since kindergarten. Although Nicole was the only student they referred to as Colored at the time, she was the most popular girl. Kimmy Stollar got up, ran to Nicole and threw her arms around her neck. She asked Mrs. Goldsmith if Nicole would have to leave, if she'd be shipped back to Africa too.

"Well Kimmy, we all like Nicole. She's a good Negro, but she is still a Negro and they're all going back."

"But my grandmother is Native American and Irish, does that count?" Nicole asked, finally finding her voice.

"I think they're sending nigger lovers there too. Your grandmother shouldn't have been a nigger lover."

Nicole had never heard any teacher use that word. In fact, if any student was caught saying the "n" word it was an automatic suspension. It was a word her mother said only ignorant people used. She gathered her books, placed them carefully in her school bag and walked out of the classroom.

When Monday rolled around Nicole's mother took her temperature and told her if she did not feel better by Wednesday she was going to school to find out the real reason for her absenteeism. Everyone in the house mourned Dr. King's death, but it was obvious to her mom and the rest of her family, that the only time Nicole's stomach hurt was when someone mentioned school. Nicole, normally the first one out of the house in the morning, loved school. She was an honor student and excelled in sports. She liked showing off her smarts to the few white students who thought all blacks were dumb "darkies" as one of her classmates called black students.

Tuesday night Grandma Kaitlan cooked Nicole's favorite dish of chicken fried steak, mashed potatoes with gravy and green salad. When dinner was served, Nicole was instead given a cup of chicken broth and crackers. She finally broke down and told her mother about Mrs. Goldsmith's announcement. If she was being shipped back to Africa, her last meal was not going to be bland soup and crackers.

Ellafare sat Nicole on her lap and told her about Shaka Zulu, the Dogon people of Mali, Timbuktu, the building of the Egyptian pyramids, and many other stories.

"Mrs. Goldsmith apparently needs to be educated about Africa and African culture," Ellafare said. "Because she is really misinformed. The majority of so-called Colored folks came here in chains to build this economy. She needs to know that if any of the Negroes in this country wished to return to Africa, he or she damn well could do so if there was the desire and means."

With every word her mother spoke Nicole sat up a little straighter.

"She'd better get used to all these uncivilized Colored folks because we plan to stay right here in America. We are just as American as any other immigrant that has come to this country. We're here now, and our ancestors gave free labor to this country. Some Black folk didn't come in chains; some came from free lineage. But we're all here now."

Ellafare told her that Dr. King did not sacrifice his life for the Mrs. Goldsmiths of the world to win. She said one day a Black man would be president of the United States.

"What about a Black woman? Mommy, can a Black woman be president one day too?"

"Sure, Nikki. We Black women can be whatever we want to be as well, with hard work, and God's grace."

In the aftermath of Dr. King's death, colored folks demanded to be called Black with a capitol B, Malcolm X became more visible, uprisings of Blacks across America streamed on TV every night, and the call for Black history classes in all levels of education from elementary through college was getting louder. With all this in mind Ellafare Crawford Jefferson walked the two and a half miles in the rain in her nurse's uniform to Sweetwater Elementary School with Nicole in tow. The meeting took place in the principal's office.

"Ellafare, what can we do for you today?" The principal, a wiry bald-headed man asked. He had been one of her patients when he was hospitalized at

Sweetwater Valley Hospital. Ellafare had run interference between his wife and girlfriend.

"To begin with, you may address me as Mrs. Jefferson, or my full name Ellafare Crawford Jefferson. I give you the courtesy of addressing you with a proper title and I expect the same. I may be divorced, and a Colored woman to boot, but we all have our luggage, don't we?"

The threat of losing her job, especially with her husband out on disability from his work as a mine worker at Bethlehem Steel, and the Principal's urging, helped Mrs. Goldsmith to find the words to apologize to Nicole in front of the class.

On the way home from the meeting the rain stopped. Ellafare smiled as she opened the door to Barlow's and said, "Let's get out of this nasty rain and get that banana split you're always asking for."

When they left the sundae shop, Nicole looped her arm through her mother's, and made sure she did not step on the cracks in the sidewalk-cause everyone knows that when you step on a crack, you break your mother's back. Sometimes when she was mad at her mother for staying at Grandma Kaitlan's when all they did was fight, or when she had to work and could not come to a school function, she didn't jump on the crack, but she stepped on it with the tip of her toe when her sister Shannon wasn't looking. But not that day—that day her mother was her hero. Of course heroes need strong backs to fight foes, like Mrs. Goldsmith. That day the shame Nicole often felt of being whole wheat toast in her white bread town lifted from her shoulders. Later that year Ellafare started a program at the school to teach all the students about African and African-American culture.

But Mrs. Goldsmith wouldn't be outdone. She found an opportunity for revenge. She gave the class an assignment to write a paper and prepare a presentation on their father's job. She had reviewed Nicole's records and did not see a father listed. Nicole wished she could share with her classmates what her father did for a living, like Tamara O'Neal. Tamara's father ran Alcoa Steel. He was the CEO, even if his face appeared on the front page of the Pittsburgh Post-Gazette for "allegedly" embezzling money. She still had a father at home, at least for now. The paper said he was out on bail. Nicole wrote and turned her paper in, but she did not present it because she had laryngitis the day of her presentation. She received an F on her paper about her father, the African king.

Shortly, after the assignment Nicole met her father for the first time. It was the summer after her twin brothers, Aaron and Arselen, who everyone called Ari, graduated from high school and before they left for college. One day while sitting on their front porch in Sweetwater, a town of rolling green hills, Amish families, steel workers on one side of town, the Heinz family (whose ketchup made them a fortune) and other rich Caucasians in the heights, and the nine black families dispersed throughout, Nicole spied a man, who looked like Ari and Aaron, walking up the hill to her house with a little boy about her age.

No one told her it was her father, but she knew it like she knew all the words in the song, "Amazing Grace", which her grandmother played every night on their small record player. She never told her mother or anyone else about the F on her paper, or that Mrs. Goldsmith called it "all lies" because Mrs. Goldsmith had proven to be a liar herself, and Nicole did not care what Mrs. Goldsmith thought period. Any teacher who purposely hurt a child was evil. Besides, when Nicole first saw her father, shoulders squared back, head held high coming up the driveway, his black coffee colored skin dressed all in white linen and a white straw hat with purple trim tilted on his head, she knew she had written the truth. Her father looked just like an African king.

Nicole ran her hand through her twists and closed her eyes remembering what happened from so long ago.

Still when Mrs. Goldsmith said Coloreds were going back to Africa, she did not want to return to the home of her ancestors, to be boiled in a pot, or forced to walk around with bones in her nose. Her mother told her those images were not a true representation of Africa, but as a child Nicole thought what if her mother was wrong. She did not trust Mrs. Goldsmith, but she did have a history degree. Nicole knew she had to conduct her own research on the continent and eventually she would have to cross the ocean to visit the motherland.

While Nicole's love of Africa started with the stories she heard sitting on her mother's lap, the love grew deep and wide like the roots of the acacia trees, which buried deep into the soil. Some say the roots went down to the center of the earth. Nicole's knowledge of Africa was almost as deep and wide. Through years of informal and formal study, culminating with her Master's degree in African Studies at Long Beach State, Nicole developed a deep and abiding love for all things African. Harvard accepted her into their PhD program in Africana Studies, but she knew before she studied one more aspect of Africa she needed to experience the magic for herself. She wanted to see the ancient city of Timbuktu in West Africa, the Serengeti with the animals running freely in East Africa, and even the slave castles in Ghana where her ancestors were kept chained. But most of all she wanted to look in the face of an African on the continent of Africa and visit the great Bettencourt Academy. She wanted to kiss the soil from where her ancestors came.

Nicole opened her eyes, and placed Dubose's handkerchief up to her nose. The ginger scent comforted her and brought her back to the present. After some time on the dusty road the driver stopped the truck and pulled up to the American Embassy.

Nicole's truck was the last one through the gate with the Peace Corps trainees. Four soldiers walked to the truck and opened the doors. Nicole, Andy and Rebecca entered the embassy through the security gates, then went down the stairs into the bunker. Other Americans already evacuated to the embassy were there. Many looked up with weary smiles. Some got up from their seats to greet them with hugs and handshakes.

By the way they were dressed, Nicole could tell who worked for United States Aid for International Development (USAID), the US embassy, or were PCVs already serving in the country. The USAID, and embassy people wore white shirts and khaki trousers for the men; some women wore khaki skirts. Some wore seersucker suits. Many of the PCVs were dressed in traditional African clothes. Some of the women volunteers wore their hair braided with beads. Nicole had never seen a white woman with beaded cornrows, or any cornrows for that matter, except Bo Derek on TV.

A man in navy blue khakis and a crisp white shirt, walked to the middle of the room, and spoke. Nicole missed his first words. She thought maybe he'd said his name. A diminutive Black woman in a dark suit, with her hair in a bun, stood beside him. The man kept looking at the woman. She appeared to be in charge.

"We are so glad all of you are safe," he said. "Understandably shaken up, but safe. The ambassador will be here with us in a few minutes. Please grab a seat and some food. We have US military offshore in ships. You can see our forces here. You are well protected."

He looked at the short Black woman beside him and she nodded. She's definitely in charge, Nicole thought as she sat down at one of the tables. She unwrapped the cellophane covered sandwich, but didn't eat it. Instead she looked around the large underground room. When they first walked into the embassy, it had been through the back, past security, and then down some steps into this huge room. She decided that the room must be the holding site for the evacuation or the secure bunker, as they called it in training. The instructor told them it was unlikely that a coup would happen in Liberia. President William Tanner, whose presidency spanned three or four decades, was popular for his lineage of the returned freed slaves.

People still poured in. Someone whispered that the short Black woman was Vera Whittaker, the ambassador's assistant. She was handing out sandwiches and sodas. There was something comforting about her, like the plaid blanket Grandma Kaitlan would place over her knees while she rocked in her chair on cold evenings in Pennsylvania. Nicole watched Vera Whittaker touch the shoulder of a weeping evacuee, an elderly Caucasian woman with a white shirt and blue skirt.

She wondered what the ambassador's decision would be. Would all Americas be ordered to leave Liberia? Not likely. Liberia was strategic for the United States in many ways. It had the largest maritime fleet in the world. Not that the ships belonged to Liberia. Businesses and other countries registered their fleets in Liberia for tax reasons. Also during World War II, the US built a base near the capital Monrovia to refuel and maintain US military aircrafts active in North Africa, the Middle East and Europe. At the height of the war, in 1943, US President Franklin D. Roosevelt stopped in Liberia on his North African tour to visit American troops.

She knew Liberia still held great importance to America with the country having the largest plantations of rubber trees in the world; as well as much of the world's iron ore, diamonds and gold, and also the only US owned satellite on the

African continent. But Nicole didn't care about any of that right now. All she wanted to do was get on the plane and get the hell back to American soil. Screw this back to your roots nonsense, she thought.

Sierra Leone

ONCE THE PLANE skidded to a stop on the wet tarmac Femi and his father, Dr. Oyami Bettencourt joined the other passengers with shouts of joy, and applause for their safe landing. The turbulent flight from Atlanta arrived three hours late to Sierra Leone. Dr. Bettencourt glanced at his watch, 9 PM. Because of the delay, instead of walking into the African sun, the night would greet them. Unlike his father, Femi who'd never been on an international flight, felt like he'd been traveling for days. When he stood up, his legs felt like he hadn't stretched enough before a football game. He felt like he was still in the air. His father explained that he was jet-lagged, which was why he had advised him to drink plenty of water. Dr. Bettencourt told him it would take a couple of days, but he would get his mojo back.

Femi didn't know what mojo was and wasn't going to ask his father right then. They joined the line to disembark from the plane, and walked down the steps onto African soil. The land he'd heard about all his life, the birthplace of his father, and the Bettencourt legacy. Stretching his over 6-foot frame he tried to take in this place, Africa. It smelled different, like the biscuits his mother and grandmother made on Sunday mornings. No, not the biscuits, it smelled like the homemade ginger lemon marmalade they put on the biscuits.

On the plane ride over, he refused to talk to his father. He still simmered about missing the high school football camp held by the Atlanta Falcons. At first he pretended to read, and then went to sleep. Didn't his father know that to make the starting varsity team at St. Patrick, his high school, was unheard of for a junior? Maybe at some other school, it might not be hard to start as an underclass man, but at St. Patrick's, it was nearly impossible. They recruited from all over Atlanta and had produced, at last count, twenty-five pro football players and countless college stars.

Femi's coach told him that with his height, broad shoulders, and good throwing arm he could be one of the great quarterbacks in high school, college, and probably even make it to the pros. He just needed to commit himself. But Femi and his coach both knew Oyami did not want Femi playing sports. Of course, Femi knew all about his family's history. They were all educators with PhDs with the exception of his father who was a MD.

Although he had never traveled to Africa with his parents, and never met his grandparents, he knew all about the family legacy. He knew his ancestors' history of a white wealthy land owner from Virginia fell in love with one of his female slaves, freed her, and bore children with her. At that time children of freed slaves had to wait until they were 13 to be freed regardless if the parents were free or not. Rather than raise his children as slaves, Anderson Bettencourt fled America with his wife and children to the West Coast of Africa. The family established a school and fought against the capture of human beings from the African coast to send to the Americas. They had fought against slavery 400 years ago, but recently the BBC said the Bettencourts no longer took a stand against anything. Femi couldn't care less. He was tired of people wanting to use his family. He decided that, as soon as he turned eighteen, he would change his last name to Williams, his mother's maiden name.

But, as soon as Femi felt the African breeze on his face, and smelled his mother's sweet potato biscuits with ginger lemon marmalade, much of his anger disappeared, like morning mist when the sun starts a new day.

For years, he had heard so many stories from his parents. His father, Oyami, was born in Sierra Leone, but educated in the United States; his mother, Esther, was born in America, but she always said her true education came from her adopted country of Sierra Leone. This was his family's homeland, and within minutes of landing, he understood why. He looked around at all the people who looked like him. Femi had never seen so many shades of brown and black in his life; cinnamon, caramel, banana brown—and the darker hues of amber black, coffee black, tar black and the blackest of them all, blue-black. Black folks truly are a rainbow of colors, he thought.

Everyone seemed to know his father. The luggage handlers and security staff smiled, nodded, or waved. A man approached Oyami, and patted him on the back. "Welcome home," he said.

When they reached the terminal, he saw more people who looked like him; but there were also Middle Easterners, and Indians. They also smiled and greeted them. He heard, "Welcome home, Dr. Bettencourt" so many times he stopped counting. Femi knew there were not that many dentists or doctors in Sierra Leone. In fact, his father had made several trips to his birth home in the last years to bring a team of traveling doctors and dentists, called the Traveling Docs, and to set up a new hospital. But everyone looked healthy and happy.

In the airport, the security guards all carried guns. Now this was something he never saw, visible guns at an airport. Many people milled around, some in the clothing of their country, some in Western clothing. The women wore lappas, the long colorful skirts, wrapped around their waists that went down to their ankles. He remembered his father saying that traditionally women in Africa did not show their thighs. The upper leg of a woman was thought sacred, for only her husband to see. But he warned him, once they were up country in the bush, there would be women with bare breasts. His father told him not to stare. Their breasts were food for their children. Even though in recent times, many African women had taken on Western ways and were feeding their babies store bought formula. Problems arose when the women diluted the formula with more water than recommended to stretch the powder.

Femi checked out one woman with a bright lime green lappa and matching top with elaborate puff sleeves. Another woman selling handmade jewelry in the terminal wore an orange wax print lappa and a matching top with a plunging neckline. Some of the other women he passed wore outfits fitted to their curvaceous bodies, while some had loosely fitted outfits. Most of the women wore headdresses. Oyami explained to him, the covering of the head for African women was part of the culture. It showed a women's modesty. Femi thought, okay they can't show their heads, but they can show their breasts. Now that was quite a cultural difference.

He liked the head wraps. Some had just a simple tie, but others had intricate twists and bows. Most of their outfits rivaled many of the fashions out of New

York, or Paris that he'd seen in his mother's fashion magazines. He would sometimes leaf through them to look at the exotic looking women. Now these women here in Africa, were really exotic.

He hadn't known what to expect, but their beauty took him by surprise. He had to keep reminding himself to breathe. He didn't want to stare, but when they smiled, he smiled back. The women stood straight, and walked tall. Even the heavier, shorter women looked regal, because of the way they carried themselves. No one appeared to be self-conscious about their weight, like American women. They sashayed as they walked by Femi and his father.

Femi thought if he were to tell his teammates at St. Patrick that he saw a woman weighing about one hundred pounds carrying a basket on her head that looked to weigh twice as much as her, no one would believe him. And the warmth he felt from them was almost overwhelming. Almost everybody smiled and waved. He didn't know if it was because his father was a Bettencourt, because he was a doctor, if this was just their culture, or a combination of all of these things. He looked around at all the faces that looked like him. Back home in Atlanta, while there were plenty of Black and brown folk, the only time he found himself in the midst of a majority of people who looked like him was at church on Sunday. His neighborhood was mixed with whites and Blacks, and most of his schooling had been at private schools attended mostly by Caucasians; but here he felt an immediate acceptance and connection.

Femi had attended many African parties in America. His parents, held one every year at Christmas. He always looked forward to the food; fried plantains, fufu-the round gooey ball some folks said looked like a big dumpling-and soup; bitter leaf, and potato greens with chicken. Jolloff rice; a flavorful rice dish was his favorite. He also liked chin chin, a West African street pastry, made with flour, eggs, cream, and butter, and then fried. His mother would add fresh orange peel and either cinnamon or nutmeg to it. When his high school buddies came to the celebrations, they headed straight to the Jolloff rice on the buffet. They said it tasted like fried rice.

At the baggage claim area, a man who did not quite reach Femi's shoulder, wearing a brown Nehru jacket with matching pants, approached Femi and Oyami. The man and Dr. Bettencourt shook hands in the traditional African way. They clasped hands, then slid their two middle fingers together and ended the handshake with a snap.

"Hi sir. Welcome home. This must be your boy we have heard so much about. The missus did not come this time?" He asked as he stepped back and bowed slightly.

"Gojo. Good to be home. How's the family?" Oyami greeted him. "No, the missus no come this time, and yes, this is my son, Femi"

Femi snapped fingers with Gojo.

"You snap like a real West African man," Gojo said.

Femi grinned, and shrugged.

"Femi, this is Mr. Gojo. He has been the family driver now for over thirty years." He said, turning back to him, "Gojo, let's get the bags, then stop for a cold drink before we go up country."

"Sir, there is a change in plans. It just happened by and by so you probably have not heard. There was an attempted coup on President Tanner's return to our neighboring country, Liberia. They say some Sierra Leoneans may have been involved. They have closed many roads going up country and to the borders. We will need to travel in the day. It will be safer. Who knows where the rebels take refuge. I made arrangements for you and Mr. Femi to stay at one of the new hotels in Freetown."

"I do not know what to say. This entire region has been stable for so long." Dr. Bettencourt said, surprise in his voice. He opened his mouth to continue, but then just shook his head.

Femi saw the worried look on his face. He knew from overhearing conversations between his parents that his father believed the Bettencourts had lasted since the 1600s in Sierra Leone because they did not get involved in politics.

Bettencourt Academy educated many of the political leaders in West Africa, but did not advocate for any faction. They saw themselves as educators. The family was recently criticized on the BBC for not taking political stands. Femi agreed with the article and showed it to his mother.

"It is more complicated than you think," Esther said. "Go and experience the country for yourself. When you come back we will talk then."

Time magazine had picked up the story and elaborated that the founders of Bettencourt Academy who had risked their lives to rescue those who had been captured from entering slavery, would be disappointed in the current Bettencourt's reluctance to take a stand against many of the atrocities occurring on the continent.

Femi knew that look on his father's face. It meant he didn't want to be drawn into a conversation about politics with Gojo, or anyone else. Oyami looked at Gojo and patted him on the back.

"Difficult times Gojo," he said.

Driving from the airport into Freetown, the capital of Sierra Leone, Femi noticed the skyscrapers in the distance. Freetown looked like downtown Atlanta with its tall buildings and crowded streets.

Femi and his father found a place to stay in Freetown, but not at a hotel. Dr. Bettencourt had many friends in Sierra Leone. Dr. Francis Momah, a fellow immunologist who had a private practice, but also worked for the World Health Organization (WHO) invited Oyami and Femi to stay with him. Dr. Momah worked at the main hospital and also taught at the University of Sierra Leone. He welcomed the company of a fellow doctor, and he wanted to catch up on the latest medical news from America. His home looked like the home of a well-to-do doctor in any country, but bigger. His house sat at the edge of town, surrounded by palm trees. There was a verandah in front, where the two doctors sipped palm wine and chewed kola nuts in the evening. Femi knew from the African parties what these things were, but had never seen his father drink anything alcoholic before.

The house, which was painted a lemon yellow with a creamy vanilla trim, stood four stories tall. The doctor, his wife, five children, and his mother and father all lived there; but Femi thought, a twenty-room house to be excessive for anyone. But he liked staying with them in the big rambling house. And good thing, because their one-day stay in Freetown turned into weeks. One of the doctor's sons, Francis Jr., was the same age as Femi. They spent their time teaching each other about their respective games of football and soccer. The doctors did rounds at the hospital in the day, taught at the University and attended meetings at the WHO. They often took Femi and Francis with them. Some nights, all four of them went to dinner in a cook shop, a small restaurant that served fresh cooked African food. Cook shops featured only one or two items on the menu. When they ran out of those dishes, the owner closed the restaurant for the day.

Finally, one morning right before the sun exchanged places with the moon, Gojo, showed up in the van. After breakfast, they loaded it, said their goodbyes, and took off up country to the Bettencourt compound. As they drove Femi, lulled by how still everything was, fell asleep. When he opened his eyes, it was dark. The darkness became even more pronounced as they traveled into the interior of the country, what the locals called up country. Femi imagined the darkness swallowed them like Jonah had been by that whale. He could not distinguish between the African night and himself. The thought soothed him. He and Africa as one. He did not know how long they had driven. Every so often, he would wake up and try to focus his eyes.

With no streetlights, and no visible stars on portions of the road where the night haze covered the stars, the van's headlights reflecting back into the vehicle was the only light on the road, aside from cars passing them on the opposite side. The roads were so narrow that sometimes Gojo had to pull the van off the road to let the approaching car go by, sometimes he went first. Femi thought there must be a lot of accidents, because how did they know who would yield first.

His father and the driver spoke in a language Femi did not understand. He thought maybe it was the pidgin English his father and mother sometimes spoke at home when they didn't want Femi to know what they were talking about. But he realized as the sounds vibrated through his ear, that although there were words he understood, and what they spoke was pidgin, this was different from what he heard at home. This language sounded like they were singing a duet. The driver made an O sound at the end of every sentence and often snapped his fingers. His father responded by clapping his hands and laughing.

Femi recalled his father saying that although he learned proper British English as a child in school and from his parents, he spoke pidgin when he played soccer with his friends, or when he negotiated for the latest record album at the market. This language held the high note of "yeaho" when the soccer ball hit the net, and the low note of "come on brother, these records came all the way from 'merica, I cain't give it to you for that price, what you final price? What you sayo?"

Of course all the Bettencourts could speak four languages at the minimum. It often left Femi with his mouth gaping when he heard his father switch from language to language without a pause, when talking to his siblings and colleagues from foreign countries. Every evening after dinner, while his mother washed dishes and fixed lunches for the next day, Femi and his dad sat at the table. Femi finished his homework and Oyami worked on research papers for his work at the Center for Disease Control (CDC). Dr. Bettencourt worked as an immunologist who specialized in tracking and curing diseases.

When a problem stumped him, he would put down his pen, rifle through his scattered papers on the table and sit with his brows furrowed. Femi knew that soon his father would leave the table and go to his study to make a call, or sometimes a series of calls, to colleagues around the globe, to brainstorm the issue. As soon as Femi's mother began humming "Amazing Grace" or "Chitty Chitty Bang Bang" he would slip out of the kitchen to stand by the slightly opened door of his father's study. Oyami would start out in English, switch to pidgin, go on to French, speak the tongue of this grandmother from the Mendi tribe, and end back up in English.

Femi wanted to join in this conversation with his father and Gojo. He had so many questions to ask about this place. The anger he felt at his parents for making him miss football camp had subsided. He did not know how to tell his father that he felt a connection with his birth place as soon as he the stepped off the plane and inhaled the African air. He felt like he was in the fourth quarter at the state championship with ten seconds to go, with his team down by five points, and he threw the winning touchdown. That is what he planned to tell his mother and his friends when he returned home; that being in Africa felt like making the winning touchdown in the championship game.

The Bettencourt compound rose out of the countryside like a castle. The massive trees formed an arch above the paved road leading to the gates. Femi exhaled sharply. The house was twice the size of Dr. Momah's home. He knew one of the buildings behind it was the school. Lights flooded the night, dimming the stars. Behind the gate was a man he recognized immediately from a picture on his father's desk, and who he had heard about most of his life. Femi looked out of his window into David's eyes. He now had the nerve to call himself a Bettencourt. David smiled, but his eyes were hard. David opened the door for Dr. Bettencourt and they hugged.

"David, go and greet your little brother, Femi."

David walked over to where Femi stood outside the car and grabbed him tightly around the waist and lifted him slightly up off the ground. Femi kept his hands firmly in his khakis. After a few moments, David released him.

"I finally meet you little brother. But I guess now I cannot call a big football star like you little. You're almost bigger than me and I have ten years on you. I have wanted to meet you since I startled your father that morning ten years ago, right there in the schoolhouse." David turned and smiled at Oyami. "He thought I was one of the rebels. But I had come from neighboring Liberia. I was making my way to Freetown to my uncle's home to tell him, my father had passed."

Femi looked at the man everyone referred to as his brother. They did resemble. The almond shaped eyes; the dark chocolate skin; the broad shoulders and big arms. Ten years from now, that's how I'll look. But that's where the resemblance will end. Femi thought.

"My parents may have adopted you, but as far as I'm concerned, I'm an only child," Femi said to David turning his back on him to follow Gojo into the house.

Peace Begins at Home

NICOLE SAT AT the table beside Rebecca, her turkey sandwich still unwrapped. She looked around the room and waited and watched. Although embassy personnel assured them that they were safe, she didn't believe them. They arrived at the embassy nearly six hours ago, and there was still no word from the ambassador. Everyone looked exhausted. Some rested their heads on the tables, others leaned against the wall. Some slept, while others sat paralyzed in fear. Many cried silently.

Nicole unwrapped the sandwich and picked out pieces of the turkey and plopped them into her mouth. She chewed slowly. Her last meal was on the plane hours ago. Under normal circumstances she used food to soothe her frayed nerves, but at the moment food did not concern her.

She looked at her backpack and saw the folder marked Peace Corps sticking out. She opened it and pulled out her acceptance letter from the Peace Corps. She thought back to when she first received the letter and the conversation she had with the receptionist, La Donna, at her old job as a Community Organizer at Centra De La Raza in Long Beach, and wondered if maybe La Donna had been right.

"You ain't gotta go cross an ocean to help people. Folks right here in Cali need help—right in Long Beach, and in Philly too, where you came from Ms. Nicole. Africans do not care about you. They sold us," La Donna said, shaking her head.

Nicole knew some Black Americans thought their African brothers and sisters looked down on them, but she also knew from interacting with Africans that many longed to connect with their brothers and sisters in the Diaspora, but did not know how. She thought often Africans born on the continent and those born in America had a hard time relating to each other. Many Blacks sought out their African roots to help them cope with the racism they experienced in America.

Nicole thoughts drifted to the long-standing rift between Blacks and cops in Philadelphia, and the Move incident where the police had bombed an Afrocentric community whose members all went by the last name Africa. When she was younger, Nicole shied away from them because they looked different, and she thought maybe they were a little too fanatical. The day after the bombing she stood in shock with hundreds of others behind the yellow police tape. The homes were now in piles of brick and dirt. It took many days to pull all the bodies from the debris.

Nicole looked around the embassy at the other volunteers she'd trained with in Bethesda. She thought about who would stay and who would leave. At this point she hadn't made her decision. She didn't know if staying was even an option. She wondered if the American press had picked up the story yet, and if her family knew about the coup. Two days before she left, her father threw her a huge bon voyage party. She knew six people at the party, including her father, his new thirty-year-old wife and her sisters, Shannon and Barron. Her twin brothers had vowed to never set foot near their father. Everyone seemed so excited she was going to Africa, especially her father. At the end of the night, he toasted her.

"To my youngest daughter Nikki, who will venture to places most of us only dream of. I am so proud of you."

Nicole had wept as she clinked glasses with him. For years she yearned to connect with him. Now as she sat in the evacuation hall, she thought about her family, and the Move people. John Africa had started the group to give Black people a piece of Africa in America. They wanted to find a place to belong, and look what happened to them.

Nicole thought about the seven-year-old girl who was killed in the Move bombing. She remembered her classmate who was shot using her body as a shield to protect the children. Her classmate also walked past those houses every day to take the L train to Temple University, but unlike Nicole, she didn't cross the street. She spoke to them every morning. After the Move bombing Nicole finished her classes at Temple, but did not wait for graduation. She packed her bags, got in her car and drove to California. She told La Donna that she came to California to work in the Black community to try to stop the violence. That she grew up in violence, and it is no way to live, but more than that to make peace with her father.

"My father and I had been estranged after my parents divorced for the second time," Nicole said. "I decided I had to make peace with him. Peace begins at home. Here I was putting applications to work in community outreach to help people, and I didn't even speak to my own father."

She Was Finished Running

EXO DUBOSE ENTERED the evacuation hall and stood in front of the room. "We understand everyone is anxious," he said to the crowd. "The ambassador will be here soon. There is plenty of food. You're safe here. If anyone feels ill, or needs anything, especially you new volunteers," he looked at Nicole, "ask one of the soldiers stationed here."

As quickly as he appeared, Dubose disappeared. Nicole sat at the table with Rebecca on one side, and Marvin Taylor on the other side. Andrew was sleeping. Nicole wondered how he could sleep with all the chaos going on. After a few moments, a white girl with beaded cornrows approached her.

"Hi I'm Jennifer. My African name is Kisi," she said, eyeing Marvin who seemed to be catatonic.

"Hi Jennifer, I'm Nicole Jefferson. Could you please point me to the ladies' room?" Nicole said staring at her hair.

"We look alike with our braids."

"I don't have braids, these are twists."

"Well, whatever," Jennifer shrugged.

"Could you please just point me to the ladies' room, or do I need to ask someone else?"

"Wow, you're hostile," Jennifer said, taken aback.

"No hostility intended. Stop with your stereotyping. I don't want to play stupid white girl games. I need to use the bathroom. And you can forget about Marvin. He doesn't date white girls. And as you can see, he's still in shock."

"Fine." Jennifer said, flipping her blonde braids. "Follow me."

In the hallway, more American soldiers stood at attention. Jennifer pointed Nicole to the restroom and walked away. Nicole saw Dubose standing with his back to her talking to a soldier in a low voice. The other soldier chewed his lower lip, and rubbed his mustache three times, just like the EXO had when he addressed the trainees the first time on the plane. EXO Dubose put his hand on the soldier's shoulder. He received a call on his radio, nodded at the man and walked away. The soldier was also dressed in military fatigues, but when Nicole came closer to him, she saw he had Liberian emblems on his uniform. She locked eyes with him and he held her gaze. They exchanged smiles as she passed him. She could feel his eyes on the back of her neck. She turned and smiled at him again before disappearing into the ladies' room. Even as she closed the bathroom door she still felt a connection to the soldier.

Nicole looked around the luxurious bathroom. So much for Americans roughing it in a Third World country.

"If this bathroom indicates the lifestyle of Americans in Liberia," then these folks are livin' large over here, and all on our taxpayer dime," she thought.

Aside from the marble counters, there were four sinks with antique gold-trimmed mirrors above them. Perched over the mirrors were amber colored glass covered lights. She placed her palms flat on the sink. The coolness of the marble moved up her arms and spread out to the rest of her body, cooling her down, at least for the moment.

After a thirteen-hour flight from Washington with a connecting flight in Amsterdam, landing smack in the middle of a coup, and seeing a white girl in braids, Nicole was definitely on edge.

She studied her reflection in the mirror. Tiny blonde and red twists cascaded down to her shoulders framing her face. People often said she looked angelic. They commented on her flawless complexion and her heart-shaped lips. But it was her unusual eyes, midnight black irises with flecks of gold or amber which made her stand out. Depending on her mood and how the light hit her eyes, men would take a second-long look and women would tell her their deepest secrets.

She had a deep dimple on her left cheek, but it only appeared when she smiled from her heart. Her mother told her when she was little that an angel kissed her cheek, leaving his mark on her to let everyone know she belonged to

God. Now Nicole prayed the angels protected her and everyone else in the Evac room. She also said a prayer for the little boy soldiers.

⤜▬◐ ◖▬⤛

Nicole looked around the bathroom. On the walls were framed pictures of the Statue of Liberty; Mt Rushmore; and the Golden Gate Bridge. These images probably helped Americans in a foreign country feel like they were home. But on the walls facing the door hung three framed color photos of life in Liberia.

The first photo showed the countryside. A young Liberian girl stood in a T-shirt with lappa material tied around her waist like a skirt. Nicole owned many lappas herself, which she purchased from various African markets in the United States. Most of the women on the continent could not afford to have the cloth made into skirts or dresses, so they simply wrapped the material around their waists. Those who had money had a tailor make them lappa outfits, fitted long skirts with matching tops. In the picture, the girl's eyes were wide and bright. On top of her head in a large white tin bowl she carried mangoes, papayas—known locally as paw paws—and tiny bananas called monkey bananas. The little girl's eyes in the photo seemed to look out in bewilderment.

An old African myth claimed that when one's picture was taken the photographer had captured that person's soul. Nicole wondered had the photographer asked permission to take the picture.

Nicole pushed open the heavy mahogany door to enter the part of the restroom where the toilets were. The stalls reminded her of the stalls in Amsterdam where they had stopped for their connecting flight. The bathroom doors reached almost all the way down to the floor. Each toilet had its own little room. Nicole didn't turn the light on in the stall. She didn't really need to go to the bathroom, she just needed some time alone. Nicole pulled the lid down and sat on the toilet seat. She pulled her feet up on the seat and sat with her arms around her knees, and rocked back and forth.

She wondered what her big brothers, Ari and Aaron, were doing right now. The three of them used to call themselves The Three Musketeers because Nicole followed them wherever they went. When Aaron and Ari started playing high school football she followed them around like their mascot. The sound of the door opening in the lounge area brought Nicole back to the present. She heard the door close.

"I checked. I've been standing by the door waiting for you. Nobody came in."

It was Jennifer, the white girl with the cornrows.

Nicole heard another voice. "Look Jen, this is the only area in the embassy without cameras. We can't be too careful. Check the stalls."

"All the lights are out. I told you no one else is in here. And please don't call me Jen. My name is Jennifer."

A bang startled Nicole and she let out a small yelp. She covered her mouth hoping they hadn't heard her. Nicole heard someone walking toward her. She crouched down on her knees on the floor of her stall and saw a woman wearing royal blue pumps approaching her. She quickly sat back on to the toilet seat, drew her legs up off the floor, and covered her mouth. She held her breathe. Sweat poured off of her. The woman kicked the door. It didn't open. She turned the knob.

"This one is locked."

Nicole pressed herself as far back from the door as possible.

"It's probably out of order," Jennifer said. "Look, I have to get back in there. If I'm gone too long someone will come looking for me. I don't work at the embassy and have diplomatic immunity like you."

Nicole finally took a breath when the blue pumps moved away from the door.

"I'll make this quick," Ms. Blue Pumps said. "Tanner is alive and here in the embassy. Those idiots, so-called rebels, couldn't kill anyone if their own lives depended on it. For years they've whined about wanting freedom. About getting rid of the Americo-Liberians, the freed slaves who came from America, and the indigenous people taking their land back. We set up the entire thing, left Tanner out their hanging, brought in troops from Sierra Leone to help, even paid those suckers, and what do they do? They try to highjack a plane full of new Peace Corps Volunteers. What idiots. We pay them to take over their own country and they still can't get it right."

"Look, I want out of this. I came to this country to do good."

"Well, it is too late for that. You should have thought about that before you started smoking dope and sleeping with rebels. You New York women are the worst. You come to a foreign country with your lily-white idealism and think you're going to let it all hang out, like the natives are waiting for you to save them. You dress like them, wear your hair like them. Well you're not one of them. You're an American. If it wasn't for me your ass would still be in jail. The jails here are no joke. You don't get three meals a day and a freaking cot. No one cares about you. Men and women stay together in the same cells. You would've been messed up on the first day."

"I am already messed up dealing with you," Jennifer said. "If you all want President Tanner killed why not it do yourself, instead of making these young men your puppets. All they want is an education and a way out of the village, where the only career choice is farming and much of the farm land is now destroyed."

"That is exactly what we're going to do," Ms. Blue Pumps said.

"What do you mean?"

"We've brought someone in to take care of Tanner. We knew your solider boys would mess up. That is why I have a clean-up team in place. It's time for Plan B."

"What does this have to do with me?"

Nicole couldn't believe what she was hearing. She braced herself against the wall to keep from slipping and bit her lip so she wouldn't make a sound. Were they actually talking about killing the President of Liberia?

"Our contact is one of the new PCVs who will contact you with further instructions."

"It took years for the Peace Corps to establish that the organization helps people and promotes peace, not spy for the American government," Jennifer said.

"Officially, the Peace Corps knows nothing about this and I don't expect they'll find out about it."

"I want to speak to the ambassador myself. I want him to tell me."

Ms. Blue Pumps moved toward Jennifer. Nicole heard Jennifer gasp. She crouched down and peeked under the stall. Ms. Blue Pumps was a white woman with thick blonde hair pulled back into a bun. She had Jennifer backed up against the wall and had a handful of Jennifer's braids in her hand. She put her pale face close to Jennifer's tan one and whispered something to her that Nicole couldn't hear. Ms. Blue Pumps then abruptly let her go, wiped her hands on her skirt, smoothed her hair, and walked to the door.

"I'll be in touch," she said, a warning in her voice. "Keep your mouth shut. You talk when I say talk. You do what I say to do, or you'll find yourself back in jail. And by the way, I received an APO communication from your father, thanking me for getting you out of jail and for not letting the American press get hold of the pictures. After all, it's an election year, and he has presidential aspirations. See you soon Jen." She said, then walked out.

A few moments later Jennifer left out of the stall area. Nicole heard her turn on the faucet. When she heard the door bang shut, Nicole breathed a sigh of relief.

"You can come out."

Nicole gasped and scooted back on the toilet seat.

"I know you're in there," Jennifer said.

"I thought you left," Nicole said, opening the door.

"Look we don't have a lot of time," Jennifer said. "Take this and keep it for me." She thrust a palm-size tape recorder into Nicole's hand.

"What's going on? I heard some crazy…" Nicole asked.

"There's no time to talk right now. They'll search me. I need you to get that tape to someone we can trust—someone who will either get it out of the country to my father, or to a reporter. It will expose the people behind the attempted coup." Jennifer looked nervously at the door. "Look, I gotta go. Go back in the stall and wait five minutes after I leave. I don't want to be seen coming out with you. We'll work this out."

Jennifer hugged Nicole, who did not hug her back, wiped the tears off her face, and then left the bathroom.

"We," Nicole said to the closed bathroom door.

Nicole looked down at the tape recorder in her hand. She couldn't believe any of this was really happening. She pulled a paper towel from the dispenser and wrapped it around the tape recorder wondering how she'd gotten involved in overturning a conspiracy to kill the president. Minutes passed, and she still stood frozen in the same place. Why should I get involved with this? I don't even know what's going on, she thought, wishing she was back in Long Beach. At least she knew the game back there. She knew what colors represented what, who claimed what turf. Here the turf was larger, instead of a street, or corner, this was an entire country being taken over.

She hesitated for a moment, then threw the tape recorder into the trash. She opened the door and walked to the sink.

"I am catching the first flight out of here" she said to her reflection in the mirror.

She then looked up into the bewildered eyes of the little Liberian girl in the picture. "Go ahead, run away, just like you ran away from Philadelphia after the Move bombing, and the way you ran away from Long Beach after Thaddeus was killed. Go ahead, get on the plane. Run away," her eyes seemed to say.

Nicole stood with the door open, staring at the little girl in the picture. Her eyes seem to follow Nicole. Her soul had not stolen by the photographer. Nicole ran back to the trash, dug out the tape recorder, and stuffed it into her money belt. Later, after she heard the ambassador's briefing she would make her decision on what to do with the recorder. For the first time since she arrived on African soil, she felt like she stood on solid ground. She was finished running.

Souleymane Guindo

DAT, DAT, DAT, dat, dat. Dat, dat, dat, dat, dat. Gunfire. Rapid fire gunshots could be heard in the distance—the sound of a German HK21. Souleymane Guindo knew his weapons. As the new Minister of Defense, the top ranking military position in Liberia, it was his job to know. Since Liberia did not manufacture guns, knowing their origin helped Brigadier General Guindo track the source of the rebels' weapons.

All official weapons used by the Liberian military were made by US manufacturers, such as the new M249, a lighter gun that made a purring sound when fired. Souleymane signaled to his number one man, Ian Pola, to stay put and keep an eye on the President. He knew President Tanner was safe in Vera Whittaker's office in the American Embassy. Marines surrounded the building and off the coast were a thousand US troops.

Souleymane grabbed the walkie-talkie clipped to his belt, and walked into the outer office. He tuned into the secure frequency connected to his American counterpart.

"Sir, the package is secure," Souleymane said.

"Bravo Zula," Dubose responded.

"Is this line secure?" Souleymane asked.

"As secure as it can be."

"The guns sound like German machines," Souleymane said. "I thought you said that this operation was Russian led out of Sierra Leone. Why would Russians use German weapons?"

"You're really going to ask that right now," the EXO Dubose replied. "If you want to ask questions let's start with why would those jackasses try to take over an American aircraft with Peace Corps trainees. That doesn't make any sense. The good news is all the Americans are safe. We're on our way to the embassy now. You personally keep the package secure until I get there. Remember this is our watch."

"Roger that," Souleymane said; then he considered the EXO's words. "All the Americans are safe." He could feel anger start to form in the pit of his stomach and rise into his chest. He took a deep breath and let it go. This was not the place or time to deal with American arrogance, even if it came from his mentor and friend. He already had a preliminary tally that thirty Liberians had been killed with twenty-one of those being boy soldiers, probably under twelve years old.

Souleymane walked back into the room where Pola was keeping guard over President Tanner. Then he closed the door. Although no one else was in the room, he knelt down and whispered in President Tanner's ear.

"Sir, the US ambassador will be here soon. Your cabinet ministers are also on their way. We need to make an announcement as soon as possible so the public will know you are alive and safe."

President Tanner sat in front of Vera Whittaker's desk. He grasped the general's hand and held on to it.

"Thank you, General. You saved my life. What does one say to the man who saved your life? I knew you were the right man for the job. So young, but so wise."

Souleymane pulled his hand from the President's grasp. "Mr. President. My job is to protect you at all costs."

He then walked to the door, opened it and left the room. Souleymane thought of himself first as a soldier. He drew his imaginary cloak around him like a shield. He could not allow Tanner's emotional display to put him off track. Soldiers did not have time for emotions in the midst of battle. When he was younger, other children in the village taunted him because he was an only child and his father Gabbe Guindo had only one wife. In a country where a man's wealth was largely determined by the number of his wives and children, Souleymane's only child status caused him many tears in the dark. He heard talk from other children, and even their mothers, that his family was witched, or that his father's great wealth of land and cattle came from making deals with nefarious people. One night, as he lay crying, his father entered his room, sat down on the bed and gathered him up in his arms.

"I think different than most men," Gabbe said. "No shame in tears son, even for a man. The shame is to allow other people to make you feel bad about whom God made you. There is a time for tears, but never in the middle of the battle. You hold your head up high with dry eyes when those people say evil things to you. God gave me you and your mother. I do not need a gaggle of wives and children to be a good or wealthy man."

"Is our family witched, daddy?" Souleymane asked.

"I do not believe in ghosts or witches. Even if other people do. I choose to have one wife. One is sufficient for me. I would have liked to have other children so you would not be so lonely. It did not happen. But that does not mean we practice witchcraft, or that I am an evil man."

The next morning, his father woke him before daybreak and they went into the bush. Every morning after, as well. On those morning excursions, his father taught him the traditional way of life.

Sometimes he took him into the bush to show him which herbs were edible, or which tree bark could heal a wound. Other times, his father just took him for a walk in the forest to talk to him.

"Many men do not understand women, Souley. They treat their women like their horses. They hit them with a whip when they run in the direction they do not want. Son, never hit a woman. Only weak men hurt women and children."

One day a man, whose skin color was brown and hair texture the same as his father's, came to the Guindo compound where Gabbe was waiting with several of the village men while his wife gave birth. The man, who said his name was Trent Dubose, took off his hat and told his father that his wife had lost another child. Although the man looked like his father, he spoke like the white men who came from America to visit their village. Hearing the news, the men left Gabbe alone with Dubose and Souleymane. Dubose sat across from Souleymane's father.

"Your chief sent me," Dubose said. "I just arrived in the village when your wife was giving birth. I don't feel like I am the one who should tell you this news, but your chief insisted."

Souleymane's father held up his hand. "It is okay, my brother. As soon as I saw your face I knew my child had not made it. Was it a boy or a girl?"

"A girl," Dubose answered.

"Chief Esi is unconventional, but she is a wise woman," Gabbe said. "She learned much from her father. He had several wives, but they were all barren with the exception of Esi's mother who died in childbirth. I am a blessed man. I continue to lose children, but my wife is still here for my comfort."

Tears welled up in Dubose's eyes. Although Gabbe told Souleymane it was okay for men to cry, he'd never seen his father or any grown man cry. Dubose was the first. At that moment Dubose became his hero. He made Souleymane feel normal, not so different.

Souleymane was nine the first time the EXO visited his village. He continued his visits every month for years. When Dubose came he brought books and games for Souleymane, his best friend David, and for Gabbe. On these visits he taught Souleymane, and David self-defense, martial arts, and how to shoot a gun. They showed him the back roads and the secrets of the bush. Sometimes Gabbe joined them on their walks.

"Kick your right leg at an angle," Dubose commanded. He demonstrated the move to Souleymane and David. David executed it perfectly. He balanced on his left leg and kicked the right one high.

"Perfect," Dubose nodded. "Now you, Souleymane."

Souleymane kicked his right leg high—then fell on his butt. This was his tenth attempt. He sat on the ground with his head hanging. David reached out to help Souleymane up.

"No, let him get up on his own."

Souleymane sat on the ground shaking his head.

"See it in your mind, Souley. See your leg lifted high, kick out. Imagine your opponent. If you think you're defeated, you are already."

Souleymane remembered the EXO's words as he stood in the inner office waiting for Dubose to arrive. He forced his mind back to the situation at hand-President Tanner's safety. He knew the American Embassy was secure, but something did not fit. The EXO was not giving him the full story. He decided to transfer President Tanner from Vera Whittaker's office to a secure bunker in the embassy. Souleymane summoned the US marines for the transfer.

With President Tanner secure in the bunker, Souleymane walked to the other side of the embassy to see if Dubose had arrived. He stood at the door of the bunker where the US personnel had been evacuated and looked into the room. Americans from all sectors in the American Mission filled the room. A little boy nestled his head on this mother's lap as she stroked his hair to comfort him.

As a young boy, Souleymane rode to the market on the public bus. Many times on the journey, his mother soothed him in the same way. He often thought of his mother during a crisis. He remembered the bus was always crowded with people and produce. Live chickens roamed around and baskets of monkey heads to sell at the market jammed the aisles. But the seats surrounding Souleymane and his mother were always empty. Other market women would stand rather than sit next to them.

Sitting with his head on his mother's lap Souley would weep silently. Blessie Guindo would stroke his head and give him slices of mango. Sometimes she would hum songs to him. The notes would leap from her soul like a gazelle running gracefully in fields. Often the market women, despite their disdain and fear, would find themselves singing along or swaying their heads and hips.

"Brigadier," Dubose jolted Souleymane back to the present. The two men saluted each other, and then embraced. When Dubose's walkie-talkie buzzed, he excused himself to take the call. That's when Souleymane saw her walking toward him. He held her gaze for what seemed like an eternity. Her eyes had the same sunflower bursts as Chief Esi from his childhood village. He wiped his mustache three times as they stood in the hallway staring at each other. He opened his mouth to speak, but all he could do was nod. She smiled at him. He lifted the invisible cloak he used to protect himself and let her in. Her smile enveloped him, like the summer breeze off Sugar Beach. She walked past him, turned and looked over her shoulder still smiling.

God Believes in Everyone

NICOLE WALKED BACK into the evacuation hall a changed woman, she vowed to herself that no matter what the cost she would help Jennifer get the tape to someone who would help. She arrived along with the ambassador, who was finally ready to give his speech. Looking around the packed room Nicole saw Vera Whittaker behind her. Where had she come from, she wondered. Did she know about the tape recorder? She kept her eyes forward as she walked to her seat.

"What happened to you?" Rebecca asked. "When that Jennifer chick came back and you weren't with her, I didn't trip. I know how you like to go off by yourself when you're stressed, to sort things out. When you didn't show up after twenty minutes I was going to come look for you."

"Shush, Ms. Whittaker is giving us the evil eye," Nicole said hushing her.

Ignoring her, Rebecca continued, "I asked her what happened to you. She rolled her eyes, and said you could hardly leave the embassy with all the security around. She claimed she walked you to the bathroom and left you there."

"We'll talk later," Nicole whispered.

"Are you all right?" Rebecca persisted.

"I'm fine. Thanks for the concern, girl," Nicole answered. "Now be quiet, the ambassador is about to speak." Nicole turned her attention to what the ambassador was saying.

"I am Ambassador Thomas Watkins. Thank you so much for your patience. I'm sure you are all worried about today's events. I want to assure you that the coup attempt was not successful and that President Tanner is safe. No Americans were hurt in the coup attempt and we have armed guards around the embassy and troops waiting offshore."

Nicole thought it was odd that he didn't mention if any Liberians had been hurt or killed. Someone asked a question about the boy soldiers; if any of them had been killed and what was the ambassador going to do about them?

"He isn't going to answer that question," Rebecca whispered to Nicole.

Nicole tried to concentrate on what the ambassador was saying, but the cassette player in her money belt felt heavy against her hip.

"We are looking into the boy soldier situation," he answered after a long pause.

Should she tell Rebecca about the cassette? She didn't even know for sure what was on it. Before she told anyone anything she needed to know exactly what was on the tape.

But when would she have an opportunity to listen to it? She couldn't chance another trip to the bathroom. Nicole looked around the room and wondered if she should give it to Vera Whittaker or the ambassador. But she was worried that they might be involved. She looked at Jennifer sitting on the other side of the room with some other volunteers. She appeared to be listening intently to the ambassador.

Maybe Jennifer had set her up. Maybe the people Jennifer worked with were trying to recruit her. Who could she possibly trust after what she heard in the bathroom? Ms. Blue Pumps said one of the new PCVs was part of the clean-up team, but who? Was it Randy Jones, Andrew McArthur, or maybe even Marvin Taylor? Most likely not Randy, since he threw up before they even got off the plane. He certainly didn't seem to have the stomach for it.

But that could have been a cover. It could be any one of them. Why did Jennifer give her the cassette? For all Jennifer knew she could be involved. Nicole looked around the room. She thought about when she watched Court TV, or read a mystery, the guilty person was always the one you least expected. Who did she least expect to be involved?

Her eyes settled on Rebecca. Of course, Rebecca. Who knew more about Africa than any other trainee aside from herself? Rebecca had referred to the Liberian rebels as freedom fighters. She'd befriended her the first day at training, and even had her room assignment changed to bunk with her. The first night of training Nicole went to dinner in Washington with a few of the other Black volunteers. They found a hole in the wall soul food joint on the west side called Henry's and chowed down on greens, mac and cheese and chicken fried steak. When she returned to the room, Rebecca was in the upper bunk with the lights off. Nicole thought she was asleep so she tiptoed in. Nicole turned the bathroom light on so as not to disturb Rebecca. After she crawled in bed, Rebecca surprised her with a question.

"Nicole. Why did you join Peace Corps?"

"I thought you were asleep."

"No, just lying here thinking."

"I answered that question in orientation."

"No, I don't mean the generic, politically correct answer, Nicole. I mean your real reason."

"I joined the Peace Corps to go to Africa," Nicole answered. Then she told Rebecca about the stories her mother used to tell her when she was a little girl, about Africa and its history and the beauty of both the land and the people, and about Mrs. Goldsmith.

"I needed to come to Africa as well," Rebecca said. "The town I grew up in Wyoming had only a few Black people. I never thought about what it was like to be a minority. I mean back then. One of the football players, Anthony, was a Black guy. When prom came I decided I was going to ask him to escort me to piss off my ex. The other cheerleaders told me it would cause trouble. My ex-boyfriend was the star quarterback. I figured it would drive him nuts."

"Is there a point to your story?" Nicole asked. "Training starts at 8:00 AM, and I want to get some sleep.

"He said no. There were only two Black girls in the school. I asked him which one he planned to go out with, he said both. That they were all going together as a group, with a bunch of others including whites, Asians and the one Hispanic guy. I got pissed, like, who is he to turn me down, a white girl. And a popular one at that. I spread the word that he tried to force himself on me. My ex found out about it. He told some unsavory guys in town that he knew, and he got them to beat Anthony up really bad."

Nicole jumped out of bed and turned on the light. She climbed the ladder up to the bunk, and grabbed Rebecca by the collar of her pajama top.

"Why the hell are you telling me this crazy story? Is this supposed to make me like you? It sounds like a modern-day Emmett Till story to me. If going to Africa was not so important to me, I'd kick your ass right now."

Rebecca started crying softly, then louder. She then started sobbing so hard that she couldn't catch her breath. Nicole let go of her and got down from the ladder. She grabbed a bottle of water from the nightstand and handed it to Rebecca.

As she remembered that day, she hoped it wasn't Rebecca. They'd overcome too many obstacles to be friends. Ambassador Watkins was finishing up his speech with a prayer. He looked more like a country pastor, with his stark black suit, his crisp white shirt, and receding hairline, he was even holding a Bible. With his blue eyes and light complexion, he could pass for white, passé blanc is what they called it here. His wide nose gave him away. As a boy, his mother probably tried to make it thinner by pinching it with a wooden clothespin.

"How dare he bring religion into this," Rebecca said angrily. "Not everyone believes in this Jesus crap. My parents tried to push that stuff down my throat. I didn't want to hear it from them, and didn't travel 12,000 miles to hear it from him."

"Then why were you praying with me on the plane?" Nicole asked.

"It was an impulse from when I was a little girl."

"Most Black folks know, that but for the grace of God go I. Maya Angelou said there are only six Black folks in America who don't believe in God."

"Not everyone believes in God, Nicole."

"No, but God believes in everyone."

Vera Whittaker shot the two women a stern look, as the ambassador finished his prayer. He then told them how the coup happened. He said one of the captured rebels turned over the information. The rebel said it was just before dawn that day on April 1, 1980, before the operatic sounds of the Muslims chanting their morning prayers and before the cocks crowed. Master Sergeant Samuel Kinkeweh, rallied his forces of Liberian soldiers, Sierra Leonean sympathizers, and German mercenaries to action. He ordered them to pick up their machine guns, their rocks, their machetes, and other weapons. Some drank beer, some smoked. All hyped themselves up for their mission.

A silence surrounded them in their Jeeps, Land Rovers, and Peugeot trucks as they sat on the window sills, and piled in the back of the truck beds. Some held their machine guns up in the air. Some waved them around, while others carried broken beer bottles, knives and rocks. They came prepared for the fight of their lives.

Kinkeweh promised them that after centuries of oppression, of working as drivers, house boys, and flunkies for the elite Americo-Liberians, they the indigenous people, the tribal folk, the ones who never left, the traditional people who were not captured and did not need to repatriate to Africa, would take back their country.

What Watkins didn't tell them, and what the rebels did not know was that, Vera Whittaker, a short, dumpy, African-American woman, who worked as his assistant, had other plans for President Tanner. Watkins did not tell them that as the renegade Liberian soldiers, and their cronies surrounded Robertsfield Airport with their vehicles and rode slipshod in circles screaming, that they rode to their deaths. Whittaker had already notified Dubose and his troops to intercept them. Watkins did not say that later witnesses would testify they yelled, "Tanner no more," "Tanner to die." Or that German and American mercenaries helped plan and execute the coup for cold hard cash and rights to diamond and gold mines.

Ambassador Watkins did not tell them that by 4 AM, the rebels had secured the guns from the armed guards at the airport and tied them up along with two cleaning people. As the rebels stashed their hostages in the back of one of the trucks Master Sergeant Kinkeweh declared, "We have made our move. The plane will land soon. We must sit and wait. We have waited many, many, many years, a few more hours—no big thing. We are not to kill anyone but Tanner and his men. No one else. Not one American is to be harmed. Do you understand?"

The Presidential plane was due at 7:00 AM. One of the soldiers, who reeked of beer and sweat, watched the prisoners in the truck. Although he had been in the military for two years, this was his first time carrying a gun. He poked the nuzzle of the gun at the cleaning woman they had taken prisoner from the airport.

"You simple child, you," she said. "You think you all goin' to know how to run a country, you think that Kinkeweh, going to give you what Tanner no give."

Sweat poured down his face, although it was only 5:00 AM, the sun came up fast and bright. The morning prayers at the mosque began. He could hear the imam leading the prayer. Crows rose from slumber and perched on fences to sing their morning songs.

The rebel soldier heard Kinkeweh on the walkie-talkie with one of his commandos at another post outside of Monrovia. Sweat streamed into the rebel's eyes. He wiped the sweat from his eyes and accidentally discharged his weapon. The cleaning woman fell back blood pouring from her head. The other prisoners screamed. A rebel grabbed the soldier around his neck and squeezed until he fell limp in his arms.

At the same time, a plane descended out of the sky and came screeching down the runway. The rebel soldiers who had left their vehicles jumped inside and rode to the plane. The plane came to a stop. Kinkeweh led the way to surround the plane. The writing on the plane read PAN AM. Master Sergeant yelled, "Retreat! Americans. Retreat! Americans."

But the rebel soldiers didn't retreat, they were too hyped on homemade alcohol and drugs and had much hate in their hearts as they sang their village songs and surrounded the plane. Peter Heweh, who had just turned nine, his eyes egg yolk yellow from lack of sleep and drugs jumped from the truck and looked up into the plane windows into the eyes of a woman who looked like Chief Esi, the Paramount Chief of his village. His lips turned up into a smile. The woman on the plane did not smile. Tears flowed down her cheeks. Her hair looked like Medusa with red and blonde snakes.

Ambassador Watkins didn't say, that the American GM Monster trucks rushed in like a herd of raging elephants, dust swirling around them as they closed in on Kinkeweh and his men. The American soldiers threw tear gas bombs at the insurgents. Gunfire echoed from both sides. Peter Heweh started shooting, not at the American soldiers, or the Peace Corps trainees on the plane, but at his fellow Liberian rebels. The Ambassador did not say because he did not know that was when Nicole flashed back to the dead bodies strewn about at the Move compound, after the attack, and Thaddeus lying dead on the street in

Long Beach with thirty-one bullet holes in his young body, and fainted. When the dust settled and she awoke, the bodies of Liberian soldiers, and the rebel soldiers from Liberia and Sierra Leone littered the ground.

The Woman with the
Sunburst Eyes

THE AMBASSADOR DID not say that Dubose signaled the pilot to open the plane doors. Then the EXO walked up the stairs made, the sign of the cross over his heart, blew a kiss to the sky, and entered. Or that Souleymane watched from his bulletproof military vehicle, and thought about Dubose his mentor, was actually more like a father. Souleymane had known him since he was nine. The EXO Dubose put him through school in America, at The Citadel. But recently Souleymane felt like he didn't know him at all. When first Souleymane's mother died and then his father, Dubose took over the role as his father. Aside from his best friend David, Dubose was his only family. The Ambassador did not say Souleymane pondered the EXOs words.

"No Americans were killed." And while Souleymane was grateful that there were no American casualties, he mourned his countrymen—especially the children. The EXO hadn't said a word about Liberian casualties-not even the children. The Ambassador did not say Souleymane watched the American soldiers as they followed the EXO on-board and started debarking the new volunteers. Or that Souleymane radioed on a secure frequency to Vera Whittaker that everyone was fine, but Kinkeweh got away. He did not say the good news was that a boy soldier named Peter wanted protection from the Liberian rebels. He would be willing to talk to the Americans if he could spend a few minutes with the woman on the plane who looked like Chief Esi. Or that Souleymane told Vera Whittaker that he was on his way to the embassy, and Dubose would complete the evacuation, and would follow. His number one job was to ensure the safety of his President.

Or when Souleymane arrived at the US Embassy, he first went to check on President Tanner, who was in Ms. Whittaker's office. While everyone told him the President was safe there he decided to move the President to an underground bunker. When he returned to Ms. Whittaker's office her secretary told him to go straight in. He opened her door, but paused. He watched her. She sat with her hands clasped and eyes closed.

"I understand you moved President Tanner to one of the bunkers. Come sit. No need to explain to me or anyone else." Vera spoke with her eyes still closed.

Her French roll was held in place by several hair pins. She opened her eyes, and pulled the pins out one by one, then fluffed her hair out. It fell down below her shoulders. Or that Souleymane reflected on the first time he witnessed her ritual. It was during their first meeting to discuss if the threats against Tanner were credible, and to construct a plan to circumvent the insurgents. In the middle of their conversation, she took her hair down.

"You may think this odd, Brigadier General," Vera said. "I inherited my hair from my mother. She had a thick, healthy bush of hair that needed a relaxer to stay straight. A straightening comb wouldn't. When anything bothers me I take my hair down and remember my mother. It gives me strength."

Nor did the Ambassador know that while he briefed the American citizens Souleymane shook off his encounter with the American woman who resembled Chief Esi. Or that Souleymane knew the ambassador couldn't brief the Americans on Whittaker's reluctance to call her superiors in Washington and tell them that she failed to capture Kinkeweh. Failure did not sit well with Whittaker, nor with him.

Souleymane knew the ambassador could not tell his evacuees that Whittaker slammed down the phone, and told her assistant to block all incoming and outgoing call from the Embassy until they made a plan to correct their mistake.

Or that on his horrific day that Souleymane scanned the room and set his eyes on the woman with the sunburst eyes and the gold and red twists, who he had encountered in the hallway, and knew that she was the one.

The Tortoise and the Hare

NICOLE DECIDED TO stay along with twenty-four other volunteers. The other trainees left the country two days later on the Pan Am plane they arrived on. Each volunteer, both new and those already serving in country, met with the Peace Corps Country Director, Dr. Beverly Brandt and Vera Whittaker, to discuss their continued service in Liberia.

Nicole knew she had to get the incriminating tape into the hands of someone who would expose the culprits behind the coup attempt, not that she agreed with Tanner being president for life. She thought fair elections should be held to avoid a dictatorship. She pondered about giving the tape to one of the evacuees going home and telling them it was a package for a friend. But she did not want to implicate anyone else. Everyone leaving the country was being thoroughly searched.

She learned that the boy soldier who had pointed the gun at her, but then killed his fellow rebels, was named Peter Heweh. Dubose told her Peter was the rebel who gave them the specifics of the attempted coup. He also played a big part in preventing the plane from being taken over. He said he saw her face against the window and something in him clicked. She reminded him of his village chief, and he wanted to meet her. Dubose told her she didn't have to do so; it was her call. Maybe she should talk to the embassy psychologist and counselor, Dr. Jade Baker about it.

In the days following the coup, those who stayed met with Dr. Baker. He wore a pair of faded jeans and a light blue shirt at Nicole's first and subsequent meetings. Nicole's mind wandered during their sessions. She looked for some type of mark on his shirt and jeans, a tear, a stain, anything to see if they were the same clothes he wore over and over again, or if he had several pairs of matching shirts and jeans.

She didn't know why his clothes occupied her thoughts while there were far more serious things she needed to concentrate on. Dr. Baker held both group and individual sessions. In the group sessions, Nicole talked about her feelings while she was looking into Peter Heweh's eyes, but stopped there. Always there.

"What happened next Nicole? What did you see after he stood below your window and looked up?" Dr. Baker asked.

Nicole shook her head.

"You don't remember what happened next?"

"She fainted." Rebecca would chime in.

"Thanks, Rebecca. But let Nicole answer for herself. What did you see Rebecca? What do you remember?"

"I remember praying."

"You prayed. Nicole fainted," Dr. Baker pressed on. "Did anyone see what happened? Does anyone want to talk about what happened?"

"I was so busy staring at Rebecca praying, since she is so anti-God," Marvin Taylor said. "I didn't see a thing."

"Shut up Marvin," Rebecca snapped.

"Let's wrap it up for today," Dr. Baker said. "Maybe we'll dig deeper in your individual sessions."

Nicole remembered clearly what happened. She had nightmares every night. She saw the smoke disappearing into the air, uncoiling like a huge snake. She remembered Peter Heweh, the thin dark boy staring at her and she remembered Thaddeus. She remembered Peter pointing his gun at her. She remembered him smiling at her, as tears streamed down his face. He then nodded at her and said something she couldn't hear. She remembered him turning the gun, and the sparks from the gun, then the bodies with holes and blood everywhere. One boy's eye was shot out and blood flowing from the socket. She remembered.

In the next group session Andrew McArthur announced he wanted to stay in the country, but didn't plan to attend any more counseling sessions.

"Look, Dr. Baker," he said "I know you think these sessions are helpful, but I think what happened is still way too fresh. I want to spend my time learning about my host country and my assignment. I decided to stay, mainly because of Nikki, I mean Nicole. She's scared, but she's staying. Well, so am I."

Days later Nicole sat in the Peace Corps headquarters, waiting for her interview with Dr. Brandt and Vera Whittaker. She wondered what Dr. Baker wrote in his report to them.

At night while Rebecca slept, Nicole relived the incident, over and over again. She looked out the window of the Pan AM plane into the eyes of the little boy with a machine gun in his hand. She remembered something different each time. Sometimes he sucked on a lollipop. Or instead of fatigues, he wore shorts and a dirty white T-shirt.

Although they had been roommates at the safe house and now at the hotel, Rebecca and Nicole did not discuss their decisions with each other. Nicole remembered reading an article in *National Geographic* magazine while still stateside about the rebels snatching children from remote villages and getting them hooked on alcohol and drugs.

The article was written by a young man who had fled from Rwandan rebels and escaped to London with help from an underground amnesty group. The young man, writing under the assumed name of Nhe, chronicled his journey from his initial capture to his final escape.

Nhe wrote about his childhood in a village with a population of about fifty. He reminisced about sitting at his mother's feet, when he was about nine, while she cooked okra soup and boney fish. He said his father used to tell him the story of the tortoise and the hare. How the hare and the tortoise set out on a race. Everyone thought that the hare would win, since he jumped so fast. But the hare kept getting sidetracked, while the tortoise kept a steady focused pace. In the end, the tortoise won. His father farmed for a living. His mother took the produce to market to sell. Nhe, the oldest of four, was to look after the other children when his mother went to market once a week.

At that time the rebels rarely entered the villages. But if they caught a lone child nearby they would take him. His mother told him not to leave the compound under any circumstance. She did not give him a reason. He heard that the bad people stole kids to take their body parts to make witchcraft. It was something his mother and father whispered about when they thought he was asleep.

The day the rebels caught him, he had left his eight-year-old sister to retrieve his soccer ball. He had accidentally kicked it over the compound wall. The soccer ball was a present from his father. It was from England and cost a month's salary. His father told him not to play with it unless he was home. That soccer could be their way out of the village. Many little African boys like him learned how to play soccer well, and as adults, they were making money to pay for food, schoolbooks, and medicine for their families. Some even traveled to England or France to play soccer and they sent money back to the village. Nhe knew he had to get his soccer ball back, before someone stole it.

He planned to grab the soccer ball, and run as fast as he could back to the safety of the compound. Once outside the compound he saw a man holding his ball. The man with his soccer ball is Nhe's last whole memory. The rest of his memories came in flashes, like lightening during a violent thunderstorm.

He described the camp where the rebels taught him how to fire a gun. Every time he hit a beer bottle, he could eat. No food until he hit his target. One day his capturers made him dig a grave for one of the other little boys. The boy was not a good shot. He received little to no food. He starved to death. Nhe became an expert shooter to survive.

Nhe wrote that he went from shooting beer bottles to bush animals. The rebels made him watch the blood ooze out of the animals as the life left them. The more kills, the more food, and candy. He liked the sweet taste of the candy. In his village he never had candy. But even the candy did not fill the void he felt. He wanted his mother, and his father. He missed his sisters and brothers too. But he told the rebels he hated his parents. He knew he had to, in order to survive. He knew they wanted him to say he hated his parents and siblings. But he did not.

At night he whispered prayers to the God his mother told him about. He received no answers. But he remembered the story of the tortoise and the hare his father told him back in the village. The tortoise won, because he stayed focused on his goal. That is how Nhe survived and escaped. He stayed focused and when he had the chance to run, he ran and never looked back. Some market women hid him among their bags of rice, and the amnesty group helped get him out of the country.

The door opened to Dr. Brandt's office, startling Nicole. Jennifer walked out with one eyebrow raised, typical nonverbal Liberian communication. Liberians communicated through pursed lips, raised eyebrows, looking down to the ground, sucking their teeth or a hundred other nonverbal signs. But Jennifer was not Liberian and often used the body language inappropriately. She looked straight at Nicole, but did not speak. As she passed Nicole, she bumped her, causing Nicole's bag to fall and some of the contents to spill out onto the floor. Jennifer helped Nicole stuff items back into her bag without saying a word. Dr. Brandt stood watching them.

"Nicole, please join us," she said ushering her into her office.

"You remember Vera Whittaker."

"Of course. Hello Ms. Whittaker," Nicole said, still trying to gather herself together after her encounter with Jennifer.

Vera held both hands out to Nicole then kissed her on each cheek in the traditional Liberian greeting. They then sat facing each other as Dr. Brandt spoke.

"As you know we are meeting individually with all American Mission personnel to ascertain if this assignment is still a good match. The US President and Tanner have agreed to keep our American operation intact in Liberia. They believe there is no credible threat to American lives. The rebels were not trying to hurt any Americans."

Nicole was starting to shake, but she never took her eyes off Dr. Brandt. Brandt explained that if she decided to stay she would have to go through further psychological evaluations, and meet with Dr. Baker on a weekly basis.

As Nicole thought over Brandt's words, Vera spoke up.

"Although we think we've captured all of the rebels, but things have now changed in Liberia. For a few months, there will be a curfew. For the time being, everyone has to be off the street by 6 PM, but the American Embassy is working with the Liberian government to get the curfew pushed." Vera smiled at Nicole before continuing. "We know that Americans are not used to these kinds of restraints. In fact, Liberians are also not used to them."

"I understand this is a time of transition in Liberia, but I came to help and I'm staying. The women in the village need to understand that breast milk surpasses mixed formula. Especially formula diluted with contaminated water. They have to understand that they could be harming their babies."

"Nicole, after all that has happened here, no one would think less of you if decide to go home," Dr. Brandt said. "Most of your fellow trainees have decided to do so."

Nicole closed her eyes, and took a deep breath. When she spoke, it was from the part of her that loved Africa and yearned to come here. She spoke from the part of her that had protected her Grandma Kaitlan, from her abusive husband, Lemuel. She spoke from the part of her that gathered the dirt off Thaddeus' grave to bring it to Africa for his final rest.

"I came to let women know that they can still enter their secret societies and learn how to conduct themselves as young ladies, without being circumcised. I came here, because in Africa, in Liberia, every day, children die from lack of clean water. Every day, a child dies, because the majority of people here do not have flushing toilets. They defecate near water streams. That if we can help to provide a source of clean water, all the other issues, malaria, and death in childbirth will subside as well. I didn't come to make a speech. I came here to tell you; I will stay the course. Let me know what day you want me to take the psychological tests. I'll be ready."

Until that moment she didn't think that she had the courage to stay. The meeting ended with Dr. Brandt telling her they would contact her with their decision after they reviewed her file, which would be within 48 hours. Nicole left the office and walked out into the courtyard of the Peace Corps building. Sitting on the bench outside, was Jennifer.

"We have to stop meeting like this," Jennifer said.

Nicole sat down beside her, but didn't respond.

"Are you staying or leaving?" Jennifer asked.

"Leave me alone," Nicole snapped.

"Well, that may be my plan."

"What does that mean Jennifer, every time I see you, it spells trouble for me?"

"When I bumped into you in Dr. Brandt's office, I slipped you a note with information about how to reach my father. I might disappear for my own safety before they get to me. If I do, please contact my father and get the tape to him, but not while I'm still here. I'm working on a plan, if it doesn't work, we go to plan B."

Nicole slipped her bag from her shoulder and opened it. A folded piece of notebook paper sat on the bottom.

"Don't pull it out. Someone could be watching us." Jennifer said, then stood to leave.

Nicole put a hand on Jennifer's arm, stopping her. "One question Jennifer, what made you trust me, or think I wanted to get involved?"

"They get background information on all the volunteers before they arrive to see who they can find dirt on, and can be easily manipulated. They couldn't read you. They knew you were an expert on Africa, especially Liberia, but they couldn't figure out if you were a back to roots Black power chick, or a Negro trying to help the natives. Or maybe someone in between."

"Who do you mean when you say 'they'?"

"This isn't a good place for us to talk. Meet me at a cook shop on the outskirts of town. Take a taxi to Bomi Road where the blacktop ends. You'll see a woman selling roasted meat. She'll tell you where to find me."

"This is like something out of a James Bond movie. Are you serious?" Nicole asked shaking her head in disbelief.

"I wish it was a movie. Meet me tomorrow at 1 PM."

⤛⊙ ⊙⤜

The next day Nicole left the hotel room early so she wouldn't wake Rebecca. The American Embassy moved everyone from the safe houses to hotels in Monrovia, while they reviewed their files and conducted psychological tests. Nicole thought that maybe those who stayed were not brave, maybe they were a little crazy. For Nicole, working and living under violent circumstance didn't scare or deter her. She realized that, for the majority of the PCVs, drive-by shootings, gang fights, and police battles were things they saw on the news, not regular occurrences in their neighborhoods. Her stint in Long Beach as a gang mediator prepared her more than she realized. But in the end, it was the daily fights between her grandmother and Lemuel that prepared her for battle.

Nicole decided to drive and not take a taxi to meet Jennifer. She didn't want to be traced through the taxi service. She drove about an hour out of town before she saw the woman with the roasted meat at the end of the blacktop. Nicole first drove by the woman to make sure she wasn't being followed. She circled around twice, then parked her truck across the street.

The woman sat by herself, out in the middle of nowhere. She wore a white Yankees T-shirt and a red lappa tied around her waist, with a matching red head-tie. They looked faded from several washes. Her feet were bare. Her skin was so dark it was blue-black-what Grandma Kaitlan called people whose skin seemed so dark that it was beyond black. Her skin glowed in the afternoon sun. She didn't have one scar or pimple. She was absolutely beautiful, Nicole thought.

Nicole could smell the roasted meat wafting up from the small makeshift hibachi. The woman kept the raw meat in a large bowl filled with water. The skewers were laid across newspapers with seasoning on them. To prepare the kabobs the woman picked up a skewer, rolled the meat in seasoning, skewered the meat and placed it on the grill.

Volunteers were warned not to eat street food because the meat could be anything from rat, dog, possum or some other type of bush meat. Tatu, Nicole's Togolese friend from the states, said bush meat could be anything from smoked monkey carcass, fresh crocodile, giant rats, or preserved porcupine. None of which made Nicole's mouth water. Eventually, most volunteers sampled some street fare. They would then share which roasters cooked beef or chicken, and whose food didn't make you ill. Nicole approached the woman who smiled broadly, and pointed to the meat on the grill. She pulled out some cash from the money belt under her shirt and handed the woman two US dollars.

"I'm looking for a white woman named Jennifer."

The woman held up her hand, wiggled her fingers, and then pointed to the meat.

"No. I don't want meat. I need to find a woman named Jennifer. She told me to see you, the woman roasting meat at the end of the blacktop."

The woman picked up several skewers and began to roll them in the seasoning, then placing them on the grill.

Nicole knelt down in front of the woman.

"I don't want meat. I am looking for a woman."

Nicole outlined the shape of a woman with her hands. She pointed to the inside of her palm. "She is a white woman from America. She is toubabu."

As the meat cooked the woman smiled. She wrapped the meat in newspaper. The juices seeped through the paper leaving a greasy stain. The woman wrapped up five sticks of meat and handed them to Nicole. She smiled and nodded.

Nicole sighed and took the meat. She thought maybe she had misunderstood Jennifer. The woman didn't speak English, and Nicole did not speak her language. She looked at the woman's T-shirt, and said, "Well at least we're both Yankee fans," she said pointing to the T-shirt.

"Yankees," the woman said.

"Yes," Nicole nodded, then she stood up and turned to walk back to her truck.

"Mommy," the woman called after Nicole.

Nicole turned around, and the woman beckoned her to come back. She handed Nicole a folded Yankees shirt then ushered her away. Back in the truck Nicole opened the shirt to find a note from Jennifer. The note directed Nicole to a cook shop off the blacktop a few miles down the road. When Nicole reached the shop, she had devoured the roasted meat. She didn't know what kind of meat it was, but hunger and nerves had overtaken her. The cook shop was called A New York Minute for Jesus. Inside, the walls were lined with pictures of the New York Yankees and Jesus. Nicole saw Jennifer sitting at a table in the corner of the room.

"I'm getting tired of all this secret agent stuff," Nicole said.

"Please sit. I'm sorry about all of this. I didn't ask for this, any more than you did."

The waitress approached the table.

"Two beers," Jennifer said.

"No thanks. I don't want to drink in front of Jesus," Nicole said.

"Believe me. You'll need it. Everyone here drinks, while watching the Yankees. What you want to eat. I already ordered?" Jennifer asked.

"Jennifer, please speak proper English. You're not Liberian. Besides I already loaded up on five sticks of roasted meat. I don't know what they were, but they were good."

"I knew you would like. It was safe, tasted like chicken, right?" Jennifer winked.

After the waitress brought their beers they sat at the table, without speaking, waiting for the food. A few minutes later, the owner busted through the swinging doors from the kitchen with a big bowl of steaming white rice, beef and gravy, fried plantains, and fried okra.

"You're going to eat all this?" Nicole asked incredulously.

"That and more," Jennifer grinned. "I also have some chicken stew coming."

Nicole sat watching Jennifer as she ate. She looked like an all-American white girl, blonde hair, blue eyes, and perfect teeth from years of braces. She stood about 5 feet 9 and looked to weigh about 120, the average size of a swimwear model. She could've been a model, but she didn't eat like a model. Jennifer stopped for a moment to take a swig of her beer straight from the bottle. Then she dove back into her beef, rice and gravy. Nicole took it all in. When Jennifer finished, she wiped the back of her hand across her mouth. Then pulled a pack of wipes out of her backpack and wiped her hands. She reached across the table and handed Nicole a wipe.

"The only way I've survived without getting sick is because I wipe down plates before I put food on them. And I wash my hands constantly. If there's no clean water, I use sanitary wipes to clean everything. Not to worry, the chicken should be coming soon."

"That's good," Nicole said. "I wouldn't want you to starve to death."

"I came here, because we can talk. The owner, Mrs. Baffoe is a friend. I saved her only son's life when he was choking on a chicken bone. I used the Heimlich maneuver," Jennifer said, clasping her hands together and pushing underneath her chest. "We're safe here." Jennifer took another swig of her beer before continuing. "So, you want to know how I'm involved. They approached me before I even got in country. They knew my father was a Senator. In college I studied hard, and played harder. One night at a fraternity party, I met some guys who talked about joining the Peace Corps. Although I'd had one too many beers I knew it was what I wanted to do. The next morning, I called the Peace Corps and asked them to send me the application."

"In a drunken stupor, you made a life decision," Nicole said.

"Not drunk, I'd been drinking, but it was the first time I wanted to do something for someone else. I majored in business and planned to go into investment banking with the firm my father founded before he went into politics."

"That one conversation changed your life?" Nicole asked.

"I don't really know how to explain it. It was as if a veil was lifted from my eyes. It was like when I was ten years old and put on my first pair of glasses, everything came in focus. I filled out an application and sent it in before even discussing it with my parents."

The owner arrived with the chicken stew. The fragrant stew, cooked in tomato sauce with the green peas, corn and carrots made Nicole's stomach rumble.

"Looks like your stomach doesn't know you're full," Jennifer said motioning for Mrs. Baffoe to bring another plate for Nicole. Jennifer dipped her napkin into her bottled water and wiped Nicole's plate and handed it to her. She opened the glass tureen and scooped some of the stew onto Nicole's plate and then on her own.

"Long story short. I joined the Peace Corps without my parents' permission. Not that I needed it. I was old enough to make my own decisions, but my parents had my life mapped out before I was even conceived. When my father heard I joined, he hit the roof. His plan to have me work at the investment firm went out the window. I told him the Peace Corps was a two-year commitment, and when I finished my assignment I'd come back and join the firm. I came here without his blessing. Jerk didn't even see me off at the airport. What kind of father does that? I am going overseas for two years and he doesn't even show up to say goodbye."

Jennifer looked down at her plate and blinked back tears.

"In stateside training, I reunited with the guys who'd told me about the Peace Corps." One of them said there was a secret force in the Peace Corps that worked with the Embassy to ensure America's security,"

"And that didn't sound like a covert CIA scheme to you?" Nicole asked.

"Maybe I'm naïve," Jennifer shrugged.

"You grew up in New York City, and you're naive. I ain't buying it."

"In stateside training, and later while in country someone took pictures of me snorting cocaine and in a compromising position. They said they were CIA but now I think they are rogue. They threatened to use the pictures against my father in the upcoming election."

"This secret organization white mailed you," Nicole said, shaking her head.

"What?"

"That is what I call it, instead of blackmail. They used the pictures to get you to do what exactly?"

"To obtain information about people. At least that's how it started."

"And then," Nicole prompted.

"Then I became part of the machine. I recruited other volunteers."

"What's your involvement in the coup attempt?"

"The woman you heard me speaking to in the bathroom used me to send messages into Sierra Leone because I live close to the border. Some Liberians, and Sierra Leoneans who hated Tanner for what they felt was his oppression of the indigenous people joined with the Americans to plan to coup."

"Who is she? Nicole asked.

"Her official title is the Information and Assistance Officer at the US Embassy. But I don't want to say any more about her. She's bad news, she'll pretend she's down with the people and then flip on you. She's evil. I was sold on the story that since Tanner has ruled the country for forty years, democracy in Liberia didn't have a chance until he relinquished his power. Since he was not resigning any time soon, they decided to help him."

"The American government propped him up," Nicole said.

"Until President Tanner started talking to China and Russia, about Liberia owning their own rubber plantations, and terminating the deal made back in the 1800s with the American tire companies. And about Liberians, Africans running their own diamond mines, and charting their own destinies."

"What you're telling me is that the American government helped plan a coup so they could help American businesses keep a stranglehold on the natives."

"Don't tell me that sounds unrealistic to you? But that's only a part of it. A lot of this goes back to the Cold War. There was no way the US would let China or Russia come in and take over Liberia. This country is strategic for the US. Liberia is the only African country America really has ties to. They have the satellite here that broadcasts throughout the continent of Africa and the Middle East."

"I know the history," Nicole said. "But how is Germany involved. I heard a BBC report that there were German soldiers involved."

"The Germans are paid mercenaries. I don't know who foots that bill. I'm not high up on the totem pole. They used me. I want out. I plan to tell my father everything. His ultimate plan is to run for the presidency. He needs to know."

After a few moments of silence, Nicole pulled the tape recorder out of her money belt and flipped it on.

She recognized the first voice as Ms. Blue Pumps.

"Here's the deal. We all want Tanner gone. We all have different reasons but it doesn't matter why. With him gone, we all win. America will support the new president because we'll handpick him."

"As long as no Americans are killed or hurt, we won't interfere," said a male voice.

Muffled sounds could be heard in the background. And then a voice came on that Nicole recognized, but she couldn't place. The sound was not clear.

"We need to be careful. If this gets out, we'll be fried."

Jennifer turned off the tape recorder.

"You have to get this into the hands of someone you trust who can get it to my father. Despite our differences, my father is an ethical man. He takes his oath as a Senator seriously and would be very upset to know that Americans are involved in trying to overthrow a foreign government."

"Why don't you do it yourself?" Nicole asked. "Besides we interfere all the time."

"I've been wrong about so many things, at this point I don't know who to trust. But I think I can trust you. From reading your profile I don't believe you'll sell out. As far as American interference, we like to call it 'support'. We can't say we helped plan a coup. That would be un-American."

"You don't know anything about me. I could be one of the bad guys."

"I wish it was as clear as that, who's bad and who's good. One thing I've learned in this whole experience is that people are complex. They are neither good nor bad. But to answer your question, they couldn't dig up any dirt on you. To them, you're an anomaly. On the wait and watch list. They also don't think you can be bought. Your friend Rebecca, however, is another story."

"What?"

"Be careful of her," Jennifer warned. "And watch your back."

"I trust Rebecca," Nicole said. "We had a bumpy start, but we've bonded. She lived a very sheltered life; but in training when I found out she knew as much about Africa as I do, we became fast friends. She even asked to be my roommate."

"She played you to get close to you," Jennifer said, looking nervously around the cook shop. "Look, you should go. If you don't see me again, get the tape to my father immediately. If they tell you I went home, don't believe them. Either I went underground, or they got rid of me. Either way, get that tape to my father. Fast."

Nicole stood up shakily from the table. She felt as if drums were beating in her head. It was all too much for her, the attempted coup, boy soldiers, and now Jennifer confiding in her that Rebecca may be involved somehow and that her life could be at risk.

Nicole took the recorder, stuffed it back into her money belt, and tucked it under her shirt. Nicole reached across the table, took Jennifer's hand and squeezed it. Then she left the restaurant.

Nicole drove and drove until she reached the blacktop. She passed the spot where she bought the roasted meat. She looked on the passenger seat. The Yankees T-shirt was gone. She looked under the seat but there was no sign of it. She remembered locking the truck. Had it fallen out when she got out to meet Jennifer, or had someone followed her, broken into her truck and taken it? Was someone following her now? Nicole looked in the rearview mirror, her eyes nervously scanning the road. There was no other vehicle behind her.

She drove past her turnoff, and headed to Monrovia. The setting sun cast an orange and pink glow across the horizon, but its beauty was lost on Nicole. She wanted to make it up country before it got too dark. The small tape recorder felt like a heavy weight on her hip. She thought about the people she met since arriving in Liberia. Who could she trust? The only person who came to mind was EXO Dubose. He'd recently left Monrovia to deploy American troops to the borders of Sierra Leone. Nicole drove to the town where her driver, Slopadoe lived. She parked in front of a shack store and asked a little boy sitting on the steps to get him. In Liberia, it seemed everyone knew everyone else.

Nicole hated to impose on Slopadoe, but she knew this was not a trip she could make by herself. First, she did not know the way, and word on the street was that the rebels headquartered near the border of Liberia and Sierra Leone.

Nicole bought a Fanta from the store and sat on the steps sipping the grape soda while she waited for her driver. Her hands clasped around the cold bottle, calming her nerves. In the states, she rarely drank sodas, but she didn't trust the water in Liberia, and bottled water cost more than soda. A few minutes later, Slopadoe came running behind three little boys. Nicole had only sent one little boy. She handed a dollar to the one she sent. The other two put their hands out for their share.

"You all leave Madam be," Slopadoe said, shooing them away.

He wore his well-worn driver's suit of brown slacks and a matching short-sleeved shirt. Because it's considered rude to stand over your boss, he sat down beside Nicole on the steps of the store, but not too close.

"Madam, what is wrong? Are you okay?"

"I'm sorry to bother you Slopadoe, but I need to get up country to see someone and I don't want to drive myself."

"Of course not. I work for you 24/7."

"I did not mean it like that," Nicole said.

"I know Madam. Please hand me the keys. The hour runs late and wherever you need to go, it must be important or you would not be here."

They got into the truck, with Nicole in the passenger seat and not in the back, where she would normally ride.

"We need to go to Sherboe, to cross the border to the Sierra Leone side, Nicole said.

"I know where it is. We will need to be careful. Once we get up country to the border, you will have to get in the back seat. No one will bother us, once they see this big American truck and know you are an American with clout. But you must act the part."

"I don't have any clout. I'm a Peace Corps Volunteer."

"Miss Nicole, you are an American. We assume all Americans have clout and wealth."

As they drove into the darkness, the night sky loomed above them, lit with thousands of stars. Nicole sat in the passenger's seat beside Slopadoe. She left word with one of the boys to go to the hotel where she was staying to ask Rebecca to cover for her if anyone from the Peace Corps or the embassy was looking for her. She sent a note saying she would be staying in town because she could not make it back before curfew. After what Jennifer said about Rebecca being a mole, Nicole thought it best not to confide in her. Although she didn't believe the idealistic ranch girl from Wyoming could be caught up in coups and espionage.

Nicole did not have a plan in mind, only that she had to find Dubose. She didn't know who else to trust. Jennifer did not trust anyone, not even herself. But Jennifer had to trust Nicole to give her the recording. What if this was a trap, or a setup? Nicole decided that she'd start with Dubose and then see what he had to say.

When they arrived in Sherboe, Slopadoe went straight to the hotel where most Americans and other foreigners stayed. Slopadoe opened the door and helped Nicole down from the truck.

"Where do you think I can find EXO Dubose?" Nicole asked him.

"If he is not in the hotel, someone will know where to find him. You should check with the clerk at the front desk or leave word for him there, and then get something to eat while you wait."

"Okay. Thanks, Slopadoe. You should get something to eat too. We had a long drive. Let's meet back at the truck in a couple hours."

When Slopadoe nodded and walked away, Nicole pulled her shirt down over her money belt with the tape recorder and looked at the hotel. It could easily compete with any five-star hotel in America. It was located near the gold and diamond mines, so the gold girding, marble floors, and large white columns in the lobby didn't surprise Nicole. She knew she looked a mess after driving hours in the truck. Her American accent would be her key to not being thrown out of the hotel.

There were many Jewish people wearing hamicos, traditional knit hats, milling around the lobby. Nicole heard German being spoken. She had picked up some German from Mrs. Stollar, her childhood friend Kimmy's grandmother. She was a first-generation German woman who lived on the farm down the road from Grandma Kaitlan. Nicole spent many hours in the Stollars' home helping Mrs. Stollar bake apple strudel and other German pastries, while singing German songs with Kimmy.

Nicole sat down near a couple speaking German. Attendants dressed in white aprons carried out trays of tea sandwiches made with peanut butter and grape jelly on whole wheat bread. Nicole stared at the sandwiches. The German couple smiled at her as if they could read her mind. She hadn't had a peanut butter and jelly "sammich" as she and her sister Shannon called them, since elementary school. She didn't even like peanut butter and jelly, but it was a rare commodity in Liberia and she was starving. The stew she'd eaten with Jennifer hours ago was long gone. She sat down near the couple and waited for the attendant to serve her.

"Sandwich, Madam?" The attendant asked, handing her a hot towel to wash her hands.

"Please," Nicole said.

She wiped her hands on the towel and set it on the table. The waiter handed her a small plate and places a few of the little sandwichs on it.

"This is wonderful," Nicole said biting into the sandwich.

"We serve them every night," the attendant smiled. "Americans love them well-all the foreigners do now. Actually, now I find that we Africans have become fond of p & j as well."

Another waiter came over with tumblers of cold milk. Nicole tried to chew slowly, but found herself, eating the tiny sandwiches in one gulp, and then licking her fingers. How unladylike, she thought. The attendant came with another round of sandwiches and slipped Nicole a brown sack of them.

"Here, take some back to your room with you. Put them in your purse."

Nicole took the bag of sandwiches and slipped them in her purse. She remembered the tape recorder tucked into her money belt and her mission.

The Germans were also enjoying their p & j and milk. Since they started eating, their conversation had ceased. The man wiped his mouth with the back of his hand and started speaking in German again. He didn't look at her, but Nicole knew he was talking about her. She tried to piece together the conversation. He told his companion, the beautiful Black woman across from them could be a decoy. A decoy, thought Nicole, a decoy for what? The woman looked over at Nicole, but when Nicole looked back. She averted her eyes.

The man asked his companion if she thought Dubose would stand them up. The woman said her contact assured her Dubose would be there. When Nicole heard Dubose's name she felt the sandwiches coming back up. She didn't want to draw attention to herself, but she had to get to the ladies' room, or the sandwiches would end up all over the marble floor of the lobby.

She grabbed her purse and hurried to the bathroom. Once inside she splashed cold water on her face. Although still a little nauseous she had to get back out there before the German couple left. She took a deep breath, rinsed her face again and walked back out into the lobby. EXO Dubose, and another man now sat across from the German couple. Dubose had his back to her; but she'd know him by his bearing anywhere.

Nicole was close enough to hear Dubose speaking German with the man. What was he doing here, and speaking German? She crossed the lobby and sat behind them, facing the German couple with Dubose' back to her. The German woman mouthed to her, "Are you American?"

Nicole nodded her head. She hoped Dubose wouldn't turn around. If he heard her voice, he would recognize it. The German man frowned at his companion, then Nicole. Before Dubose could turn around Nicole hurried out of the hotel. Now she understood what Jennifer meant. She couldn't trust anyone, not Rebecca or even EXO Dubose. She saw Slopadoe sitting on the bench in front of the restaurant across the street from the hotel. She pointed down the street corner, indicating for Slopadoe to meet her there.

"Where's the truck?" she asked.

"Around the corner. Did you see Dubose? He went into the hotel."

"Did he see you?" Nicole asked.

"No, I do not think so. He was busy talking to the man he was with; but he is a very observant man."

"How would you know?" Nicole asked.

"I have been a driver for the Peace Corps for a long time. I know many things Madam. Liberia is a small country. Everyone knows everyone, or knows of them. EXO Dubose lived in Sierra Leone before coming to Liberia. He practically raised that young man, David, the man who is with him. Long before David started calling himself a Bettencourt, he lived with EXO Dubose as a boy."

"The man he was with is a Bettencourt?" Nicole asked.

"In a matter of speaking, the Bettencourts adopted him as a teenager. He lives there now at the academy, but he, well there are many stories concerning him."

"Let's get to the truck," Nicole said.

Safely inside the truck they rode in silence back to her hotel in Monrovia. She felt the tape recorder in her money belt. She couldn't believe that such a small little thing could bring down governments.

Chief Esi

A FEW DAYS later, Nicole pulled off the blacktop road and onto the gravel. She had been sleeping badly, feeling the weight of the attempted coup, and the near encounter with Dubose weigh heavily on her. But what really shook her to the core was the possibility that Rebecca could be working with a covert group sanctioned, or not, by the CIA.

She was following directions her Peace Corps Officer, Ed Hawk left in her mail box at PCV headquarters. Her PO wrote on the front of the envelope, "Follow the instructions to find your new living quarters in Logantown. Inside are directions and the key."

The wind blowing on her face made her nose tickle. She felt safe off the main road, or the blacktop as the locals called it. She had arrived to PCV headquarters late due to a training session at her work assignment, the Liberian Communication Network (LCN). They had started work on the Clean Water Initiative, a joint project between USAID, United Nations and the African Organization of Unity. She missed meeting with PO Hawk, but she was thankful he had left her directions. Dr. Brandt and Vera Whittaker had found her fit to serve out her assignment in Liberia. They also approved Rebecca, Andrew, and Marvin. Only Randy Jones was sent home. They deemed him not mentally fit for duty. Nicole wondered if he was sent home, did that mean he wasn't the CIA operative.

When she told Slopadoe that she was late and had to drive out to her new place without her PO, he looked down at the ground and shook his head. He said he had eaten some bush meat for lunch that didn't agree with his stomach and the runny belly kept sending him to the toilet. He didn't protest too much when Nicole told him she would find her new home on her own. By now Nicole felt she and Slopadoe understood each other. He told her one day, "You do not act like other Americans, Madam Jefferson. You wish for me to call you by your first name, you sit up front with me. Sometimes you insist on driving yourself."

Nicole also greeted him every morning, and asked about his family, unlike most Americans. Many learned the customs in time; even with business greetings, small talk had to be made before anything else got done in Liberia. Sometimes Americans would rush through the greetings to get to the business. She also wore African clothes, though she didn't wrap her head, and she looked everyone straight in the eye and gave them a big smile. Slopadoe told her that big smile matched her big heart.

When they traveled around the countryside on their research expeditions, the village children ran to hug her and she did not tell them to go away. She never gave them candy or money as a bribe to ingratiate herself with them, as many other foreigners did. Often she gave them books to share with each other, or some nuts and local fruit. She told them that when she came back she would bring more books and read to them, and she actually did. She made sure to include books about their country written by African authors.

Nicole explained to Slopadoe that she didn't have a husband waiting for her in America. But in order to gain the respect of the Liberian men, she had to wear a wedding ring and pretend she was married, to ward off their advances. Some Liberian men still tried to make their moves, but Nicole would just giggle with her hand over face and feign shyness.

Before she left Slopadoe, he told her that Logantown was about an hour away, and most of it was on the blacktop, but when she went far enough the gravel road would start. Once she drove off the blacktop, he told her she would have to use landmarks, since there would not be street signs.

Life off the blacktop showed the other side of Africa, the one hidden from the world. Back there the women could still walk around bare breasted without foreign gawkers, or westernized Africans staring. Their babies could suckle, without them covering up. Nicole learned on the National Geographic Channel that a woman's thighs had to be covered in most parts of Africa, but their breasts could be uncovered in traditional areas of Africa. In the Muslim countries, women had to cover from head to toe. But in traditional Africa, the thighs and lower body were considered sacred. A woman held her diamonds between her legs. Her husband was the only one who should be able to see her most precious part of her body.

In stateside training, the Cross-Cultural instructor role played with the trainees, over and over again, where to place their eyes when they saw a bare-breasted woman. She instructed them to never stare at an African woman's breasts. It was considered rude and disrespectful. Also looking at local non-westernized African women in the eye was considered bad manners, unless you knew them. The instructors told them to look at the ground or above the person's head, but not at their breasts, or directly in their eyes.

Off the blacktop, Nicole noticed everyone seemed to be more relaxed. Women and children offered her kola nuts or a tin cup of water, when she entered their villages. Although many of them had little to nothing, they shared. When she tried to pay them something, they smiled and shook their heads. They freely took the books and fruit, but not any money. The giving of kola nuts showed one was welcome. She hadn't been in this particular village, but she found it universal off the blacktop how the people greeted her. She felt like a long-lost relative returning home. The kids ran alongside the truck waving at her, or gave her a shy smile, hidden behind their hands. The older villagers sat on the ground or on handmade wooden stools and shouted a "Hey Mommy" greeting.

She drove until the gravel ended and there weren't any people. She thought she must have missed the big boulder landmark drawn on the map, because she was lost. She stopped and got down from the truck. No one walked on the road, which she found unusual. On African roads, someone was always journeying somewhere. Walking was their main mode of transportation.

She walked a quarter of a mile to a village, but before she could enter the town, three boys who looked to be around ten years old ran to meet her with kola nuts, and paw paw. Then several of the children seemed to appear out of nowhere and surrounded her. They walked her into the village circle. Two girls took each hand and pulled her into a little hut, made from grass and mud. Inside, a woman who looked ageless lay on a mat on the floor. The coolness of the hut surprised Nicole. The woman waved the little girls away and held her arms out to

Nicole. Nicole bent down and embraced the woman. She sat on the floor beside her.

"My Misu. You came home," the woman said in English, very good English. Not American, but with a British lilt.

Nicole held her breath. She didn't know what was happening. Here she was in a village off the tarred road in Liberia and this woman called her Misu and spoke to her in perfect English. The old woman wiped tears from her face with the palm of her hand.

"Misu, you do not have to say anything. I know it's been a long time. It is me. Your mother, Esi. I do not know how many years, at least twenty since your father took you. I imagined you would look just like you do now. Well, not the hair. But your eyes, of course. Those eyes, just like mine. How you have grown into such a beautiful lady, to be expected because you were a beautiful child. I never gave up hope that I would see you again."

Nicole looked at the woman whose eyes revealed she had lived a long life, but her banana colored skin was smooth and unlined. She tried to look away from her gaze, but she couldn't. In a flash, Nicole found herself walking with the woman around the pyramids of Egypt and across the Sahara Desert, to find their way to this village in West Africa. Nicole traveled with the woman through her past. Although her father had three wives, none conceived. Then her mother, the fourth wife, had a little girl. The mother died in childbirth and left her daughter to be reared by the chief's three barren wives.

The chief noticed that when he would come to see about his daughter, that none of his wives had bothered to clean or feed his only child. He began to take her everywhere he went. No one dared to ask the chief why he took his daughter with him. She grew into a beautiful, but peculiar child. Her dark eyes, almost black, had flecks of amber in them. She would sit for hours at her father's feet, while he resolved palaver; listened to complaints, and helped to find a resolution. He rarely gave direct advice. Many times he told stories about how their ancestors handled a particular problem. Other times, he just listened and allowed them to come to their own conclusions.

One day, a professor from the Bettencourt Academy in Sierra Leone traveled to see the chief concerning research on African folklore. The professor brought his young son with him. The son soon discovered Esi. The two of them played together, running up and down the compound. Soon, they became quiet. The chief and the professor went to investigate what mischief they had gotten into. The little boy was reading to Esi. Thereafter, every few weeks, the professor showed up and learned about the African customs and history from the chief; and the professor's little boy helped Esi to read and write English, and French.

The chief knew his time to cross over was coming soon. He sent for the professor, and told him he wanted to betroth Esi to his son. The professor said he wished for his son to have his own choice in choosing his wife. However, when they were older, the son chose Esi. They married in the village. The chief lived to see the wedding and his only grandchild Misu, born.

As the chief's time came to an end, he summoned the elders of the village and told them he was not going to name Esi's husband as the chief, but Esi. He needed all the elders to support his decision to name a woman chief. If the elders didn't agree with his decision, the villagers would oppose him as well. The chief turned to the elders and spoke from his heart. He addressed them as "brother" and in the singular, to emphasize the importance of unity.

"My dear brother, where did you spend the first days of your life, I ask in earnest. If woman is good enough to carry you in her womb, born you, feed you, she can lead you too, no? Have you not read of the great queens of long ago, of Nefertiti, Nzinga, of the great Harriet Tubman from America whose relative became the first President of Liberia, and of many, many more? Esi has had the fortune to learn at my feet, but also to learn book. Her husband will soon graduate from the great Bettencourt Academy across the border. The two of them together can bring the good of the new and respect our traditions, but throw out those traditions which harm our people."

They knew he referred to the circumcision of young ladies, which still occurred in the secret society for girls called the Sande. After discussing it at length with the professor, he decided not to make Esi go into the secret society and follow the traditional rites of passage. The chief enlisted some local women to teach Esi things she had to know as a woman that he could not teach her. But he warned them, that his daughter was not to be circumcised.

Many of the villagers felt that the chief had gone too far. But the professor came back with a film showing girls bleeding to death, getting infections and not being able to enjoy their marriage vows because of female circumcision. The chief was successful and Esi became the first female sitting chief in her village, one of few in Liberia. Her father, the sitting chief died a month after she was seated. His granddaughter, Misu, was six years old, when he died. She too, sat at the feet of the chief, her grandfather, to learn from him.

Esi did not conceive again. Her husband, a book smart man from Sierra Leone now a teacher in their village, became restless. When he trained at Bettencourt Academy, there was a vital, active, academic life, with people from abroad coming to visit, or guests coming to lecture on a regular basis. When he received an offer to study in America for his master's degree he jumped at the opportunity. He left, for what was to be a year, to study abroad. One year turned into two. He wrote to Esi to say he needed to stay longer, because he had started a PhD program. Meanwhile Esi continued to sit as chief. The advice she gave and her great wisdom became legendary.

Esi's husband returned to the village during his winter break. He told Esi he wanted to take their daughter, Misu to America to visit for a while. He said he missed her too much, and felt life in the village did not offer her the opportunities she needed to become an educated woman. Esi thought this would be a great opportunity for both her and Misu to see America, but her husband discouraged her from coming. He told her the invitation was for Misu only. That she needed to stay in the village and take care of her responsibilities. So she packed a bag for Misu, looked into her eyes one last time, the same eyes that Esi had, jet black with amber specks, and she kissed her daughter goodbye.

That was over twenty years ago. In those few moments her eyes told Nicole the story of her life, whom she had mistaken for her daughter Misu, stolen away by her husband. Nicole did not question the journey she took with Esi. It did not send her into a cold sweat like the little boys with guns. She sat quietly for a few minutes just looking into Esi's eyes, then she took Esi's hand in hers and smiled. She did not have the heart to tell her she was not Misu. Instead, she sat on the mat beside her and stroked her hair.

Nicole didn't know how long they sat like that. She didn't think about her truck a quarter mile back on the gravel road. She didn't think about the darkness enveloping them, or about the attempted coup, the tape recorder she still had in her money belt, or anything else. She thought only about Esi's life and about Misu. One of the young girls in the village came to offer them a bowl of fufu and soup, but Nicole smiled and motioned to her to put the food on the table. Darkness descended around them. Another girl brought lanterns. Esi opened her eyes, smiled and squeezed Nicole's hand.

"You will find your way," she said.

She then took her last breath with her eyes still open. The skin on Nicole's arm became hot and she felt a surge of power go through her as Esi died still looking at Nicole.

She ran Esi's last words through her mind. "You will find your way." What did she mean? Nicole didn't have time to think of these things for long. Chief Esi was dead.

She did not know what to do, so she sat holding Esi's hand until one of the girls looked in. Thirty minutes later Dubose entered the hut. With him was the Liberian soldier she saw her first day at the embassy. Esi's last words didn't make sense to Nicole. She knew she had her confused with her daughter Misu.

"Ms. Jefferson. Sorry, we keep meeting under these types of circumstances," Dubose said. Kneeling down beside her, he put his hand on her shoulder. Nicole knew she had misjudged him at the hotel. He wanted to protect her. She leaned her head on to his chest and pulled her handkerchief out from her money belt to wipe her eyes. The tape recorder fell out. Nicole reached for it at the same time as the Liberian soldier. Their hands touched. Nicole felt a rush of heat travel up her spine. She held her breath until Dubose spoke.

"This is Brigadier General Souleymane Guindo. He is the Minister of Defense, here in Liberia."

"Shouldn't you be protecting the President, especially after what happened," Nicole asked, holding out her hand for Guindo to shake.

"Glad to finally meet you. I saw you at the embassy the night of the attempt."

He held on to her hand and looked deeply into her eyes as if to study her.

"Oh, I'm so sorry. I don't remember meeting you," she lied slipping her hand out of his grasp.

"I did not say I met you. I said I saw you."

"Well, I don't remember seeing you."

"The General came with me because he grew up in this area. When I received the call at the embassy that Chief Esi passed, I thought of him. He knew Chief Esi as well. His family hails not too far from here, in Logantown," Dubose said.

"Logantown. That's where I was going when I got lost."

"Well you're a good twenty miles off. How did you get out here?" Dubose asked.

"From the map left by my PO."

"Can I see it?" Dubose asked.

Souleymane knelt down beside Chief Esi. He looked up at Nicole and back at Esi.

"She thought you were her daughter Misu, no?"

"How did you know?"

"Your eyes."

Dubose helped Nicole stand, then they all left the hut. Outside, the villagers had gathered. The women brought pots of rice, dishes of potato greens with chicken, and palm oil stew. The men carried jugs of palm wine. A hole had been dug in the ground to roast a goat.

"They know Chief Esi has passed," Souleymane said. "The celebration of her crossover or what you would call her home going begins immediately. She'll be buried tonight. For the next three days there will be food and festivities. On the fourth day, the village will mourn. Some women will shave their heads. Others will wail. Some will sit silent. Normally, they wait until the end of the month for all funerals. The families join their money together and have one big ceremony. But with a sitting chief, she will be honored in her own right. Chief Esi's line ended with Misu, whose father took her away."

"Misu didn't have any children?" Nicole asked.

"No one knows. Her father never returned to the village, or even contacted Chief Esi," Souleymane answered.

"What happens now? Who will take over as chief?" Nicole asked.

"Like many other places in Africa, there is a mayor and other officials who will govern now. Many areas that had chiefs, once their line dies, the chiefs are not replaced." Souleymane said. He took Nicole's hand to help her into the vehicle he'd arrived in with Dubose.

They drove Nicole back to her truck. The men insisted the General accompany her to Logantown to see her new place, and then escort her back to Monrovia since it was now nightfall.

"It is too dark for you to see," Dubose said. The General knows this area well. I don't know why PO Hawk would give you such a map. It's as if he wanted you to get lost. I'll talk to him. May I keep the map?"

He folded the map and stuffed it into his front pocket, without waiting for Nicole to answer. Nicole and Souleymane rode in silence in her truck to Logantown. As he drove, she snuck glances at him. Although he was dark, like Hershey's Cocoa dark, the full moon allowed her to see his features. He looked to be in his early twenties, no gray hair like Dubose. His close-cut hair framed his face. The dark hair and mustache glistened on his dark skin. She didn't think military men were allowed to wear facial hair. He'd pulled out and was chewing on a cinnamon stick, a long reed, traditional or country people used to keep their breath fresh and clean their teeth. It looked like it was working, because he had the whitest most beautiful teeth she'd ever seen.

"Why did you say you did not see me at the embassy?" Souleymane asked, surprising her.

"Because you were staring at me."

"And."

"It's rude to stare."

"Not, in Africa. It is a compliment. What could be any more interesting than a person, especially a lovely person such as you?"

"Thank you. But we learned in stateside training that it's rude to look anyone in the eye, unless you are friends with them."

"Well, I intend to be your friend," he said, giving her a long look.

"You'd better watch the road."

"I know this road. I walked it, rode it, skipped it, and ran it for years. It is you I want to know better."

"What if someone runs out onto the road? What are you going to do then?"

"It will not happen."

"How old are you?" Nicole asked.

"Twenty-five."

"That is very young to be a Minister of Defense."

"No one wanted the position. The last three died under suspicious circumstances."

Souleymane turned off the blacktop and onto the gravel. Nicole felt the tension start in her legs, her entire body seemed to stiffen as he parked the vehicle. She spoke almost in a whisper.

"Why would you take such a dangerous position?"

"I am a soldier. I obey orders."

"Any order. What if the orders are unjust, like using little boys to kill?"

"That is against military policy. Children cannot join the military."

Nicole felt the anger of the last few weeks overtake her. She balled her fists up and pounded on the dashboard.

"You know exactly what I'm talking about. I saw them. You had to know the rebels had boy soldiers. You killed them. You allow those so-called rebels to steal children and turn them into killers."

Souleymane pulled Nicole across the seat into his arms. She struggled against him but he held on to her. Finally, she stopped struggling and cried against his chest. When he kissed her forehead she felt tears on his cheek. They sat for what seemed like hours in each other's arms.

"I took the job because of those little boys. I was an orphan at ten. My mother died giving birth to my sister. It was her seventh miscarriage. My father died when I was twelve. If not for Dubose, I could have been one of those soldier boys."

The full moon found them still entwined in each other's arms. In front of them stood a white stucco one-story house with turquoise blue trim. On the porch sat a handmade rattan mat outside of a turquoise painted door. Coconut trees surrounded the house, and across from Nicole's new home sat a two-story version of her house with a green door, and trim-her landlord's home. Peppers, the white star-shaped national flower of Liberia and white orchids of different shapes and sizes surrounded both houses and created a path from one house to the other.

Nicole looked at the house and said, "It reminds me of my grandmother's house in Pennsylvania. She painted her doors turquoise. I heard it's supposed to be a custom here in West Africa."

She slipped out of his arms, jumped down from the truck, and ran to the door. She then remembered that she'd given the envelope with the keys to Souleymane back at the village. She turned to go back to the truck and bumped into him. She hadn't heard him approaching. They stood looking at each other on the porch of her new home. He took her face in his hands and brought his face close to hers and whispered, "Nicole. You are a serious woman. You need a serious man."

Their relationship began that night under a full moon in front of the turquoise door, in a yard of white flowers and coconut trees. They decided for the time being to keep their relationship private. Her position required traveling into the bush country, which had no electricity or running water, although some people had generators. She spent many days in the field, meeting the indigenous people. Telephones in homes were rare in Liberia. Only the very wealthy had them. As a PCV, she was not issued a phone, so she kept in touch with Souleymane through notes. He often left notes on her porch under the mat, or he had one of the village boys deliver notes to her. They would often meet in a private room at a restaurant in the city, or at a local out of the way cook shop to share a meal and talk. They often held hands, or walked together, arm in arm, at one of the secluded beaches. The closest they came to a kiss was that first night on her porch, when he leaned down to whisper to her.

Nicole had not forgotten about the tape recorder she still kept in her money belt next to her passport, or about the attempted coup, Jennifer Giles, Rebecca's possible involvement, Esi's words or Peter Heweh, she just wanted to enjoy her time with Souleymane while she figured out her next move.

Bettencourt Academy

FEMI WOKE AND for a moment didn't know where he was. In the darkness he could not see his own arm. He switched the light on and lay in bed staring at the ceiling, remembering that he was no longer in Atlanta but in Africa.

Bettencourt Academy was as foreign to him as people calling soccer, football. He thought of the years his father and mother had spent here. The first year his father left for the trip the changes started. His mother no longer took long walks with Femi down their street, hand in hand greeting the neighbors, and stopping at the store run by Mrs. Gardner and her husband. Sometimes Esther purchased huge cucumbers Mrs. Gardner had pickled herself. The store owner kept them in a jar on the counter to entice all the little kids, but the parents loved them too.

When spring bloomed Femi looked forward to having his mother all to himself. He didn't have to share her with the students at Spelman. Although Esther's students called her Dr. Bettencourt, in their neighborhood everyone called her Mrs. Bettencourt. Sometimes Oyami would tease her and call her the real Dr. Bettencourt, since she was a teacher, and of course all Bettencourts were teachers, except for him.

That first spring his father left for Africa signaled the end of his long walks for pickled cucumbers with his mother, and the start of his father's yearly trips to Africa. Femi started kindergarten the following year. Grandma Elizabeth, Esther's mother filled in. She now practically lived in the Bettencourt's home.

The first day of kindergarten, Femi refused to leave the house until his father came home. His grandmother helped to dress him. The night before she filled the huge clawed bathtub in his parents' master bathroom with bubble bath. It was always a special occasion when he was allowed to use the big tub. Afterward she read him his favorite stories, *Green Eggs and Ham*, and "The Tortoise and the Hare" from *Aesop's Fables*. The next morning, he bounced out of bed and dashed down the hallway to his parents' bedroom. The door was open, but they weren't there. He slid down the winding ebony staircase to the first floor, and ran into the kitchen. He found Grandma Elizabeth pouring pancake mix into her sizzling cast iron skillet. She always bought her own cookware when she came to visit.

"Grandma, why do you bring your own pans to cook in?" Femi asked her one day. "What's wrong with Mommy's pans? Don't you like them?"

Grandma Elizabeth picked Femi up and sat him on the counter.

"Honey, there is not a thing wrong with your mommy's pans. I cooked in these pans for your grandfather, rest his soul, for over twenty-five years. You see this pan here. It's a magic skillet full of love. I want you to feel all the love when I cook for you in these same pans I cooked in for your grandfather. One day I'll pass these pans down to you and your wife."

Wife, Femi thought. He would never take a wife, because his Grandma Elizabeth and his mother were the best women he knew, and they'd be too old for him by the time he was ready to marry. Besides he thought, he could not could marry his mother or grandmother. He looked around the kitchen. Maybe his father was hiding like he did sometimes when they played. He opened the pantry door, but no one was there. Today he started school with the big kids. He needed to put his hand in his father's hand. He needed to look into his dad's eyes and see his reflection. Just then Esther walked in and Femi asked her, "Where's Daddy? I start school today."

"Sweetie, when I arrived at the airport last night, the airlines said the storm was so bad in London where your Dad connected from Sierra Leone that the flight had to be delayed. Daddy is on the plane now. He'll be here in time to pick you up from school. Grandma and I are going to cook a big feast for you in her magic pots and pans."

"Daddy's not home?"

Esther reached for Femi to hug him but he pulled away. At breakfast he was silent. Esther and Elizabeth tried to get him excited again about his first day of school, but he looked down into his plate of smiling pancakes. Grandma Elizabeth had made a happy face on the pancakes with a whip cream smile and chocolate chips eyes. Femi used his fork and smashed the eyes and grin into the pancakes without eating them.

Femi came back to the present with a tear sliding down his cheek. This was stupid, he thought. He was too old for tears. But he knew his tears were not for that one time his father missed a big day in his life. It was for all the missed parent-teacher meetings, the missed doctor appointments, and mainly the one thing that meant the most to him-his football games from Pee Wee to varsity.

The first two years Oyami traveled by himself to Africa. In the third year he recruited other doctors to help him staff a free clinic at the Bettencourt Academy. He contacted his mentor, Dr. Turner, who now taught at Meharry. Dr. Turner helped him to contact other doctors, and form the nonprofit group Traveling Docs. As soon as Oyami arrived home from one trip, he started planning for the next one. He made calls from his study to colleagues to request they join him at the Academy to offer free medical care. Those who could not were asked to donate. Esther headed the fundraising and donations. People at church gave money, books, and clothes for the needier students at Bettencourt Academy.

Femi lay in the same room his father slept in as a boy, drifting back to sleep with thoughts of football, his parents, David, and Bettencourt Academy in his head. In the dark night, on the Dark Continent he fell back to sleep, dreaming African dreams.

She Felt Like Home

SOULEYMANE PULLED HIS shirt over his head, untied the drawstring on his pants and stepped out of them. His chiseled muscles revealed his years of Taekwondo, running, and military training.

"First one in the water wins a much-needed foot massage," Souleymane yelled as he ran to the water.

Nicole sat on their blanket with an unopened picnic basket, her sun dress still on. He saw Nicole looking at him. She pulled out two bottles of iced Italian sodas, a container of fried chicken, and some homemade bread. Souleymane knew the effect he had on women. Things had changed a lot since his childhood. He was no longer the scrawny little village boy.

Through years of training, first on Liberian soil with Dubose and then at The Citadel in the US, Souleymane was what women thought of as a heart-throb. His quiet smoldering good looks caused respectable women to sometimes squeeze a little tighter when they hugged him, before they caught themselves. The brazen ones held on to his arms tighter or put their hands places where they didn't belong. Souleymane would push back from their embrace or gently remove their hands. As the Minister of Defense, that rarely happened now, although every once in a while, a diplomat's wife's hands wandered. Souleymane's father had taught him well.

"Find a good woman, Souleymane, like your mother or Chief Esi. Your mother was my partner, my equal. She worked right alongside me. When I felt weary or defeated, she comforted me. I taught her what she didn't know and she taught me what I didn't know. When I was discouraged, she listened and then talked words of encouragement into my soul. Who you mate with is important. Hold out for the one for you."

At that time Souleymane didn't really understand what his father meant, but now he understood. From the first moment he saw Nicole, he knew she was the one. Being with her felt both comforting, like the beach breeze, and exhilarating like jumping into the ocean from the surrounding cliffs. She felt like the family he'd lost as a child. She felt like home.

"Come on in," he beckoned to Nicole.

"It's too cold."

"Sugar Beach is known for its warm water. Come on."

She slipped out of her sundress and walked to the water. Then she stopped and looked around. Souleymane's security was always in tow. Today was no exception. She looked at Souleymane and shook her head. Then she walked back to the blanket and slipped her sundress on. Souleymane joined her.

"Everything okay?"

"Can we ever be alone?" Nicole asked.

Souleymane pulled her up and took her in his arms.

"It never bothered you before. What is the real problem Nikki?"

"I do not know how to swim," she answered.

Souleymane pulled her closer to him.

"I will teach you. What I know and you don't, I will teach you, and what you know and I don't."

Nicole finished the sentence, "I will teach you."

Not the Paradise I Dreamed About

NICOLE CROSSED THE border into Sierra Leone gripping the steering wheel to calm her nerves. She couldn't let the soldiers at the checkpoint know she was scared. Until she opened her mouth they would think she was just another rich lady from across the border in Liberia coming to buy things at the market. Jennifer warned her to let them know that she was an American on a research mission so they would know she was not going to grease any palms. The border guards demanded money from the locals, or they would find a reason not to let them cross the border.

Nicole passed through the border checkpoint without incident. She had offered the guards two ice cold Fantas from her cooler. They took them, looked at her passport and waved her through. Relieved, she parked the truck outside of the market to walk in. She gave a few coins to some local kids to keep an eye on the truck. With her backpack slung over her shoulder and her money belt tucked under her shirt with the tape recorder, she walked to the market.

She knew it was dangerous to meet Jennifer at all, but the idea of meeting at a public market made it seem safer. People came from all over to shop at the Cotton Tree Market in Sierra Leone. It was held once a month and attracted people from all over the continent of Africa, and elsewhere. The market was a riot of colors, sounds, and scents. It overflowed with fresh produce, avocados the size of melons, mangos, paw paw, all types of spices, from pilau mix to melegueta pepper. As well as tie-dye, batik, and handwoven fabrics from mud cloth to kente. Nicole didn't know where to look first.

The market women started their pilgrimage to the market days ahead. The vendors trekked from all over West Africa, not just Sierra Leone, with loads of goods for their booths. They came with anything from Western clothes to books, electronics, cameras and tape players. On the side stalls, the farmers sold their fruit and produce. In the outside stalls hung salted, cured and fresh meats. When Nicole saw the dried monkey heads hanging on strings for sale, she almost lost her breakfast.

Nicole waited just inside the gate, where Jennifer told her to meet her. She waited and waited. Jennifer was late. She scanned the crowd looking for her and saw some gorgeous royal blue dyed fabric with white block wax cutouts calling out to her. She didn't like to barter or haggle, but the welcoming ceremony for the new PCVs would take place in a few weeks. The PCVs decided they would buy material and have African outfits made to wear on that day.

Nicole looked around again for Jennifer. She was nowhere to be seen so she decided to go over to the fabric stall.

"How much Mamma?" Nicole asked.

"Okay Mommy, I give it to you for a good price."

Nicole knew she'd never get the same price a local did, but she was going to try to barter for a better deal. Nicole and the woman went back and forth a few times and finally came to an agreement. The woman wrapped her material in newspaper.

Holding her package Nicole turned and bumped into a young man.

"Excuse me, ma'am. I heard you haggling with the market woman. I don't mean to be nosy, but you speak English like an American," Femi said.

"'Ma'am?' Little brotha, I'm too young to be a ma'am," Nicole said.

"At six feet six and two hundred and ten pounds, I know I'm definitely too big to be called 'little brotha'."

"My name is Nicole, and yes I'm from the US," Nicole said, holding out her right hand in greeting. Femi slipped his hand into Nicole's, sliding his middle finger along hers, then snapping the traditional West African handshake.

"You snapped like a real West African woman."

"And your name?" Nicole asked.

"Femi Bettencourt and I believe I'm in love."

"Are you one of the Bettencourts, who built the Bettencourt Academies, the first schools for the indigenous children; and are raising money to build low cost health clinics in Sierra Leone and Liberia, and a new hospital?"

"Yes, the very same," Femi grinned "That's why I'm here when I should be home working out with the football team. I made the cut for the varsity team. My father, Dr. Oyami Bettencourt, is heading the clinic project. He wants me to work in the clinics."

Nicole watched Femi beam with pride, as he spoke.

"Right now, I love being a Bettencourt," he said.

"Reading about the work your family has done and is doing in West Africa is the reason I joined Peace Corps. I read about your great, great, great grandparents. Your family is the reason I fell in love with Africa and dreamed of coming here one day."

"I guess both of our dreams have come true. Here you are standing right in front of me under the African sun."

The market women continued hawking their produce and other items for sale. Little kids tried to sell them cassette tapes, cold drinks, or tin cups, but Nicole and Femi stood grinning at each other, in the middle of the market. Femi broke the silence.

"I met some Peace Corp Volunteers at the school the other day. Where are you assigned?"

"I'm across the border in Liberia, and I'm not a teacher. Not all volunteers are teachers."

"No offense. I happen to like teachers, as you know. I come from a family of teachers." Femi was silent for a moment; then he said, "Look, do you want to grab something to eat? I was on my way to the cook shop Mommy's Real African Food, on the corner. I hear the potato greens and chicken makes you wanna slap your momma. My dad told me to try that shop. I'm not into the more exotic stuff like goat or bush meat."

"Goat meat isn't really exotic," Nicole laughed. "But I'm with you on the bush meat thing. I'm supposed to be meeting someone, but she's late. I'd like to hear more about the clinics and hospital your family plans to build. I'll ask one of the little guys to keep an eye out for her. She's toubabu, and easy to spot. Her name is Jennifer, but folks here in the market know her as the toubabu Peace Corps teacher from across the border. I'll tell them to let her know we will be in Mommy's."

After Nicole delivered her message to a few of the little boys, Femi took her backpack and threw it over his shoulder, then they walked to the cook shop. He opened the door for her, led the way to the table, and then pulled out her chair.

"You're quite the gentleman, Femi Bettencourt. A lot of your older brothers could learn from you. Speaking of older, how old are you anyway?"

"I'm seventeen."

"Really."

"I'm no kid." Femi said with a big smile. He then placed the Walkman he'd been listening to when he spied Nicole at the market on the table.

"What were you listening to?"

"That new cat Prince. He premiered on American Bandstand right before I came over here."

"He plays a wicked guitar," said Nicole

"Yeah, you know him?" Femi asked.

"I saw him on ABS too. What did you think, you don't sound too impressed?"

"I liked his music. But he appeared very cocky, like he didn't want to talk to Dick Clark," Femi said.

"Oh, look who is talking about being cocky. I think he's a genius."

"Really."

"Yes, really." Nicole laughed.

"*Really.*"

"Definitely," Nicole said.

"Are you going to tell me why?" Femi asked.

"He's nineteen years old now, but remember what Dick Clark said to him. Prince had a chance to sell his music at fifteen. He was a kid. What fifteen-year-old would say no to that? But he didn't sign the contract because he wanted to produce his own music. Dick Clark seemed to think it was amusing, and that Prince was cocky as well, but I tell you that brother is not going to be a one album wonder. He'll be timeless. Thirty years from now he'll still be around, producing, creating and selling his music."

"Good. Then we can reminisce about how we first discussed his music the day we officially met. At our 30th anniversary we can still party to his music."

"Oh, now we are getting married." Nicole said as the waitress approached the table.

"May I order for both of us?" Femi asked.

Nicole nodded.

A few minutes after taking the order the waitress who was also the cook brought bowls of Jolloff rice, potato greens and chicken, and a side platter of fried plantains for them to share.

They ate in silence for a few minutes enjoying the food; then Femi said, "I heard the plane with the volunteers landed right in the middle of the attempted coup."

Being with Femi relaxed Nicole, she'd almost forgotten about the dangerous start to her trip. Now she felt her shoulders becoming tense and her mouth go dry. Her appetite vanished. She began to shake a bit and grabbed the sides of the table.

"I'm sorry. I probably shouldn't have brought it up." Femi said, seeing her reaction.

"The volunteers who decided to stay after the attempted coup, made a pact not to discuss it, unless it's during counseling, and even then, we have a hard time."

"When we were in Freetown, I heard my father and his friend talking about the coup. They said that President Tanner took a stand against multimillion dollar foreign companies that made agreements with the Paramount Chiefs over a hundred years ago to lease the land where the rubber plantations were, for a dollar. He's also opposing the companies that mine for diamonds and gold. Tanner wanted to null and void those old contracts to make sure that some of that money stayed in Liberia."

"Traditional Africans think about land so differently," Nicole said. "Back then, they didn't think that anyone could really own land. The land belonged to everyone. They had no idea what they were selling."

"My father said it was very complicated. Tanner had it from all sides, the international corporations, the indigenous people, the Americo-Liberians, and the American government. Then Tanner started talking to China and Russia.

Everyone thinks the Cold War is over. It isn't. My father thinks that Tanner is an honest man. Many of his cabinet ministers took money that was intended to clean the water supply and provide healthcare to the villages. They used the money to buy new vehicles and homes in Liberia and abroad. Several of them have villas in Europe."

Nicole looked around the cook shop. She noticed two men seated near the door of the restaurant staring at them. She then saw another man a few tables from them, glancing their way.

"Let's talk about something else," she said. "You play football huh? Let's see, I believe you must be a quarterback."

"Now, how would you know that?"

"Your arms. The way you're built. I love the game. One of the things I miss about America is not being able to watch American football. I have twin brothers whose lives are all about football. One still plays for the Steelers, and the other-"

"Is a coach for the New York Jets. Your brothers are Ari and Aaron Jefferson. The famous Jefferson twins. You're their sister."

"Yep."

"Wow. Now I *know* I'm in love."

Nicole looked over and saw the men still watching them.

"You know; I think I'll go look for my friend. If she's not here, then I better head back. It's a long drive."

When the waitress/cook brought the bill, Nicole reached for it, but Femi slid his hand under hers and grabbed it.

"You can't pay on our first date."

"Look young blood, this is not a date. I don't rob cradles."

"Okay, whatever you say." Femi shrugged. "But I invited you, so I'll pay."

Femi paid the bill and they left the shop. Femi handed Nicole her backpack as they stood outside. He then pulled her into his arms and hugged her tightly. The two men from the shop followed them out, and started screaming at each other. Nicole and Femi moved out of their way, but not fast enough. One of the men snatched the backpack from Nicole and ran. The other man took off in the other direction.

"Rogue, rogue, rogue," shouted a vendor. Market women, and shoppers all started shouting "rogue", and running after the man with the backpack. Suddenly feeling light-headed, Nicole swooned and fainted. Femi caught her before she hit the ground. He picked her up and carried her back into the cook shop. The waitress motioned for him to take her in the back and lay her on a mat. She gave him a cold bottle of water. Femi held Nicole in his arms and placed the bottle on her forehead, cooling her down. She opened her eyes.

"You okay?"

"What happened?" she asked looking around.

"You fainted."

"How long was I out?"

"Just a few minutes. Someone stole your backpack."

"Oh crap!"

"People chased one man down and caught him," the waitress said. "But the one who took your backpack got away. They have instant justice here you know. They don't wait for the police. People will chase a thief and if they catch him, they'll beat him. The police usually arrest the person for his own safety. They arrested the man after they pulled the market woman off of him. The police want you to come to the station when you are able."

"Thank God, he didn't get my passport, or money. I keep those in my money belt."

Nicole felt for her belt under her shirt to make sure the cassette player was still there too.

"But they took my new fabric I bartered so hard for." Nicole shook her head and got up. "I better get back over the border. At this point, I don't care if my friend comes or not. It'll be dark in a few hours, and there is a curfew in Liberia."

Femi helped Nicole to her feet, but she felt dizzy and lost her balance and fell against Femi.

"You're not in any condition to drive yourself anywhere. You're coming back with me to Bettencourt Academy tonight. There's no way I'm letting you cross the border by yourself in this condition. The academy is only a few hours from here, and a lot closer than Monrovia. Let's get your truck."

"How did you get here?" Nicole asked.

"David, um this guy who works at the academy dropped me off."

Nicole insisted on walking with Femi to the truck, but she started to feel dizzy. Femi picked her up and carried her the rest of the way.

When they reached the truck one of the little boys she asked to watch it ran up to her.

"Mommy, Mommy. You owe us more money. Some rogue tried to get into your truck. We threw rocks at him. Mommy, please no mad at us. The mirror got broke with the rock. But we saved your truck."

Femi reached in his pocket and gave them a few US dollar bills. The boys ran off squealing with joy. Femi took Nicole's keys, unlocked the door, and then helped her into the passenger seat. They rode in silence for miles, then the skies darkened and huge drops of rain fell. Thunder boomed in the horizon and lightening lit up the sky like fireworks.

Nicole slid closer to Femi. She knew thunder couldn't hurt her, the lightening was the dangerous one, but she'd been afraid of thunder since she was a child. It would send her hiding in her closet. She felt safe as she snuggled closer to Femi. If he was only five years older, she thought. But if he was, what about Souleymane?

An hour later they reached the entrance to the academy. Femi watched Nicole's reaction as they drove through the natural arch made by the silk cotton trees. Her mouth dropped open and her eyes widened as he pulled up to the gate and pressed the code to enter. Inside, the silk trees were replaced with acacia trees. Among the acacia trees stood two giraffes with their necks intertwined.

"Giraffes. Are those really giraffes?" Nicole whispered. "I studied Africa. There aren't giraffes in West Africa, well there used to be in Nigeria. But mostly they live in East or South Africa among the acacia trees where they eat the crowns of the trees."

"There are giraffes at Bettencourt Academy," Femi smiled.

"I know. I see them, but how? I thought they were extinct in this part of Africa."

"My grandmother believes in the impossible," Femi said. "Everyone told her that giraffes could never survive in West Africa because they live off of the acacia trees and there were none here. She said she would plant them. Twenty years ago she did and she had giraffes brought in first from Kenya. They died, but then she found a reserve in Nigeria where the giraffes thrived for a while, but eventually they died off. She brought some of the giraffes from Nigeria. They were sickly, so she nursed them back to health. Now there is an entire giraffe reserve here, the only one in West Africa, on the south side of the property. But these two always wander to the gate. I think they like to surprise visitors who have no idea there are giraffes on the property, or for that fact in Sierra Leone. It's one of our many surprises here at Bettencourt Academy."

Before they could stop, Dr. Bettencourt, David, and Gojo hurried over to the truck.

"Femi, what happened son?" Oyami asked. "Your grandma, well everyone is worried. David looked for you, and was told by Ma Jan at the cook shop that you left with an American girl, and that a rogue stole her bag."

Femi got out and opened the door for Nicole. She stepped out of the truck and onto the grounds of Bettencourt Academy. She closed her eyes for just a moment and took it all in.

"Father, this is Ms. Nicole Jefferson. She is a Peace Corps Volunteer."

"Welcome Ms. Jefferson." Dr. Bettencourt greeted Nicole with the traditional handshake, and she returned it."

"Welcome to Bettencourt Academy," David said. He held his hand out to Nicole. "I am Femi's older brother David."

Nicole turned to look at Femi who looked down at the ground. She didn't take David's hand, but she nodded and smiled. She recognized David as the man who was with Dubose at the hotel with the Germans.

"Let's get out of this rain," Femi said, pushing past David, almost knocking him down.

Grandma Bettencourt met them at the door with towels.

"Grandma Julia, this is Nicole Jefferson from the US. She is a Peace Corps Volunteer."

Nicole felt like she was in the presence of royalty. The elder Bettencourt was regal and inviting at the same time.

"Welcome, Nicole, you may call me Grandma Julia. You are very welcome to our home."

Nicole shook Grandma Julia's hand in a traditional greeting. Then Julia told Femi to change into some dry clothes. When Femi left, Julia led Nicole through the foyer and up three flights of stairs to her bedroom. The room looked like something out of a magazine. There was a handmade armoire made from local wood, with a matching bed. The end tables were carved from local cotton tree trunks. The bed sat on a round raised area in front of a huge window that faced a forest of silk trees. The bedspread, made from mud cloth, had hand dyed designs. Julia went to the closet and took out several lappa outfits, one in the royal blue color that the thief had stolen earlier. She told Nicole to select the one she wanted to wear.

"I believe my grandson is smitten with you." She said as Nicole looked at the lappa outfits.

"I believe you're right," Nicole smiled.

"He carries his feelings on his face, much like his father. I am just getting to know my grandson. When he was little, his father thought him too young to be away from home, and his familiar surroundings. I just met him for the first time a few weeks ago. In this short time, I have learned he feels things deeply. He is going to be a great man. I am not saying that just because he is my grand." Julia smiled broadly and walked to the door.

"Well, here I am rambling on about things and you are drenched. We serve hot beverages, cocoa, tea and coffee, downstairs in the parlor any time of the day. We will get one of the guest rooms ready for you. Until then feel free to use my suite as your own. Supper will be in about an hour. The bathroom is to your right."

After Julia left the room, Nicole stood in front of the mirror with the blue lappa outfit. In the reflection she could see a Bettencourt family portrait on the wall behind her. She turned to look at another picture of Anderson Bettencourt, Femi's deceased grandfather, and Femi's father, Dr. Bettencourt. She thought it must be hard to keep all these Dr. Bettencourts straight. She heard a knock on the door. Still holding the lappa, she walked over to the door and opened it. She was surprised to see David standing there.

"I came to see if you needed anything," David said.

Nicole looked at him, then shook her head.

"My little brother sometimes acts very American."

Nicole noted the strong resemblance between Femi and David, but Femi said he was an only child.

"He is American, no?" Nicole asked cocking her head to look at David. He was definitely the man with Dubose that night.

"I meant no disrespect. I understand you are American. I just meant we Africans are a very hospitable and communal people. When you arrived I was trying to greet you and Femi, and his behavior was disrespectful."

Nicole didn't answer. She continued to study his face. No, they were not true brothers, even if they were biological brothers. The eyes gave it away. David's eyes were hard.

"I will not keep you any longer. See you at dinner," David said with a slight bow.

Nicole nodded then shut and locked the door. She didn't like David, and she didn't quite know why.

A few minutes later, she was standing under a hot shower. The cascading water was luxurious, like satin floating against her skin. In her new home in Logantown, she didn't have hot running water. Few PCVs did, or for that fact, few Liberians. She missed hot water, it was something she'd taken for granted in America. There were many things she noticed the average Liberian didn't have, like indoor plumbing, refrigerators, medication for the simplest headache or minor pain. As a PCV she had all these things with the exception of hot water. Now they all seemed like luxuries to her.

She sometimes missed her life in America. Nicole thought of herself as a coward. She ran when things got tough, first from Philly after the Move shoot-out, then from Long Beach after Thaddeus' death. Did she also plan to leave Liberia? She thought to herself, do I miss America now, because Africa is not the paradise I dreamed about?

Your Brother David

WHEN THE DINNER bell rang at the Bettencourt home it was like a scene from "Little House on the Prairie" when all the children came running down the hill to the farmhouse for dinner. The sound of the bell evoked a feeling of comfort and peace that soon good food and camaraderie were to follow. Dr. Bettencourt and Dr. Momah emerged from one corner of the house with several other doctors from the States. David stood at the table waving Nicole over to sit beside him. But Grandma Bettencourt intercepted Nicole and directed her to the opposite side of the table.

"Nicole, you and Femi sit on the side by the wall so you can look at the view. The mango trees are in full bloom this time of year. A lovely sight to rest your eyes on. Sometimes the giraffes walk out there," she said.

Nicole was now next to Femi and across from David. Nicole took the cue from Femi who remained standing behind his seat until everyone came to the table. Femi nodded a greeting to two men, one looked Greek, or maybe Italian. Another was from an African country. They spoke French to each other. From her three years of French in college, Nicole could recognize some words, but was not fluent.

Nicole was highly intelligent. She graduated from high school at barely sixteen, from undergrad at nineteen. But when it came to languages, she lacked the gift. She took Spanish from elementary through high school and could not speak a word. She could read it, but not speak it. The same for German. She heard the Stollars speak it and could understand it, but she couldn't really speak it. She understood languages, but had difficulty speaking them.

As people poured in for dinner, she smiled and nodded at them, as Femi did. She had never seen a table that seated so many people in anyone's home before. She counted ten seats on David's side of the table, so she knew there had to be as many seats on her side. As soon as everyone was in place, Grandma Bettencourt took her soup spoon and hit her water glass for attention.

"It always lifts my spirit to enjoy good food with good folks. I welcome a new guest tonight, Ms. Nicole Jefferson, from the US. She is a new volunteer across the border in our sister country of Liberia."

Grandma Bettencourt smiled at Nicole, and everyone welcomed her in a multitude of languages.

"It is our custom here in this home to bless the food. Nicole, as our newest guest, will you please bless the food. Grandma Bettencourt asked.

For a moment Nicole's brain stopped transmitting to her mouth. She prayed in her own way, but she was not raised in church. Before she went into a full panic, she heard Femi talking and felt his hand in hers.

"Let's all pray together Grandma. Dear Lord God Jesus, we thank you for the food we are about to eat for the nourishment of our healthy bodies. We pray for those who do not have, that you bless them, and we thank you for all of our blessings, and fellowship. In Jesus Christ's name."

In unison everyone said, "So be it."

"Well said son," Oyami said. "Now let's eat."

The sound of the chairs all being pulled out at once sounded like a choir of off key singers. It delighted Nicole. She sat with her eyes wide open taking in the sight and sound of all the people speaking in so many different languages. As Femi passed each dish to her, he whispered the name of the cuisine and its origin. If it was a dish she never had before, and there were many, he ladled a little on her plate to taste.

"This one is dried boney fish with cassava leaves, this one is fish soup. We eat it over this round ball that looks like a dumpling, but it is called fufu. The next dish you know is our favorite, Jolloff rice. And this next comes in as a close second for our favorite," he smiled as he spooned out a helping of potato greens and chicken. "This one is beef with pepper sauce over rice, and this is just a simple platter of grilled local vegetables."

He passed a fruit salad with sliced bananas, mangos, pineapple, and paw paw with toasted coconut on top to Nicole. This she could identify. She spooned a large helping on her plate.

Femi explained that Madam Kumah, the head chef, at Bettencourt Academy orchestrated her kitchen as a conductor did her musicians. Dinner took most of her time. Breakfast was usually, a simple meal of hot and cold cereals, eggs, fruit, and chicken patties, and of course, rice. In Liberia, like most West African countries, rice was a staple in every meal. On Sundays, waffles or pancakes, fried chicken, and plantains topped the menu. When she finished one meal, her staff of thirty people started the next meal.

Her staff prepared all meals, seven days a week, three times a day, with an afternoon tea every day for the teachers and students. Sierra Leone, although no longer colonized, still followed many of the British ways, afternoon tea being one of them. The Bettencourts said they took the good from both the traditional and foreign cultures. As the head chef, Madam Kumah's responsibilities included, not only the Bettencourt household, but the teacher's cafeteria in their lounge and the four cafeterias throughout the school. The cafeterias were divided by age group. There was also a campus café open from 6 AM to midnight, Sunday through Thursday and 24-hours on the weekends.

The evening meal consumed most of her time. With 3,857 students at last count, 257 teachers and teachers' aides from different countries and cultures, with different tastes and the Bettencourts themselves feeding all those people nutritious, quality food on an ongoing basis challenged Madam Kumah. She prepared the old recipes, but attempted to sneak in something new. Every month they featured a food from another country. Last month it had been France, with sweet potato frites, skirt steak with béarnaise sauce, and crème brule for dessert.

The wait staff for the Bettencourt household consisted of two students, in the teacher's training class, who earned pocket money, by serving dinner and cleaning up afterward. One of the young men bustled through the door holding a white tray with three huge platters; one with stewed beef, one with a fresh-made gravy and chicken, and the last with one of Nicole's favorite's, baked breadfruit. Nicole looked at Femi, smiled and whispered to him.

"This is the Africa I dreamt about for so long. Here, at this table with your grandmother, your father, the rest of your family and friends."

"Then we are living our dream." Femi laughed. "I know we will be very good friends, I hope maybe even more than that."

"All joking aside, Femi. I'm eating a fresh mango from mango trees I can see from this table, and collard greens grown from a garden that your great, great, great—and probably another great on top of that—grandmother started. I feel like this is the home I never had. The way I dreamt life could be."

"What makes you think I'm not serious? Are you talking about that age thing again? I'm seventeen and never had a girlfriend. I mean I have had lots of girls who are friends. In fact, my best friend Lauren is a girl. Don't be jealous. She has a boyfriend. But, you're a woman. I know what I feel. I know what I want and that's you."

"I am trying to be serious. This is why I came to Africa. To finally feel like I belong. Being here with you all makes up for landing in the middle of a coup, for Chief Esi dying in my arms, and my backpack getting stolen. Even the conversation I overheard between Jennifer and Ms. Blue Pumps in the bathroom at the embassy about another coup attempt and the people involved in the first one. If none of that happened, I wouldn't be sitting here with you and your wonderful family."

While Nicole was talking, David was listening closely. Now he put down his fork and squinted at Nicole, then he looked over at Femi with a scowl. His smooth dark skin went ashen and he started coughing. One of the teachers, who sat beside him, patted him on the back. David stopped coughing. All the clatter and chatter stopped in one collective breath.

"I am fine," David said. "I swallowed too quickly. Sorry to ruin everyone's meal. Excuse me." He rose quickly from his seat threw his napkin on the chair and stormed out of the room.

"I will check on him," Dr. Momah said to Dr. Bettencourt.

"No, I will," Oyami said, placing his hand on his friend's shoulder to stop him from leaving the table.

"Let's retire to the parlor for dessert," Grandma Bettencourt said. "David and Oyami will join us soon. I'm sure he's fine."

The guests rose from the table and followed Grandma Bettencourt into the parlor. Femi nudged Nicole and motioned for her to follow him in a different direction. They slipped through the kitchen and out to the courtyard. They walked to the trail leading past a student cafeteria. When Femi was sure no one was around, he veered off the trail and started climbing a short hill. After about fifteen minutes, they stopped in front of the Giraffe Reserve. He turned to Nicole.

"What was that about?"

"What?"

"What you said at the table. Who is Ms. Blue Pumps and why did David almost choke to death when you mentioned Jennifer's name. That's the woman you said you were going to meet at the market."

Nicole looked up at Femi. The sun had started its descent in a glorious purple orange glow across the sky. They stood under a grove of acacia trees watching the two giraffes eat the crowns of the trees. Femi sat down and leaned against one of the trees. Nicole perched herself on the grass in front of him.

"I have a question of my own," Nicole said. "What's the story with you and David? I might be overstepping a boundary here, but is he a blood relative or adopted? Why did you tell me at the market that you were an only child, and David was someone who worked for your family? Is he your brother or not?"

Femi shrugged his shoulders. "I honestly don't know Nicole. No one has told me the truth about David. I can't explain it to you because I don't understand it myself. You see our family is not the storybook fable you read about. We're flesh and blood; real people with problems, and secrets."

"But I don't understand Fem, how can you not know if he's your brother."

"The story, as I've been told it, is that my father found David asleep in one of the schoolhouses, he said he was hiding because his family had been killed by rebels. My grandparents took him in and eventually adopted him. I was very young at the time. I met him for the first time a few weeks ago when I arrived in Africa. The bottom line is I don't trust him. The question you just asked me, I've been asking myself, before I even arrived in Sierra Leone. Part of the reason I'm here missing football camp is so my father, David and I can get to know each other before I go off to college. My dad and I were really close until my grandfather became ill."

"Anderson Bettencourt?"

"Yes. I'd just started kindergarten. My dad started coming to Sierra Leone every spring. At first, my mom didn't go with him; but then my grandfather became ill and she left me as well. Not all summer like my dad, just for a month. The only good thing about that is my mom's mother, Grandma Elizabeth took care of me when my parents traveled." Femi smiled.

"I overheard you telling your Grandma Julia that your Grandma Elizabeth used to read you letters, the letters she and your grandfather wrote to you. She sounds like a very loving person."

"Yeah. She took care of me after my dad started traveling a lot and my mom was busy teaching. But I missed my dad. I started playing football and was really good at it. It was only Pee Wee league, but I loved the game. I wanted my dad to come watch me. My dad, mom and I used to be together all the time. We'd eat breakfast and dinner together every day."

Femi looked out over the plains at the giraffes. He thought about them sitting around the table. His dad telling jokes. His mom flipping her braids back and laughing at his father's corny stories.

"On Saturdays we went to the Woodruff Museum, the aquarium, some poetry lecture, or even horseback riding. We were always together." Femi sighed. "On Sundays we'd go to church together, where my mom taught my Sunday school class. Afterward, we went to Grandma Elizabeth's house, or people came to our house for a big family meal. My dad showed me how to play chess, swim before I was five; how to do a somersault, ride a bike, everything. Sometimes I just sat in his office while he made phone calls and spoke in other languages. I can speak French because of him. He started speaking both French and English to me from birth. Sometimes, I even think in French."

"Sounds wonderful. My childhood was nothing like that. What changed?"

"My grandfather died."

"You never got a chance to meet him?"

"No, I spoke to him on the phone every Sunday after he became ill and received letters and pictures from him. But I never met him in person. After he died, my dad changed. When I woke in the morning he would have already left for work. Then he no longer showed up for dinner. He started traveling to Africa more. I always played in his office with my trucks, or football, or just sat on the floor while he made calls. One day I went to his office, but it was locked. He never locked the door. Who the hell was he trying to keep out, me and my mom?"

"Did you ever go into his office after that incident?" Nicole asked.

Femi didn't answer immediately. He closed his eyes and leaned his head against the tree.

"I met my father when I was nine. At least you had your father for a while when you were little," Nicole said.

"Once," Femi said.

"What?"

"I went into his office once after that."

"And."

"He called me in to have a heart-to-heart with me. I had just made the newspaper for being recognized as an up-and-coming football player in junior high."

"You've been a superstar for some time, huh?"

"Girl, stop interrupting. To be a good wife you have to learn how to listen."

"Okay sorry. My mouth is closed," Nicole laughed.

Femi imagined kissing Nicole, drawing her into his arms, and feeling her skin against his skin. Nicole put her hand on his shoulder bringing him back to the present.

"That's when I saw David's picture on his desk. I'd heard his name before, but didn't know who my dad was talking about. I thought he was calling me in his office to tell me he was sorry he missed my football games and was proud of me. Instead he wanted to tell me that Bettencourts do not play football. While he talked, I looked around the office. I hadn't been in there for a while."

Femi opened his eyes and looked at Nicole.

"I saw the pictures of us on his desk. The ice in my chest started to melt. My dad did still love me. There was proof, the picture of my mom, him and me. Then I saw another picture. It was my dad, and this guy who looked like me, only older. I asked him who it was. At first he didn't answer. Then after a long time he said, 'your brother, David.'

Nicole placed her hand on top of Femi's.

Worrisome Times

GRANDMA BETTENCOURT MADE decisions for people all the time, and they followed them. They thought that after careful consideration and discussion with her, they had made their own decisions. The next day, when it was time for Nicole to return across the border to Liberia, it was no surprise to anyone that Femi drove with Nicole in her truck and Oyami and David followed them. Dr. Bettencourt said he wanted to visit the new malaria clinic in Liberia, only after Grandma Bettencourt suggested it would be a good time for him to see the clinic and to assure their guest returned to Liberia safely. Grandma Bettencourt let it be known she thought Nicole was a wonderful young lady, and did not want her to be ambushed by rebels lurking around the borders.

Nicole Jefferson reminded Julia of herself when she was young. Julia had come to Sierra Leone for a summer teacher's conference and ended up falling in love with one of the Bettencourt men, and made Sierra Leone her home. In her brief visit with Nicole she saw the hope and energy she once had. The way Nicole almost bounced when she walked, her bright smile and big eyes that looked almost black but with a golden sunburst in the center. She noticed when Nicole laughed, it was a full open mouth laugh, which came from her gut. She liked a woman who laughed from her soul.

Julia watched her grandson. Femi's smile stretched from ear to ear, and his face opened wide to this wonder of a young lady. She knew Nicole was an adult and her grandson was still a teenager. But in a few years he would be an adult, making his own decisions. He reminded her so much of his father, Oyami. After all she was seven years older than her husband. Why couldn't the woman be older than the man?

That day Oyami came home from Dr. Turner's office and told her he was going to be a medical doctor. She encouraged him, although she knew her husband would be against it.

"Oyami, in life you have to decide if you are going to live your life, or someone else's life. You might as well decide now. I love your father. He is a good man. The Bettencourts are good people. Their legacy goes back before slavery. You are a Bettencourt. If you decide to be a teacher, everyone will be happy, but will you be happy? You make sure whatever you decide to do, seek the face of God. If God says so, then let him fight your battles."

Sitting in her parlor she looked at the picture of her late husband on the wall, then at David's pictures. She knew her son made a promise to his dying father about David, which is why palaver existed between David and Femi before they even set eyes on each other. That first evening Femi walked into the parlor and met his grandmother for the first time she saw his face tighten with the pain he felt because he'd never met his grandfather; but from the family photos on the wall, David clearly had a relationship with him.

She knew it was important that first night for her to talk to the heart of her grandson. She told Oyami to go see the new addition on the elementary school while she spent time alone with Femi. They sat together on the brown suede sofa facing the bay window watching the giraffes. She told Femi that, although he'd never met his grandfather, his grandfather loved him and thought of him often.

"Your father and grandfather wasted years not speaking to each other because they both have that Bettencourt stubbornness; it is a sword that cuts both ways."

That night, Femi shared with Grandma Julia, that when his grandfather died, his father shut him out. The reason they came to Sierra Leone was an attempt for them to reconcile as a family.

"Grandma, I don't even know how to talk to dad any more. He might as well be a stranger to me. Maybe, if from the beginning we did not spend so much time, then I would not have known what it was like to have a father. Many times, I felt just like the other boys in the neighborhood whose parents were divorced, who only saw their fathers once or twice a month. My dad lived right in the house with me, but after grandpa died, he spent more time in Africa than at home. When he was at home, he spent all his time at work, or recruiting people to go to Africa, or raising money."

Julia rose from the sofa and picked up a leather-bound hatbox that sat beside the fireplace. She opened the box and pulled out a bundle of kente cloth. She sat down beside Femi and opened the fabric revealing a diary. She held the diary in both hands to her chest.

"This is one of your grandfather's personal diaries. He wrote in it every day in his final year. You were the only grandchild he never met. He so deeply regretted it. But he knew you in here," she said, pointing to Femi's heart.

She opened the book to read the inscription on the first page. A picture of Femi in his football uniform from when he played PAL football was glued to the front page. Femi looked at it and grinned. Julia read the inscription.

"Femi, I never met you, but I know you through the stories I heard about you from your grandmother and in my final days the conversations I had with your father, and telephone conversations with you. These Bible verses, stories, poems, and thoughts I wrote for you, are a guide on how to live a purposeful life. I hope in these pages you will get to know me. Even if I have passed on to Glory when you receive this, I am always with you, and I never forgot you. Love, Grandpa."

Julia wrapped the diary in the kente cloth and handed it to Femi. He didn't read it the first night, the second night, or even in the weeks to come. The first time he read it was the night Nicole came to the academy. After the house quieted and all lights were out, Femi knocked on Nicole's door and asked her to join him in the parlor for some bush tea. He told her that unlike the tea from Kenya, or England, this tea came from Sierra Leone. The legend said bush tea was made for conversation, because after one drank it, no lies could slip through your mouth. The tea tamed lying tongues.

Nicole pulled the robe that Grandma Julia had given her, tightly around her waist, and joined him in the parlor. Maybe she could take some of that tea back to Liberia and have all those involved in this coup attempt drink up and confess. He then showed her the diary, and asked her to open a page at random and read it to him.

"I think it should be your choice Fem. This is sacred."

"I know, that's why I want you to read it."

Nicole opened to the middle of the book and looked at the title, which was Love. Then she read the inscription below it out loud.

"1 Corinthians 13 1 Though I speak with the tongues of men and of angels, and have not love, I am become as sounding brass, or a tinkling cymbal.

2. And though I have the gift of prophecy, and understand all mysteries, and all knowledge; and though I have all faith, so that I could remove mountains, and have not love, I am nothing.

3 And though I bestow all my goods to feed the poor, and though I give my body to be burned, and have not love, it profiteth me nothing.

4 Love suffereth long, and is kind; love envieth not; love vaunteth not itself, is not puffed up,

5 Doth not behave itself unseemly, seeketh not her own, is not easily provoked, thinketh no evil;

6 Rejoiceth not in iniquity, but rejoiceth in the truth;

7 Beareth all things, believeth all things, hopeth all things, endureth all things.

8 Love never faileth: but whether there be prophecies, they shall fail; whether there be tongues, they shall cease; whether there be knowledge, it shall vanish away.

9 For we know in part, and we prophesy in part.

10 But when that which is perfect is come, then that which is in part shall be done away.

11 When I was a child, I spake as a child, I understood as a child, I thought as a child: but when I became a man, I put away childish things.

12 For now we see through a glass, darkly; but then face to face: now I know in part; but then shall I know even as also I am known.

13 And now abideth faith, hope, love, these three; but the greatest of these is love." 1 Corinthians 13

Femi,

This verse is one of my favorites in the Bible. Not that I have always lived by it. A man has three loves in his life. His love of God, his love for his woman and his family, and his love for his purpose, which some equate as his career. At your age, I dreamed of being a great soccer player. I could kick a soccer ball up to Heaven. I never told anyone that dream but your grandmother, and I told her only a few months ago when I lay in my hospital bed reliving my life. When I examine my life I have few regrets, but the few loom in my mind. The blessings in my life overwhelm me. I married a woman who loved me despite my stubbornness and hard heart, and whom I love with every cell in my body. Until this day, even as I lay in my hospital bed, when I think of your grandmother, the birds chirp louder, the sun shines brighter, and my soup tastes like a T-bone steak.

As the old folks here would say, a ruin of nations begins in one's home. The opposite also applies. The foundation of a nation begins at home. Your grandmother took care of me and our home. She left her country where she did not need a generator to have electricity, where all the latest conveniences were at her fingertips. Your grandmother showed me how to love despite differences. But, I do have regrets. My biggest regret is I did not love your father unconditionally. I was caught up in a dream of our ancestors to build schools to educate people to not go out in the world to obtain material things, but to be in service to others. Your father's calling is to do what he is doing, but I in my concern about the Bettencourt name, and dishonoring our history, I did not seek God's face, but tried to make your father fit into the Bettencourt mold. I lost years with him, your mother and with you. I want you to do what you are called to do in this life. I understand you love American football, and you are good at it, and that your love of football has become a wedge between you and your father. In whatever you decide in your life, seek God's face first and go forth in love.

Love, Grandpa

Nicole closed the diary and gave it to Femi. He wrapped it back in the kente cloth. In the morning, Grandma Julia found them still in the parlor. They had watched the sunrise, and fell asleep with their heads touching. She took two big blankets and covered them. When she returned to the parlor a few hours later she carried a break-fast tray of kiwi and mango, grits and shrimp, and scrambled eggs.

As the time neared for Nicole to leave, she felt like she had lived a lifetime at Bettencourt Academy, instead of a few days. Grandma Julia gave her a box wrapped in mud cloth, but made Nicole promise not to open it until she arrived back in Monrovia.

Nicole and Femi pulled out of the gates of Bettencourt Academy to start the trek back to Liberia, with David and Dr. Bettencourt leading the way in David's new jeep. Although it was not quite 6 AM, students were milling around outside. Some in groups going on a morning jog, some walking to the cafeteria for an early breakfast, some heading to class early. The two vehicles moved on to the blacktop. Men walking to their farms moved to the edge of the road and waved as they passed by. The women walked in groups to the smaller daily market with their yams, cassava and other produce on their heads.

Nicole drove closely behind David. She smiled over at Femi, but her mind turned to Jennifer. She wondered what had delayed her. The last time she met with her at a cook shop in Monrovia, she left looking more nervous and scared than she had that first day in the embassy bathroom. She asked Nicole to meet her at the market in Sierra Leone again.

Nicole asked why they had to travel that far. Jennifer told her it was a good cover, the market was huge, and many people traveled over the border to go to market. But the main reason was there was someone in Sierra Leone Jennifer trusted who could make a copy of the tape and smuggle it into America to her father.

Jennifer also said the market was close to her teaching post, which was right over the border. Nicole had never been to Jennifer's home, but she knew the lo-cation of the school where Jennifer taught. She didn't want to get Femi involved; she almost told him the entire story at the foot of the acacia trees while they watched the giraffes.

But she didn't want to endanger Femi. The tape recorder still felt like a heavy weight on her hip. She thought again of confiding in Dubose, Souleymane, Rebecca, or Vera Whittaker, but it all seemed too risky. She was going to have to figure this out on her own.

All of a sudden, a truck came up behind Nicole and slammed into her bumper. She skidded off to the side of the road and then back on to the blacktop, dust swirled up around them. The truck hit their bumper again. The driver shouted for Nicole to pull over. Femi leaned out and looked at the passengers in the other vehicle. Nicole's hands had a death grip on the steering wheel. She turned the wheel to drive off the blacktop.

"Nicole, listen to me. Don't stop." Femi said. "That man in the truck is the same man who stole your backpack. Speed up."

Nicole didn't ask any questions. She stomped on the gas pedal. Her truck had a V8 engine that could outrun the other vehicle. Dust rose around them as she gave the engine more gas and pulled away from the other car. She swerved just in time to avoid hitting David and Dr. Bettencourt who were now right next them. Femi rolled his window down and waved to David to pull over. Nicole followed David off the road. David jumped down and ran to Nicole's window with an angry furrowed brow.

"What is going on? You almost hit us!" he yelled. Before David could finish, Dr. Bettencourt had reached the driver's side and pulled him away from the window.

"Back off David. Get back in the truck," Dr. Bettencourt said.

"Femi, you should ride with David, I will ride with Ms. Jefferson. We have had enough excitement for the day," Femi's father said.

Back on the road Oyami did not say anything for a while.

"Ms. Jefferson."

"Please call me Nicole."

"Nicole."

"What happened back there?"

"Some men tried to run me off the road. I thought at first they wanted..."

Oyami pursed his lips, and turned to Nicole.

"My son is quite taken with you. I can see in my mother's actions that she is also quite taken with you."

"How do you feel about me Dr. Bettencourt?"

"I don't want my family hurt."

"You think I want to hurt your family?"

Nicole knew Dr. Bettencourt was right. It was evident that trouble was following her and Femi might be in harm's way if he continued to spend time with her.

"It's not a coincidence that someone stole your backpack and now someone is trying to run you off the road. If they wanted to hurt you they would have done so already. Either they want to scare you, or want something from you. It has to be someone with money, power or both. You may be an African American, but you are still an American. People around here do not mess with Americans."

Nicole glanced over at Oyami. She gripped the steering wheel to stop her hands from trembling. She focused on the road, and tried to steady her hands. Part of the Bettencourt legacy sat next to her. They did so much for others. Nicole did not want anyone in his family to get hurt, least of all Femi. He may seem like an old soul, but he still was only seventeen. He had his entire adult life in front of him. In their brief time together, he had rescued her twice. Dr. Bettencourt was right. Someone did want something from her, and she didn't want to involve this family who had given so much to Sierra Leone, to Africa, actually to the world, in what looked to be a major conspiracy. It was now clear to her that someone besides Jennifer knew she had the tape.

"Dr. Bettencourt, what would you do if you had information about someone involved in something illegal, something horrific, but you didn't know if that information was true, and you did not know who to trust? And, if that the information got into the wrong hands the consequences can't even be imagined."

"I would find out if the information was true and then turn it over to the proper authorities."

"How do I, I mean how would you find out who the proper authorities are, especially after the attempted coup and with so much unrest going on politically?" She was suspicious of everyone including the authorities. And what if there was a lot at stake-money, access to information and secrets, and political power.

"You will know. It would have to be someone you trust. We do have an inner guide or conscience. If you listen to it, you will learn much. The elders call it discernment. Discern by watching, listening and turning inward. People always show you who they really are, we just don't pay attention, or we deny what we know and what we see. Pay attention to the true voice."

They sat in silence for several miles.

"Dr. Bettencourt, I need to stop to see someone in a village on the way to Monrovia. Please do not ask me any questions. Let's just say I am taking your advice and using discernment. She gave me something that has put me and everyone around me in danger," Nicole said.

Twenty minutes later Nicole drove off the blacktop and onto a dirt road that led to Jennifer's village. Not many vehicles drove into this village and to have two arrive at the same time, caused a stir. Children ran to the trucks shouting hello. The village mothers were not far behind them. Nicole and Oyami slid down from the truck but David and Femi stayed in their truck with the windows rolled up. They seemed to be having a heated discussion. Femi finally emerged from the truck slamming the door.

The chief sent one of his wives to bring the visitors to his home. Nicole excused herself to use the only indoor toilet in the village, Femi stayed back with her. When David and Oyami made their way to the chief's compound, Nicole noticed the schoolhouse and instead went to the schoolhouse where Jennifer taught, to the headmaster's office. This was no Bettencourt Academy, just a two-room schoolhouse, with an office off to the side. Femi didn't ask Nicole any questions. He walked with her in silence.

The headmaster was a thin man in his fifties with smooth wavy gray hair. He welcomed them into his office and did not seem at all surprised to see them. He greeted them with the traditional Liberian handshake.

"Welcome, I am headmaster Adu. We were starting to worry. In fact, just this morning we decided if we did not hear something soon I, myself, would travel to Monrovia to see what happened to Ms. Giles."

Nicole and Femi looked at each other, not understanding what he meant.

"You are here concerning Ms. Giles, our Peace Corps teacher, no?" The headmaster said, seeing their confused looks.

"Yes, we're here about Jennifer. I mean Ms. Giles. May we see her?"

"She is not here. That is why I thought you all came. She left over a week ago. Actually, she went missing. One morning she just did not show up. This is not like her. Not like her at all. The entire time she has been here, she never missed a day of school. She took her vacations during school breaks. I thought she had an emergency or something. We sent a note by one of our students traveling to Monrovia this past Monday, but we have not heard anything yet. Now that you all have shown up officially, quite frankly I am worried."

He thinks we were sent here by Peace Corps Nicole thought. I have to act calm, normal. This is what Jennifer was talking about. If she went missing. Now I have to get the tape to someone.

"Mrs.... what did you say your name was?"

"I didn't, but it's Ms. Jefferson, and this is Mr. Bettencourt. But we're not here in any official capacity. Ms. Giles is a friend of mine. I just dropped by to see her."

The headmaster looked at Femi.

"I am sorry. I do not mean to stare. But you say you are a Bettencourt, but you look like one of the men from across the border in Sierra Leone who frequently visited Ms. Giles. Not that I am nosy, but this is a small village, and not much goes on here that is kept secret." Femi had not spoken, so the headmaster had not heard his American accent.

"No sir, I have never been here before, in this village, or even to Africa. This is my first visit. My father is Dr. Oyami Bettencourt. He is a medical doctor who lives in the United States."

"Of course. I can hear your accent now. We all know your father. Besides, the man who came here was older than you. I thought he may know what happened to Ms. Giles.

"The man who looks like Femi, do you know his name?" Nicole asked.

"No, sorry. I only saw him a couple times, and I was never introduced to him," the headmaster said.

"She may have had an emergency. We were driving through and I remembered this is the village where she taught. I am a new Peace Corps Volunteer. I have only been in country for about a month."

"You came in right around the coup attempt."

"The very day."

"Worrisome times. Worrisome times," the headmaster said, shaking his head.

"Thank you Mr. Adu, we won't take up any more of your time."

"It has been a pleasure to make your acquaintance. Please send word back to me about Ms. Giles."

"We're on our way to Monrovia, when we get there, I will go to the Peace Corps Office to let them know that she hasn't been at her post. They probably know where she is. Someone will contact you. Could you point us to her home? I want to go by and leave a note on her door."

"Better than that, I will have one of the students take you."

The headmaster went into the hallway and came back a few seconds later with a student.

"This is Sissy. She will take you to Ms. Giles' home."

Nicole and Femi thanked him, then followed the student through the village to the outskirts where a dome style house sat in a small compound. A little girl greeted them at the door in her language.

"English. These people are friends of Ms. Giles. Is she here?" Sissy asked the little girl.

The little girl nodded.

"She is here?" Nicole asked surprised.

"No, ma'am. She is not here. I mean I speak English. My name is Ana, and I am Ms. Giles' house girl."

"Where did she go," Nicole said.

"I don't know. I live with Ms. Giles on school days. When school is not in I go home to help my mom. She has been gone about a week. My mom still sends me each day. Ms. Giles needs me to cook and wash her clothes, and she pays my school fees. My mom said she hopes she comes back soon because the school fees are due," Ana said.

"Can we go in?" Nicole asked.

"I will go ask the chief," Ana said.

"Headmaster Adu sent them, are you questioning his authority?" Sissy asked.

Sissy walked past Ana inside, then stood back allowing Nicole and Femi to walk in. The circular room had a rolled-up mat against the far wall, which Nicole assumed was Jennifer's bed. The only furniture in the place was a table with four chairs, a bookcase, and another smaller table with a hot plate on it. To the right of the table, sat a small refrigerator run by propane. The cabinets attached to the walls did not have doors. Boxes of Captain Crunch, Kraft Macaroni and Cheese, and Star-Kist tuna fish lined the shelves.

"Femi, American food, was sent to her, or bought at a high price here in Liberia," Nicole said.

Books spilled out of the case on to the floor. Nicole looked around the room, trying to find a clue as to what happened to Jennifer, or where she might have gone. Femi watched Nicole.

"Are you going to tell me what's going on?" he asked.

"You're much like your father."

"Answer the question, please."

"Not right now, but I will. Can you take Ana and Sissy outside and make conversation with them? Distract them for a minute."

"Are you trying to distract them, or get rid of me?" Femi asked.

"Both... please," Nicole said.

When Femi left, Nicole searched Jennifer's room. She could tell someone had already gone through her things. The books hadn't fallen out of the bookcase by themselves. Jennifer, although, kind of a throwback from the hippy days, appeared to be a neat freak. The few times they dined together she always lined up her flatware when sitting at a table, and she was always sanitizing her hands with wipes. It was clear that her place had been rifled through.

Nicole tried to think where she would hide something if she did not want anyone else to find it. It would be somewhere obvious. She opened a can of coffee and dug down into the can; nothing. The refrigerator was completely empty. On the shelves she saw a box of Wheaties with a picture of the NY Yankees-a collector's edition. Thinking back to the T-shirt with the Yankees and the restaurant they ate in with the Yankees' theme, she opened the box and found a cassette tape. Was it a copy of the one she had, or another one? She heard the tires of the truck screech outside the compound. She pulled out her money belt and slid the new cassette in.

"Hey Dad, we're ready." Nicole heard Femi yell.

Back on the road to Monrovia, Femi once again joined Nicole in her truck.

"Well," said Femi.

"Soon. I will tell you all that I know, soon. Right now we need to get to Peace Corps headquarters to let them know Jennifer has disappeared."

When they reached Monrovia. Femi and Nicole went straight to the Peace Corps office, while David and Oyami went to the hospital to meet with a doctor friend of Oyami's.

Vera Whittaker

THE LAST PERSON anyone would suspect as being an agent for the CIA was Vera Whittaker. How could she be? Everyone knew CIA agents looked like Harrison Ford, or Michael Douglas, or at least like Gene Hackman, back in the day. Of course, secret agents were Caucasian men who never smiled, wore serious wrist-watches and cool dark Ray-Bans.

Vera Whittaker, an African-American woman in her late forties, worked as the Executive Assistant to Thomas Watkins, the US Ambassador to Liberia. He handpicked her himself, or so he liked to tell people. Truth be told she picked him for his assignment.

Every American who entered Liberia legally had to have a passport. Because of this, Vera had a file on all of them. As for those who entered illegally, she kept tabs on them as well.

The CIA recruited Vera right out of her Yale Master's program on African History. She dreamed about teaching and knew the most obscure things about Africa. She knew that four of the five fastest land animals lived in Africa, the cheetah, the wildebeest, the lion and the gazelle. And that more people in Africa are killed by crocodiles, than by lions.

Born in Youngstown, Ohio, Vera looked like a spinster, middle-age, librarian. She wore her hair in a neat French roll. And the only makeup she wore was red lipstick and matching rouge on her cheeks. But she always carried a fully-loaded makeup kit with mascara, eye shadow, lipstick and powder. She often shared her stash with other women as a way of bonding, and getting information.

Many of the women she worked with in the embassy laughed at the dumpy gray suits Vera wore with her white shirts and sensible black pumps. She stood not quite five feet, even in the pumps. But when she pulled out an unopened tube of Shiseido waterproof mascara, or Origins lip balm and offered it up to a woman, with raccoon eyes from using cheap mascara, or dry lips from inferior lip balm, she became their confidante. Not many people could afford or obtain expensive makeup in Liberia, even if you worked for the American Embassy. And even then if you could afford it, you, had to wait for weeks for someone to ship it to you. Vera always had a supply to exchange for information. She thought it was amazing the types of sensitive information women would give up to look beautiful.

In school, Vera always made the honor roll, and won The National Spelling Bee contest four years in a row. No one was surprised when she was granted a full scholarship to Yale, after getting a perfect 1600 score on her SATs.

But Vera had a secret. She didn't think she was smart at all. She had a photographic memory. What she saw, she remembered. Everything. At least, she couldn't remember ever forgetting anything. She aced all her tests, because she remembered everything the professor said in class, every book she read, and everything written on the board.

The CIA showed up on campus in the fall of her second year of graduate school. She took the written test for fun. She thought it might be an adventure to be an agent in Africa. They contacted her exactly 48 hours after she took the test and offered her a position after graduation. Vera jumped at the opportunity. She trained in McLean, Virginia at CIA headquarters, or what the agents called Langley, after the name of the neighborhood the complex was in.

When it came time for her assignment after training, Vera's superiors knew her placement would be in Africa. They also knew, with her vast knowledge, she would be a key player with the National Clandestine Service (NCS). The NCS was the division of the CIA that recruited people from all walks of life, different ethnicities, educational backgrounds, and religions to have a network of trained people to collect human intelligence that informed them of possible threats to US security.

At least that's what the brochure they gave to Vera said. Looking at Vera, no one would have thought she was a CIA agent, and certainly not the Chief of Station. But that is exactly what she was. Dumpy, spinster, nondescript Vera

Whittaker was the head CIA officer in Liberia, who worked undercover as the ambassador's assistant.

She was the HNIC, the Head Negro in Charge. She oversaw the collection, analysis and dissemination of information back to her superiors in Washington. She sought out intelligence on foreign terrorist groups and individuals to share information with US friendly governments. She reported directly to Ronald Cheney, the Director of African Affairs of the CIA.

Vera Whittaker, an American spy-now everyone back home in Youngstown, Ohio would get a laugh out of that one. Not only was she a spy, but she was the head spy in the West African region who recruited both domestic and foreign agents, or as they were known in house as, operation officers, or operatives.

That is why it was not a surprise to her that on April 1, 1980 right before dawn, a group of disgruntled Liberian soldiers from the Army, coupled with rebels from across the border in Sierra Leone with guns from American and German mercenaries tried to kill William Tanner, the long-standing President of Liberia.

Therefore, she acted without consent from her superiors in Washington to crush the coup. It is the reason she had to reveal her identity to EXO Dubose to get his help to stop the coup attempt. She was now wondering if Nicole Jefferson would make a good operative?

Vera unlocked her bottom cabinet drawer and pulled out the files on the new volunteers. Without opening the file, she remembered every word in it. Nicole Jefferson, African American. Graduate of Temple University with honors at the age of nineteen. IQ of 150-Categorized: Genius. Graduate School Cal State Long Beach. Accepted in the Harvard PhD Program for Africana Studies. Deferred until after the Peace Corps. Political affiliations: voted Democrat. She worked after college in Long Beach with reformed gangbangers. In undergraduate, at Temple, she worked full time and went to school full time. No known ties to groups. Knowledge of Africa: Superior. Mother and father divorced when mother was pregnant with Nicole. Her parents remarried later. Two older sisters and twin brothers, in the NFL: one as a coach and one as a player.

By all accounts, the brothers were squeaky clean, but the sisters were another matter. Family history may be useful. Oldest sister involved in some criminal behavior, cleared. The middle sister ran with a fast crowd, drugs, parties, but she seemed to just enjoy the ride, not get caught up in any crime. The intelligence investigator marked Nicole with a big red question mark. She *was* a big question mark. Maybe Vera needed to read the file again. She'd never missed anything before.

Vera flipped the file open. Looked at the Peace Corps ID and the copy of Nicole's passport picture. She saw it. Why didn't she think of it before? Of course intelligence would mark her as a big question mark. Her hair. Her untamed hair. Even more untamed in her picture than in person. Negro women who did not tame their hair, scared the establishment. Braids, twists, bantu knots, big Afros, and God forbid dreadlocks, all made them ask questions.

"Why can't they just wear their hair straight like Thelma on "Good Times", or cut it short like her mother, Florida? At least it was neat."

That was the question the higher-ups wanted to know when they interviewed Black women with so-called wild hair. Vera wanted to answer them back on behalf of those women and tell them "Thelma and Florida were characters on a defunct TV program. We are real people with real blood running through our veins. And that many of our hairstyles are tied to our culture."

It was okay for the young Caucasian ladies to come into the country and wear braids. When they returned to America and their corporate jobs, or teaching positions or got married, their hair would be tame again. But Black women with untamed hair sent a message—I do not buy into your idea of beauty. I will define myself. You don't own me or define me; therefore I will not conform to your standard of beauty. Vera knew how to conform, but also how to rebel in subtle ways.

Vera studied Nicole's picture. She could tell the brown twists with red and blonde highlights did not come out of a bottle. From her bio she knew Nicole's maternal grandmother was part Native American and Irish. She noticed Nicole's dark colored eyes with what appeared to be sunbursts in the middle. She had only met one other woman with those eyes, Esi, the first woman Paramount Chief in Liberia. Of course they would proceed with caution. This one, they could not figure out. Vera pulled the hairpins out of her bun, shook her head and let her hair fall down past her shoulders. She liked this young lady. She had watched her at the Embassy after the coup, when many of the other volunteers, including the ones who had been in Liberia for years, sat in the evacuation room with furrowed brows, or hardly breathing. Some had panic attacks. Most opted to go home on the first flight out. Not Nicole. She sat quietly. She seemed to be saying a prayer with her eyes. When the planes arrived to take those who wanted to leave back to American shores Nicole hugged her friends goodbye and told them she would keep in touch.

Vera also saw Nicole when she left the ladies room at the embassy, with her sunflower eyes shining brightly, fiercely. Jennifer Giles had walked out fifteen minutes before her. Courtney Brimmer, the woman who wore those tight blue suits with matching blue shoes, had stormed out of the bathroom a few minutes before Jennifer. No cameras were allowed in the bathroom. And for whatever reason the audio had malfunctioned that day. The surveillance technician told her that they often disconnected the audio because the constant flushing of toilets disturbed the security personnel. She would make sure to send a memo to have the manager of the security personnel replaced immediately.

Her intelligence sources informed her that they may be able to move in on Ms. Brimmer. Then she would really have the blues. Care had to be taken, she was protected by diplomatic immunity since she was the Information and Assistance Officer for USAID. Now Nicole, with her untamed hair, and bright eyes had entered the picture. Was she mixed up with these people? Dubose didn't think so. They talked about her and he vouched for her, but he'd just met her. How well could he know her? Ms. Jefferson had the X factor. The thing that made people trust her almost immediately. Vera considered it a gift much like her own photographic memory. Her superiors in the CIA wanted to exploit Nicole's gift. They wanted Vera to recruit her for that ability.

She shut the folder, slid it back in her cabinet drawer and locked it. She had fifteen minutes before her meeting with Dubose and General Guindo. She picked up the hairpins, and twisted her hair back into the French roll.

Five minutes later, the three of them sat at her conference table. She studied Guindo's face. He was definitely a man of consequence. At twenty-five, he was the closest man to President Tanner. Educated at The Citadel in United States with a master's degree. He understood the political tensions between

America and Liberia, between traditional people and the Americo-Liberians, between Western and traditional African ways. Now he was the youngest ranking Minister of Defense in any country.

The position was a new one for Souleymane. When the former Commander of Liberian Armed Forces was killed in a suspicious auto accident, President Tanner appointed Souleymane to the position. Guindo was the only child of a cow herder, and farmer. His mother, Blessie Guindo, came from the Kpelle tribe and his father, Gabbe Guindo, the Mano. Gabbe dreamed big dreams for his family. Blessie died during childbirth when Souleymane was still in short pants.

Souleymane's father lived a traditional life of a farmer, but did not want to take more than one wife. Trent Dubose arrived in their village the day Souleymane's mother had yet another one of her miscarriages. Dubose, then a soldier, protected the area. In traditional Africa when a stranger came into a village, they first met with the Paramount Chief. To Dubose's surprise, the chief was a woman, but this day she did not have time for formalities because one of her villager's babies decided to arrive early.

The women gathered at the midwives' hut to pray and sing the baby into the world. The men waited back at Guindo's compound for the news. When the midwife sent for the chief, she arrived with Dubose. Together they received the sad news that the mother made it, but the baby had not.

"Mr. Dubose. You must be an important man for your country to send you here to represent them, and a smart man," Chief Esi said. "You know when a man loses his child he needs another man to tell him. I think of myself as a wise woman, not because of anything inside of me, but because of the masters I studied under and those I studied from books. There have been great women leaders in Africa, Yaa Asantewa, from Ghana, Queen Nzinga, and many more. My father, one of those masters, was one of the best. He always advised there are times even as a woman in power, you have to let men handle other men. I need your help."

Esi then took his hands into her own. A few minutes later Dubose stood outside the Guindo compound. When he entered, the look on Dubose's face told Gabbe everything he needed to know. They would have three more of these conversations over the years. Their last conversation was the hardest. Dubose had to tell his friend that neither his daughter nor his wife survived the birth. In those years, Dubose and the Guindos became family, and Souleymane became like a son to Dubose. Vera knew about their relationship, and although the two men were not father and son, they resembled each other in mannerisms.

Souleymane was six feet four with muscles that strained against his fatigues. He had his mother's dark espresso skin color, with eyes so dark that it seemed they didn't have irises. Souleymane carried himself like he'd grown up in a castle, and not on a cow farm.

EXO Dubose seemed more African than American. He loved all things African. He once told Vera that when he was a little boy he had dreams of running in open fields among elephants, and lions. He felt that military service in Africa was his destiny. One of the reasons he served in the military, and specifically in Africa, was because he didn't think of his tour there as merely an assignment. He felt a higher power called him to duty. Although not a churchgoing man, he believed in the God his mother introduced him to as a child. He first tried an assignment stateside. While on assignment, he married for a while and fathered a little girl. She would be around the same age as Nicole Jefferson.

"Gentlemen, we all know the problem," Vera Whittaker said. "We must protect President Tanner. This coup attempt should never have happened. We must catch all the rebels. But we also need to discuss having open fair elections. The time is past due."

"Some of the soldiers say that this attempt came from outside of Liberia," Souleymane said. "They believe that, in some way, not only are Sierra Leoneans involved, but Americans too."

"I know the world likes to blame America for everything, and we deserve our share of blame," Dubose said. "So do many other countries. It could be the indigenous people wanted more than someone telling them their someday will come. Much like the Civil Rights Movement of the sixties, there comes a time for change."

"Dubose, if I didn't know you as well as I do, and understand your love for this continent, I would think you are defending the coup attempt," said Vera.

Dubose looked at Vera. A smile broke out on his face, almost involuntarily. They stared at each other in silence for a few minutes, two veteran American expats who loved both continents of their ancestry—Africa and America. Vera knew that no matter how much she loved Africa, she was an American first. She hoped that Dubose had not crossed that line. She prayed that when it was all said and done she would not have to order his arrest. She had surprised him several weeks ago by revealing her position as the head of the CIA in the country, and now maybe he was going to surprise her.

A rapid knock at the door interrupted their discussion. Vera had given her secretary strict orders not to disturb them.

"Excuse me," Vera said, as she walked to the office door and opened it. Her secretary whispered something to her. Vera nodded, then turned to find Dubose leaning forward in his chair.

"Gentlemen, if you'll excuse me for a few minutes. I need to take care of something."

"Did I hear Nicole Jefferson's name. If this concerns her I'd like to sit in on that conversation,"

"Me too," Souleymane said standing up.

Vera took a deep breath, then nodded.

"Come with me gentlemen."

In a conference room on the first floor of the embassy, Vera, Souleymane, and Trent entered the conference room to meet Nicole and Femi. Nicole's eyes widened when they walked in. She stood up to greet them. Femi stood up as well. Nicole felt like the room was closing in on her. She felt faint. Before she could move, Dubose greeted her in the traditional West African way, hugging her lightly and then kissing each cheek. Nicole held out her hand to Souleymane and shook hands with him. His hand lingered in hers. She ended the handshake with the traditional finger snap.

"This is Vera Whittaker, the assistant to Ambassador Watkins." Dubose turned to Femi. "I'm Executive Officer Trent Dubose. You look very familiar."

"I'm Femi Bettencourt," Femi said, as he shook Vera's hand.

Dubose and the general exchanged a look that Nicole caught, but could not decipher.

Femi shook hands with Dubose, and then shook hands with the general.

"You must be one of the Bettencourts from Sierra Leone." Vera said.

"I am a Bettencourt, but I live in the US," Femi said.

"I am honored to meet you," Vera smiled. "I know your grandmother Julia. Your family has done so much for this continent." She turned to Nicole. "But I'm sure that's not what you came here to discuss."

"I'm looking for Director Brandt, but the receptionist ushered us in here," Nicole said.

"What do you want to see Brandt about?" Dubose asked.

"I came to see her about another volunteer. If she's busy I can wait, or see her later."

"The director is in Tonga for a meeting," Vera said. "Your PO Mr. Hawk isn't available; that's why they sent you here. I happened to run into these gentlemen." Vera gestured to Dubose and Guindo. "The EXO said he knew you, and wanted to say hello, so I invited them along."

Nicole looked at Femi then back at Vera. She could see that Femi wasn't buying her story either, but they had to find out what happened to Jennifer.

"I just came from up country near the border conducting research for work at the Bettencourt Academy. Since Jennifer Giles taught in the area I stopped at her school to see her. The headmaster thought the Peace Corps had sent me because she hasn't been to work in a week. I asked him why he didn't report it sooner. He said he sent someone to town a few days ago, but he hadn't heard back from him. But he didn't think it unusual because the student planned to visit family along the way."

Nicole paused to look at Vera and Dubose who exchanged glances. She also noticed Souleymane looking over at her and then Femi.

"How do the two of you happen to be traveling together?" Souleymane asked.

Before they could answer Vera said, "Everyone knows the Bettencourts. They are interwoven into the history of Africa, much like the kente cloth with its blue, purple and yellow strands of silk."

"If I may interrupt," Dubose said. "I believe the more urgent matter is finding Jennifer Giles."

"There is probably nothing to worry about," Vera said. "Ms. Giles probably took some time off without telling anyone."

"Is it customary for volunteers to take off from their assignment and not tell anyone?" Souleymane asked.

"Of course not," Vera said. "It is absolutely against Peace Corps policy, but this would not be the first-time Ms. Giles has done something like this."

Nicole remembered the headmaster saying that Jennifer never missed a day. Either he was lying or Vera Whittaker was lying. There was no reason for the headmaster to be dishonest, but Vera Whittaker might have her own reasons for not telling the truth.

Vera stood up and walked to the door. "I'll look into it. Thank you for coming."

"Hold on for one moment Ms. Whittaker," Dubose said.

Vera took her hand off the doorknob and turned back to look at Dubose.

"Nicole, when did you last see Jennifer?" Dubose asked.

"Two weeks ago. I ran into her in Monrovia. We ate at a cook shop."

"Anything unusual?" Dubose asked.

"Not that I could tell, but I don't know her that well." Nicole said, trying not to give too much away.

Dubose stood up and walked to the door, stopping next to Vera. "Thanks," he said to Nicole and opened the door for them to leave.

Back in the truck Femi grilled Nicole again.

"Nicole, I'll ask you again. What's going on?" Femi asked after their truck cleared the embassy gate.

"I'm going to tell you, but not right now. I need time to think."

"I've lived with secrets my whole life. I don't want secrets between us. Whatever it is I can handle it. I can help."

They drove the rest of the trip back to the clinic in silence. Nicole turned the day's events over in her mind. Someone knew she had the tape. Now Jennifer was nowhere to be found. She had to get the tapes out of Liberia and to Jennifer's father. By the time they reached the clinic she knew what she had to do. She hoped Dr. Bettencourt would help her. She pulled up to the clinic to drop Femi off.

"I can't leave things like this between us," he said.

"Fem, it's okay. I'll let you know. I'm still trying to figure it out myself."

"I can help."

"I want to come in with you to talk to your father about these headaches I've been having since I passed out at the market," Nicole lied.

"I thought you said you were fine. You're having headaches?"

"Not all the time."

They found Dr. Bettencourt and David leaving the Medical Director's office.

"Dr. Bettencourt, may I speak to you in private?" Nicole said.

David looked at Nicole.

"I only have a few minutes. We need to get back on the road and over the border."

"It won't take long. I've been having headaches and I've been fainting and feeling dizzy."

"You two go along to the truck," Oyami said.

When Femi and David were out of range, Nicole said, "I need to ask you a favor."

"I am sure you know, since you have studied my family's history that we do not get involved in politics. Does this have anything to do with Miss Giles' disappearance?"

"There's no one else I can trust. Did the village chief tell you she went missing?"

"Of course. He knows everything that goes on in his village. Does Ms. Giles have something to do with the situation you told me about earlier?"

"I have a tape I need to get to her father."

"Senator Giles."

Nicole nodded. She couldn't believe she was asking him to do this, but she didn't know who else she could ask. He frequently traveled from Africa to the US. No one would expect a modern-day Bettencourt of becoming involved in anything political.

"I will not put my family in jeopardy, or risk what we have worked so hard for with the clinics. Too many people need medical help. No. I am sorry. I cannot get involved. Please do not involve my son. He is smitten with you, as you well know."

"Dr. Bettencourt, with all due respect, the legacy of your family began with your ancestors' protests over slavery. I don't have to tell you your family history.

But it isn't true that your family doesn't get involved. That's how Bettencourt Academy started."

"I am sorry," he said, shaking his head. He then turned away from Nicole and walked toward the truck where Femi and David waited. She called out, but not loud enough for David or Femi to hear. It was wrong. She knew it was wrong. But she could not let Ms. Blue Pumps or the others involved get away.

"Then I'll ask Femi."

Dr. Bettencourt stopped, turned around, and walked back to Nicole. He spoke softly, his voice trembling.

"You would use my son like that?"

"This isn't about me. It's bigger than both of us. I didn't ask for any of this, but it's now my responsibility. I am asking you to do what is right. To get the information out of the country to Senator Giles. I have no other option."

I will help you, Ms. Jefferson, but there is price."

"Name it."

"Promise you will leave my son alone. Don't break his heart, but let him know he is too young for you."

Nicole felt a real headache coming on. Her temples pounded. She took a deep breath to steady herself. She then pulled the original tape out of her purse and shook hands with Dr. Bettencourt, slipping it into the palm of his hand.

President Tanner

FOR PRESIDENT TANNER, the day started as most days start for him in the capital city of Monrovia. He ate a breakfast of scrambled eggs sautéed white onions, along with rice, whole wheat toast, and ham. The cook prepared the food. Ever since the coup attempt, he did not trust anyone. He used a food taster. The cook would bring the food, then President Tanner would have the cook's husband taste the food before he ate it to make sure it was not poisoned. Souleymane told the President he had better hope the cook loved her husband.

One particular morning, the cook explained to the President that her husband had taken ill. He wouldn't be able to taste the food today. He fired her on the spot, but did not allow her to leave the palace. He sent troops to the woman's house to bring her husband to him, but the guards returned without him.

"Mommy, we went to your home to bring your sick husband but he was not there. Why would a sick man not be home? Please explain," the guard questioned her.

"I beg you. I do not know anything," she pleaded.

"Throw her in jail," the president ordered.

The cook's arrest was only one of the many random interrogations, and imprisonments by the president's authorities. A few weeks later, Tanner's security detail imprisoned two professors from the University of Liberia for teaching a course on democracy and free speech. A few days later, Serita Conrad, a reporter, with the *New Liberian Newspaper* disappeared on her way to work. The day before she had written a column with the headline: "Was a Coup Inevitable?"

Vera suggested to Ambassador Watkins that he call an immediate meeting with President Tanner to address these human rights violations. Her concern was when the American press finally got wind of the illegal detainments, of people for speaking out in a country that claimed to invite free speech and democracy, they would exploit the situation, and within a matter of weeks, undo all the goodwill Ambassador Watkins and others took years to build.

The meeting took place in the Presidential Palace. The Liberian Palace resembled the American white house, but smaller. The President's office in Liberia was also oval. Although he had a conference table with comfortable chairs, President Tanner preferred to conduct this meeting at this desk. He knew the Americans called for the meeting, but they also needed to understand that he ran this country, not them. He intended to listen to their concerns, but there had been a coup attempt, people wanted him dead and they still did not have all of the culprits arrested. The Americans told him they would have everything wrapped up in a few weeks, but months had passed. He intended to take matters into his own hands.

They arrived on time, as usual. President Tanner thought Americans loved to show off by being on time. He knew for this meeting he would be on time. He was usually so involved with other matters that he often lost track of time, and ended up arriving late to events, but never with the Americans. They had their views on Africans, but not all Americans were condescending. Ambassador Thomas Watkins and his assistant, Vera Whittaker, treated him with respect. Over the years, American diplomats came and went, but these two he liked. Sometimes he wondered who really reported to whom; in many of their meetings, it seemed Ms. Whittaker took over, but pretended to make suggestions. But in reality, she guided the Ambassador's decisions.

Vera arrived at the meeting with Watkins and EXO Dubose in tow. The Brigadier General was already in the office, along with Douglass Jones, the Liberian Secretary of State. The President sat behind his imported oak desk, in his huge black leather chair.

"Welcome, my friends. I hope the beautiful sunshine here in Liberia finds you all in good health."

Normally a man of good manners, the President usually stood up when women of any significance, such as Vera Whittaker, came into his presence. Today, he did not. He sat behind his imported handcrafted desk from America.

The three Americans greeted the President first, then Souleymane and the Liberian Secretary of State.

"I am so glad you all sent word, you wanted this meeting." President Tanner said looking at Vera. "Months have passed since this coup attempt and those rebels from across the border are still on the loose. Just the other day, my guards had to put my cook in jail for trying to poison me. This is very serious."

"Yes, we heard of the incident," Vera said. "Please know that we are concerned with your safety. We did hear as well, that there may have been a misunderstanding. The guards thought that since the woman's husband was not at home when they arrived, that he was involved in some type of conspiracy to harm you. But we found out that her husband really was sick and at the hospital."

President Tanner looked to his Secretary of State and then to the Brigadier General Guindo. "Sir, we have already taken care of the matter," Souleymane said. "They released the cook and her husband a few days ago. I didn't bother you with details, due to your busy schedule."

The truth was that on a constant basis Souleymane ran interference trying to make sure the president was not violating citizens' rights. He understood the president's concern about the rebels, but there needed to be a balance between security and abuse of power.

"See, we have things under control," President Tanner said, leaning back in his chair.

Ambassador Watkins spoke for the first time. "Mr. President, we came today to offer further assistance to you. We believe if we put our resources together, we can track down the leader of the coup. I've been in touch with the US Ambassador to Sierra Leone, to see what information they have on the rebels from there. We hope that you utilize your relationship with your counterpart in Sierra Leone. In order to secure our assistance, we want your word that fair democratic elections will take place in Liberia."

"Thank you so much for the concern and support the United States continues to show for our country. I have already reached out to the President of Sierra Leone to request his assistance, but now I ask you to hear me out. I think instead of talking here in this stuffy office, let's take a walk in the gardens."

The three Liberians and three Americans walked out to the courtyard.

"I hear rumors that this attempted coup had help outside of Liberia. I don't mean, just Sierra Leone," the President said.

Vera walked closely behind the President and Ambassador. She appeared to admire the new purple morning stars that recently bloomed, but she was listening intently. President Tanner directed them to a sitting area. This time he waited for Vera to sit down. He'd made his point earlier. Everyone took a seat. A few moments later a houseboy appeared with a tray of fresh mango juice, and tea.

In the cool breeze on a perfect Liberian day, with the bright blue sky overhead, and the black birds singing an afternoon song, the Liberians and Americans crafted a plan to capture the remaining rebels at large. When they were finished, Vera repeated the plan for clarification. Nothing was put in writing. They then shook hands and the Americans departed. Of course, American troops couldn't actually arrest a Liberian citizen, but they could detain any American citizen involved, and extradite them to the US.

The next day each player put his part of the plan into action. General Guindo traveled up country to the area where Jennifer Giles was last seen. They thought he would have more success feeling out the locals, since he was a local himself. Souleymane often dismissed his driver. He shunned pomp and circumstance, preferring to drive himself.

Other drivers gossiped about their boss's escapades with the loose women on La Rada Street, or with a college student. Not Souleymane's driver, he never shared any information. Not that he had much to share. The one exception was the American Peace Corps girl his boss often visited.

Souleymane changed out of his military fatigues, into black slacks and a shirt. He told the driver to meet him back at his compound tomorrow night after dinner. He often changed cars, so no one could follow him. Today he chose his Peugeot with tinted windows. On the drive from the military headquarters in Monrovia up country, he thought about the events of the last weeks, especially the last few days. Dubose told him that his childhood friend David Kumah had recently contacted him. It had been over ten years since either of them had heard from David. They assumed he was dead. He and Souleymane grew up together as best friends. Dubose mentored both boys, but could only afford to pay for one's education. After Souleymane's mother died, his father went into a deep depression. Dubose saw that his good friend could not take care of his son, and sent for Souleymane to come to America. Gabbe died a few years after his wife died. Dubose became his legal guardian.

Dubose and Souleymane wrote to David, but he didn't respond. Then word came that David and his family had been massacred by rebels trying to recruit children. Everyone assumed that all the Kumahs had been killed, but now David was saying that he had escaped across the border to Bettencourt Academy in nearby Sierra Leone, and had been in hiding out there for the last ten years under the name David Bettencourt.

During one of his visits home, Oyami found David asleep in the elementary school. David stayed on helping Oyami's father, Anderson, doing odd jobs and repairs around the school, as well as helping to run the farm. After Anderson died, Julia became more dependent on David; and even though he was a teenager at the time she adopted him, and gave him the last name Bettencourt.

Although David kept a low profile, many rumors surrounded him. Some said he hadn't escaped from the rebels, but he was a rebel himself who killed his own parents and hid out at the Bettencourt Academy. Others say he looked too much like the Bettencourts and David was actually Anderson's illegitimate son.

Since David's resurfacing, Souleymane heard many of those rumors, but dismissed them. David Kumah-or David Bettencourt now-his childhood friend, was alive; and Souleymane felt like God had reached down and restored a part of him that he'd lost. Dubose told him that David wanted to see them. What Souleymane did not understand is why it took him so long. Why had he surfaced now?

Before going up country to investigate Jennifer's disappearance Souleymane needed to talk to Nicole. He pulled the Peugeot off the road and out of sight to walk to her house. Since the embassy meeting, he hadn't seen her, but his security forces kept tabs on her. When he arrived he didn't see her truck, but the driver could have dropped her off. He walked to the back of the yard, and found Nicole on her knees with a small hand shovel digging a hole. She wore a royal blue lappa tied around her waist, and a white T-shirt. Her twists were pulled into a pony tail which sat on the top of her head. She wiped her hand across her face, and left a smudge of black on her cheek.

"Grab the big shovel," she said. "I need to dig deeper to get these seeds in the ground. I want big leaves of potato greens."

He kissed the top of her head, and then knelt beside her to wipe the dirt off of her face.

"The first time I saw you at the American Embassy, you had dirt on your face."

She smiled at him. The two of them sat facing each other on the ground, holding hands.

"That dirt you just wiped off, is from a hard day's work. The dirt I put on my face when you first saw me was my mark, my declaration, my statement, I am here. I returned to claim the history, the land, the dignity of my ancestors who left here in chains over 400 years ago; time, chains, slavery, poverty, racism, death, all did not stop me from returning. I came home."

"Sometimes I forget your age. Do you always have a speech prepared?" He shook his head. "And everyone says I am an old soul."

"I think we are both old souls; that is why we click," Nicole said leaning into Souleymane's arms.

"Let's go inside. I want to talk to you."

"Do you want to ask me more questions about Jennifer's disappearance?"

"No, I want to talk to you about us, Nikki. Right now, I just want to talk about us."

Our African Dreams

FINALLY, AFTER ALMOST ninety days in country the twenty-five volunteers who remained after the coup attempt gathered for their official welcoming and induction ceremony. It would take place in Monrovia at the Moore Centre for Africana Culture, named after one of Liberia's most noted poets and authors, Dr. Bai Tamia Johnson Moore, or as he was most affectionately known as Bai T. Moore.

Nicole looked forward to the festivities because Dr. Moore, the king of the written word in Liberia, was the main speaker. The oral tradition of storytelling and parables wove itself into everyday life like the trademark handmade silk and cotton kente cloth worn throughout West Africa. Bai T. Moore wrote the history and the stories of Liberians to share with the world, which made him famous. The kente cloth, produced in neighboring Ghana on looms with its bright blue, orange, and multicolor strips of cloths signified the rich oral history of Africa. Liberia was no exception. Africans had a parable for everything, including the recent coup. A common saying Nicole heard often about the coup was "To cure a bad sore, you must use bad medicine."

Another saying, which came from the Kpelle tribe, was "The stones that you throw into the well to kill frogs are the same stones that will cause you to suffer when you drink the dirty water."

Nicole loved the parables and proverbs, but being a journalism, and film major in undergrad at Temple, the written word resonated with her. One had to be a great storyteller to be a griot; the traditional storyteller in Africa. But with written stories the reader could live anywhere and experience Africa. The written word transported one to another world without physically going there. Before she came to Liberia she read many African writers, Wilton Sankawulo of Liberia;

Wole Soyinka, from Nigeria; J. M Coetzee, of South Africa; and of course any well-read person of world literature had to read Chinua Achebe of Nigeria, who wrote the most widely read book in African literature, *Things Fall Apart*. At last count, there were ten million copies in circulation.

Nicole arrived early at the venue to look for Rebecca, who she hadn't seen since they departed for their respective assignments. In her hand she held two copies of Bai T. Moore's *Murder in the Cassava Patch*, one for him to sign for her and the other to send back home to Shannon. But her thoughts were on Souleymane and their last meeting.

"Nikki, you know my responsibility to protect the President, and this country is more than just a job."

"I know Souleymane. What is it you want to talk about? I feel like this is a breakup speech, and if it is I don't want to hear it."

"It is not a breakup Nikki, just a break. I know this has been tough for you, guards always around. Broken dates due to national security. Keeping our relationship quiet."

"You mean secret."

"For your protection."

Even though Nicole understood the secrecy, sometimes she wished they could be more open with their relationship. But she understood and they left it at that.

The next day Nicole came home and a yard full of newly planted white morning stars, birds of paradise and red roses greeted her. There was a picnic basket on her porch with Milky Way candy bars, cans of tuna in olive oil, and a stack of *New York Times* newspapers. Souleymane was nowhere to be seen, but she knew it was from him. She also knew that he had his security people watching her. Sometimes she caught plainclothes security following her, or saw them outside her house.

She was glad that she'd given the tape to Dr. Bettencourt weeks ago. He told her it would be in Senator Giles' hands within 48 hours. Since then she'd had no contact with him, or Femi, and Jennifer was still missing. She hoped Dr. Bettencourt kept his promise.

After their recent talk, Nicole had no contact with Souleymane. She'd wanted to tell him about the tape, but she couldn't. They worked for different governments and the boundaries stood firm, or at least in theory. She asked him was everything okay. He told her everything was under control, but he could not go into details, that he hoped this coup business would be put to rest soon, so everyone could go back to the Liberian way of life. Maybe that was the problem, she thought. He also told her that, until they caught Samuel Kinkeweh, the rebel leader she would not see much of him. His duty to protect the President of his country had to be his priority.

Nicole knew Souleymane was right, but it still felt like rejection. If only she hadn't already fallen in love with him. She had fallen in love with Souleymane. The thought froze Nicole. She stopped, tripping over her royal blue and gold lappa outfit that Julia Bettencourt had placed in the box and given to Nicole the morning she left the academy. The realization of her feelings about Souleymane made her stomach churn. They would never work. It was not possible.

"I love Souleymane," she said out loud.

"Excuse me ma'am," a maintenance crew member said.

"Oh. Talking to myself. Sorry."

"It's all right. I talk to myself all the time," he laughed.

Nicole smiled and walked on to the stage. In a few hours she and the other volunteers would receive their welcome into the country and officially begin their Peace Corps assignments. Some came to teach under the Minister of Education. Others to work with the Ministry of Agriculture, to help the farmers produce healthier crops, and to stop the slash and burn method the farmers used to till the land. Some came to work with the Minister of Parks and Recreation, to clean up and maintain the white sand beaches and to set aside national parks for the next generations.

Realizing her love for Souleymane made her think of Femi. She knew he had feelings for her, but she made a conscious decision that she wouldn't cross that line, and she had made a promise to Dr. Bettencourt to not encourage his advances. He looked like a man, but at seventeen he still had his whole life ahead of him. And to be honest, she wasn't sure if part of her attraction to Femi was because he was a Bettencourt.

Nicole focused back on the matter at hand. She hadn't seen Rebecca in months. Although she'd left several notes in Rebecca's mailbox, she never got a response. She knew she was still in country. Her suspicions about Rebecca were in full force. By this time, everyone knew about Jennifer's disappearance. Ambassador Watkins had even issued a formal announcement, saying that Jennifer had been recruited by the rebels and was no longer a volunteer and that anyone with information about her should speak to Vera Whittaker.

Nicole didn't believe for one moment that Jennifer just disappeared, or that she was recruited by the rebels; it was more like she was involved with rogue Americans. Nicole jumped when she felt a hand on her shoulder. She turned around to find Vera Whittaker dressed in African attire.

"I didn't mean to startle you, Ms. Jefferson. Do you have a moment to talk?"

"Of course. We have almost an hour before the ceremony starts. You didn't startle me, as much as I was surprised to see you in African clothes."

They sat in chairs on the side of the stage.

"Normally, for these types of events, I dress like the locals to fit in," Vera said. "However, I always remember I'm an American first, and an African second. For some people the hyphenation of African-American bothers them. Some prefer to be called Black. Not me. I think African American describes exactly who I am. Truth be told; we are all Africans. This is where it all began."

"What did you want to talk to me about?" Nicole asked, a little surprised at Vera's response.

"I know you received the memo concerning Jennifer Giles, but I wondered if you'd heard anything from her, or from anyone connected to her?"

"No. As I told you at the embassy, we weren't friends. I met her that first night after the coup in the evacuation hall. Then I saw her in town and she invited me to lunch at a cook shop. She isn't the only volunteer who's invited me to lunch. The volunteers already in country made it a point to look after the new volunteers. I am sure you know the Peace Corps teams each trainee with a volunteer already serving in country."

"Who was your teammate?"

"Janet Rivers, but I only met with her once. She returned to the States."

"Do you know who teamed with Jennifer?"

"No"

"That's odd, because I understand, during stateside training the two of you became good friends."

Nicole almost let out a gasp. Do you mean Rebecca Downs?"

"I do."

"I haven't had any contact with Rebecca since the first month, when we went to our prospective assignments," Nicole said, digesting this new information.

"She's the last person who saw Jennifer."

"Rebecca?"

"You seemed surprised," Vera said, looking intently at Nicole.

Nicole didn't answer. She was feeling overwhelmed by the events of the last few months. Tears started sliding down her cheeks, onto her chest and the lappa outfit Julia Bettencourt had given her. Vera took out a white handkerchief with VW embroidered on it and handed to Nicole. The gesture calmed Nicole. She wiped the tears away.

"Thank you," Nicole said. "I'm a crier. Normally it's under control, but with recent events, all bets are off."

They sat there in silence again, while Nicole tried to compose herself. Rebecca's name kept coming up. Nicole now knew there was a reason for it. She wondered if she knew where Jennifer was, or about the tape?

Nicole stood up, and smoothed her lappa. "I'd better fix my makeup."

Vera Whittaker reached in her purse and handed Nicole a small plastic makeup bag.

"I always have a backup makeup kit. Take this, there's waterproof mascara and a new lipstick color my cousin sent me from New York. It's all the rage, a brownish copper tone, called of things, Luscious Copper Rage. I think it suits you better than me."

"Oh, thank you. But I couldn't take it."

"It's okay," Vera said. "Go now, get ready, before everyone arrives."

Without thinking Nicole reached and hugged her. Vera hugged Nicole back, and held on. Nicole thought it had been a long time since anyone had hugged Vera. Nicole left Vera alone among the empty seats.

From the side of the stage, Dubose watched Vera and Nicole. He wondered what they were talking about. The highest ranking American, the Ambassador, several American businessmen, the volunteers and several members of the American Mission would be attending today's ceremony. There were rumors that President Tanner himself would attend. Dubose had to make sure security was tight. The next few hours would be crucial to the Liberian security and to diplomatic relationships between the US and Liberia. Everything was in place to capture the rebels. Today was the day.

A few minutes after leaving Vera, Nicole walked into the bathroom, and looked around at the sinks with running water and the brand-new flushing toilets, things she took for granted in the states, everyday necessities in America, were luxuries in Liberia.

Nicole walked to the sink to wash her face. The sound of flip flops smacking on the tile floor made her look up in the mirror. Rebecca was standing behind her. The two women looked at each other in the mirror.

"Where have you been Rebecca, I haven't seen you in months and you haven't responded to any of my messages?" Nicole said, not knowing if she should be happy or worried about seeing her.

"I know I owe you an apology. I could lie and say I've been busy, which is true. But I didn't know what to say. This whole coup attempt thing, traumatized me. I think the only reason I stayed is because I didn't want you to think I was wimp. The first little thing that happens, I want to hit the road."

Nicole had so many questions to ask her, but they heard the opening ceremony music and rushed out to their seats. Nicole didn't know if she should believe Rebecca or not, but they'd have to finish their conversation later.

The program started with the new Peace Corps Director, Dr. Beverly Brandt, welcoming everyone. On the platform behind her sat Ambassador Thomas Watkins, Vera Whittaker, and next to Vera sat a woman wearing blue shoes. Nicole gasped when she saw her. It was Ms. Blue Pumps herself. She appeared to be staring at Nicole, but since her sunglasses were so dark, Nicole couldn't be sure.

On the left side of the stage sat several Liberian officials. The main speaker, Dr. Moore, sat regal in his robin blue grand boubou, the flowing wide-sleeved robe worn by men throughout West Africa.

On the stage, the empty seat next to Dr. Moore caused much conversation among the attendees, as to whether or not President Tanner would show up. Having been the target of one coup attempt, a few said he would be foolish to be out in an open public area.

As Dr. Brandt was about to speak, American and Liberian soldiers entered. A group of military men with General Guindo entered the auditorium. The orchestra started playing "Hail to the Chief" when President Tanner, flanked by his soldiers, took the stage. As everyone stood and cheered, he shook hands with Ambassador Watkins, hugged Vera Whittaker, shook hands with his cabinet members and whispered in the ear of the Minister of Education, whose smile froze. He placed his arm around Dr. Brandt's shoulder and smiled at her.

"Please sit down everyone. Thank you." President Tanner turned to Dr. Brandt.

"My dear lady, I did not mean to steal your thunder. Since these volunteers came all the way from America, I wanted them to know that we Liberians are not violent people. We love our country just as they love theirs. What happened here last month doesn't't define us. This country was settled by former freemen and slaves who came from America to repatriate to the land of their ancestors. That is my lineage. My ancestors arrived in those boats, but this country also consists of people who never left these shores. There are those who want to divide us along lines of ancestry, Americo-Liberians and indigenous people, creole people and tribal people. We must not give into these types of divisions, because in the end we are all Liberians. Liberians work together for the good of their country. That is all I came to say. Now I will sit and listen to this poet of a man, Dr. Moore."

The crowd stood and cheered as President Tanner took his place on stage beside Dr. Moore.

While the ceremony took place in Monrovia, up country near the border of Sierra Leone, Liberian soldiers and international aides, who some described as mercenaries, opened fire on the rebel camp. Peter Heweh fingered the key members from an armored truck supplied by the United States Marines. Military intelligence had traced the rebels to a camp near Sherboe. They watched the rebels for days. David Kumah Bettencourt had called a meeting at camp, the morning of the ceremony, to tell the rebels that President Tanner planned to attend the Peace Corps ceremony the next day; and they had the opportunity to finish what they started. But David had given them incorrect information. Rebel leader, Samuel Kinkeweh, spoke to his men.

"We didn't succeed on our first try. But no worry. One thing about a poor man, is he is used to losing and trying again. In one hour, we leave for Monrovia to complete the mission we failed. To unseat an unfair government. A government who has ignored the poor man, the country man's needs. We hear too much talk, and see no action. While they live in big compounds, with house boys and cooks, we try to till the dirt to plant our rice, but it has been burned too many times. We want a say in our own lives. Today is that day. We want fresh clean running water in our villages, today is that day. We want roofs overhead so when the rains come we too can be warm and dry. Today is that day!"

As Samuel spoke the first bullet hit him in the neck. He wiped the back of his neck with his hand and saw blood. His mouth opened, but no sounds came out. Liberian soldiers and foreign mercenaries sprang from the bush and ambushed the rebels. The forty or so rebels with machine guns fought fire with fire. Those without guns picked up rocks, tree branches, pulled out knives, anything to rage their fight.

The little boys with the hard-yellow eyes lay in pools of blood, some with their bodies in the fetal positions, as if trying to return to their mother's wombs. Some rebels dropped their guns and ran into the bush where Liberian military waited to capture them. Clouds of smoke from the gunfire swirled around the camp. David covered a boy solider with his body trying to protect him. In the midst of the fire, a car pulled up with a group of mercenaries and whisked David away. They guarded him until he reached his jeep parked at the edge of the village. He rode over the border to Sierra Leone.

In the distance, the gunshots could be heard in the surrounding villages. A woman started to walk toward the sound. Was her son there, in this storm of bullets? Had she not seen him, night after night, hanging out with the rebels? With that man who claimed to be a Bettencourt, but everyone knew he, and his late father hated the descendants of these so-called Black people who returned to Africa, to their homeland. When they returned, did they not know someone was already living there? They whispered among themselves. Had this mother not told her son that no good would come to him, that hate creates more hate? As she walked toward the sounds of the gunfire, other mothers joined her. The men tried to stop their women. One man grabbed his wife by the arm as she rose to join the other women marching toward the loud booms.

"Woman, this is not our battle. You go, you go by yourself."

She answered him. "Your son is out there. His battle is our battle. You don't wanna go. Stay."

"When did you begin to farm for the family? Am I not the man of this family?"

"My only son. He is my only son. He is our only son," she answered.

He released her arm. Another woman grabbed her hand and they ran to join the others. The man sat for a moment on the stool outside his hut. He didn't understand any of this. His son's hatred of people he never met. His wife disobeying him. Other men stood up from their stools to join the men gathered in the middle of the village. The Paramount Chief strapped his sandals on and followed the women. The other men took their knives, their machetes from their farms, the clubs they used to kill bush meat and followed the women. When they reached the battle site, the mother found her son in a ball, with bullet holes in his body. The Liberians soldiers remained with guns drawn. The mercenaries were long gone.

◦‣▬◐ ◑▬◂◦

Back at the ceremony, Ambassador Watkins finished his speech. Vera Whittaker then took the stage and introduced Dr. Moore. Dr. Moore who stood about six feet tall with white bushy hair like Frederick Douglass and eyes the color of topaz, took the stage. If ever a poem could be humanized, it would be Bai T. In his long flowing blue grand boubou, the audience lost itself in the twinkle of his eye, the smooth rhythm of his voice and the movements of his hands. Nicole, like the rest of the audience, sat mesmerized, listening as this great poet of a man shared his love of Africa.

"I want to tell you a story. I will make it real for you, by personalizing it. I see my good friends, the Bettencourts, from across the border of Sierra Leone honor us today with their presence. Let us say, the young man Femi Bettencourt who, I just met the other day, let us make him part of the story. He was born in America, but his legacy is from here in Africa."

Until that moment Nicole didn't know Femi or Dr. Bettencourt were at the ceremony. She looked to where Dr. Moore gestured and saw them in the first row. Femi turned to look at her and smiled. She smiled back. Dr. Moore fluttered his arms out like wings, and began his story.

"We dream of Africa. The Africa of our ancestors. The cradle of the beginning of civilization. We are all Africans. We are all one. The beginning was in a garden with flowers of all colors and kinds. Orange roses like the sun, navy blue calla lilies, and morning glories of red, white, yellow-all mixing together their aromas. The different trees, some with fruit, some just for shade-the vegetation that spread throughout the garden. The waterfalls that streamed blue green and crystal white up the mountains. The animals that lived in the garden. Most are extinct today. The land- rich black soil in some places, in others the red clay never needed tilling or fertilizing. Oh, and the African night. Stars over stars that lit up the sky at night as the sun did in the day. One man. One woman. Then they disobeyed." Dr. Moore s voice dropped an octave and he looked solemnly around the audience before continuing.

"The streaming waters from beneath the earth's surface ceased. Rain now came from the sky. The rich land stopped producing, without being tilled or fertilized. Trees were no longer protected from the sun. The man and woman knew each other, and the woman produced their seed in pain. These were Femi's ancestors. Their ancestors still lived communal, after the fall. No one owned the diamonds, the rubber trees, or the people. The diamond poachers, neither the rubber tire families, nor had the slave masters raped the land yet. The people lived communal, ate communal, and lived their lives in dignity."

Dr. Moore paused for a moment to let his words sink in, then he continued, "The people. The coffee, coco, coconut, and copper-colored people lived in harmony. At least for a while. They farmed, hunted, and fished. The land belonged to all. They worked and lived off the land. Village women sold their crafts in the market. The handmade baskets of rattan. The beaded bracelets. Hand dyed and waxed fabrics of all kinds. The men farmed on the same land, on which former slaves would return as free men and women. The farmers grew rice, corn, okra, collard greens, and more. But the people's eyes revealed their entire lives. Their lives, the lives of their ancestors; but more crucial, the lives of their future generations. Then the capture occurred. The Dutch arrived in ships of disgrace and death. The people prayed for divine intervention. Instead they felt the restraints around their arms and ankles. The taping of the mouths. The screams. The push. The shove. Some were kidnapped and dragged to the holding place by their own tribesmen. Others walked into their captivity, unknowingly."

He closed his eyes and continued. "Our ancestors were kept on the coasts in slave forts, enclosed areas with no windows, and no room to stand up. That today, these sites called slave castles, are part of the United Nations historical sites never to be destroyed. Never. These castles stained with the blood, broken hearts, but with freedom dreams of their ancestors. They saw their ancestors fight to survive, pray for strength. Their ancestors fought not for themselves, but for future generations. We dream of Africa. The Africa of our ancestors."

As Dr. Moore spoke, Vera ran her hands over her bun, and removed the hair pins from her hair, and placed them in her purse. Nicole looked up and saw Vera removing the last hair pin and shaking her hair. It fell past her shoulders. She smiled broadly at Nicole who smiled back. Vera then stood up, walked behind Ms. Blue Shoes and whispered in her ear. Ms. Blue Shoes stiffened, and looked around. She stood up with Vera behind her, and they walked off the stage. On the other side of the stage, the Minister of Agriculture stood up and walked to the Minister of Education, unlike Ms. Blue Shoes, he began to shake uncontrollably. A soldier walked over to the Minister of Education and escorted him off the stage as Dr. Moore continued.

"All of us. We. Together. The descendants of the returned slaves and free men, the indigenous folks who never left, and our friends in America, must work together to save this land. This land that stands strong in the face of all that has been taken from her, Africa stands. Liberia, one of this continent's daughters, needs your help, your love, and your support to thrive... Thank you."

Everyone stood to their feet, cheering Dr. Moore, who graciously bowed. The Ambassador joined him at the podium and asked everyone to take a seat. Dr. Brandt handed the Ambassador a plaque, which he read out loud. "To Dr. Moore. Who epitomizes the spirit of Liberia, on behalf of the Peace Corps Volunteers: Director, Dr. Beverly Brandt; The President of the United States, and the American People, we present you with this plaque and a check for $100,000 to continue to help run this center. America is interested in helping Liberians grow crops to feed themselves, but we understand that the artistic soul of a country must also be nourished."

The crowd once again stood to their feet and cheered. President Tanner took the podium again. This time, the guards walked on both sides of him and lined up on either side of the stage.

"Before I leave, I wanted to thank Ambassador Watkins, Dr. Brandt, your great American President, and the American people, but especially you Peace Corps Volunteers who despite landing in the middle of a coup attempt made a decision to stay and work with us Liberians. We know you were scared, but you stayed. I promised the citizens of Liberia, and all of you who left your homes to come help us that we would track down the rebels who tried to take over the government. I am proud to announce that as you hear my voice right now, we are arresting the coup leader Samuel Kinkeweh, and his group of rebels by the Sierra Leonean border. I also promise you that in the next year, we will hold democratic elections."

A gasp went up from the crowd, then thunderous applause. Nicole looked over at Rebecca, who had turned ghostly white. Nicole laid her hand on Rebecca's shoulder, as President Tanner exited the stage. A medic appeared and Rebecca was carried away. She seemed to be more shaken by the rebels being caught than her initial baptism in country during the attempted coup. Nicole tried to go with Rebecca, but her PO Hawk, ordered her back to her seat. He told her he would get word to everyone later about Rebecca's condition. Rebecca urged her to stay and receive both of their certificates.

To end the ceremony, Dr. Brandt called each volunteer to the stage and presented him or her with a certificate of completion of training. Nicole watched as each volunteer's name was called and that person went to the stage and accepted the certificate. She took a deep breath as Melissa Edwards went to the stage. But instead of saying Nicole Jefferson, they skipped her name and called Andrew MacArthur. She wondered why they skipped her. Surely, they didn't think she had anything to do with the coup. Maybe they knew she gave the tape to Dr. Bettencourt. They called the last volunteer's, name, Marvin Taylor. Now all the volunteers had received their certificates, except for her and Rebecca.

Nicole then heard Dr. Brandt call her name.

"Nicole Jefferson would you join us onstage?"

Surely, they were not going to arrest her in front of everyone. Nicole felt her legs move. She didn't know how she got on the stage, but there she was, standing next to Dr. Brandt.

"As part of every new commitment ceremony, the new volunteers vote for the one person they believe exemplifies the spirit of what it means to be a Peace Corps Volunteer. The person who encouraged everyone else, who studied the country she was to serve in. The person who became part of the culture. I am proud to announce that the volunteers selected Ms. Nicole Jefferson as that person."

Andrew MacArthur stood and led the cheers. Others joined in. Nicole shook hands with Dr. Brandt, who handed a kente cloth scarf to Dr. Moore. Dr. Moore placed the scarf around Nicole's neck so the kente cloth draped across her shoulders. To be given a kente cloth by a chief or prominent person in traditional Africa was the highest honor. She looked out into the audience of fellow volunteers and smiled until the dimple appeared on her cheek.

Femi, and Dr. Bettencourt stood in the front row, clapping. Souleymane, whom, she thought had left with the other soldiers guarding President Tanner, leaned against a palm tree at the back of the center, a wide smile on his face, and Dubose appeared at the side of the stage and saluted her.

"Ms. Jefferson, it pleases us to present you this honor," Dr. Brandt said. "Time and time again, I had the opportunity to travel into the interior to talk to the volunteers, to see how they were holding up, to look them straight in the eye, and ask them were they okay. Is this still what you dreamt about? Because we know to be a Peace Corps Volunteer one has to be a dream warrior. I asked every single trainee, do you still wish to serve here after the coup? They all answered yes. When I asked what the biggest factor in their decision was, they did not say because I want to serve in Liberia, although they did and still do. They did not say because I feel an obligation to finish what I started. What the majority of them said was that I fell in love with Africa, with the Liberia that Nicole Jefferson told us about every night. She shared the stories of her youth that her mother told her about Africa. So today while we understand why those who left did, we honor all of you who stayed, and in particular your unofficial leader Nicole Jefferson," Dr. Brandt finished.

Dr. Brandt planted kisses on both of Nicole's cheeks. Dr. Moore followed suit and then presented her with the plaque. Dr. Brandt stepped aside to give Nicole the microphone.

The crowd encouraged her, by shouting, "Speech. Speech."

Nicole stood there for a moment looking like a lost little girl. She tried to speak, but nothing came out. She shrugged her shoulders mouthed thank you and started to walk away from the mic when she looked back into the audience. Femi stood up touched his heart and said, "From your heart. Speak from your heart."

She smiled back at Femi and touched the kente cloth to her lips, and walked back to the microphone.

"As a little girl I dreamed of coming to Africa. I imagined stepping off the plane and kissing the ground from which my ancestors were snatched. My mother, Ellafare Crawford Jefferson, would sit me on her lap and read to me the great stories of Queen Nzinga, the great Ashanti society, about the Dogon people and so many other accounts of this continent's greatness. She told me about all the natural resources here, the diamonds, gold, the wild life, tigers, giraffes, and more. But most of all she told me about the people. So, despite landing in the middle of a coup, despite the fear we felt, despite the rumors of another coup on the horizon, we volunteers who stayed made a statement. We said we believe we can make a difference. We said we understand those who need to go home, but we hope they understand that we need to stay. Across color lines, age lines, gender lines, the twenty-five of us who decided to stay represent America. The hope, the faith, that we came humbly, not to save anyone, well maybe we did. Maybe it was to save ourselves, and to save America. On behalf of all the volunteers, those who left and those who stayed, I thank the Liberian people for allowing us to work beside you in your endeavor to make life better for all Liberians, Americo-Liberians, indigenous people, and us expats who live here. Thank you for allowing us to live out our African dreams."

They Lived So We Could Live

NICOLE HADN'T BEEN to the Robertsfield Airport since the day she arrived in country a year ago. She now stood in line to board the plane to Ghana where she was to join Femi and his family on a trip to the slave castles in Elmina.

She couldn't't help from thinking about the coup attempt and the aftermath of the capture of the culprits. Of course it never came out about the role Ms. Blue Pumps played. After Vera Whittaker walked her off stage, Ms. Blue Pumps, was never seen again in Liberia. A memo circulated throughout the American community that a family member of hers fell sick in the United States, and she returned home. Jennifer Giles was also never seen again, but the word on the grapevine or in the bush was that her father sent her to Spain and she was living there under an assumed name. Nicole believed it was true and that Jennifer was fine. She had received an unsigned postcard from Barcelona. On it was written, "Thanks, from on Yankee fan to another."

Nicole still had the tape she found in the cereal box at Jennifer's. She didn't't know why she decided to hold on to it. Once on the plane, she closed her eyes and fell asleep. When she woke the plane had landed in Accra, the capital of Ghana. The Bettencourts and their team from Sierra Leone were to meet her at the baggage claim area, but when she descended the steps from the plane she saw Femi's smiling face. They kissed cheek to cheek, and hugged each other. Nicole broke the embrace first.

"How did you get past security on this side?"

"Good to see you, too."

"Oh don't tell me, it was the Bettencourt name."

"Wrong, don't think my family name is a pass to everything."

Nicole remembered when she spoke to Femi a few days ago he told her he couldn't meet her when she disembarked the plane because of heightened security.

"Girl, look at these guns on me," Femi said flexing his arms. "I talked to the manager of the terminal, a woman who, kept looking at my arms. I think she almost fainted. But I did tell her if she did faint, my dad was the famous doctor, Oyami Bettencourt. She let me through."

They drove from Accra the three hours to Elmina Castle. Their party consisted of fifty students, Dr. Bettencourt, Femi, several teachers, Dr. Momah, Francis, and David. Elmina Castle sat along the shoreline of what used to be called the Gold Coast, now called Ghana. Although everyone in the group had studied the history of the twenty slave castles on the coast, nothing prepared them for the emotions they experienced standing on the same land where the capture of their ancestors took place over 400 years ago. The tour guide gathered the group in front of the castle. From the outside, it appeared to be just another old whitewashed building. The guide explained that the Portuguese built the fort in 1482 as a haven for the traders. The area traded heavily in gold, spices and textiles. The heavy stone foundation, bricks and mortar came on ships sent by King Joao, in Portugal, along with 600 men to build the fort.

When the rest of the group followed the guide to enter the castle, Nicole and Femi stayed outside. Nicole pulled from her backpack the jar of dirt, she'd brought from the states. She walked to the beach in front of the castle. Femi followed her.

"This dirt came from the front yard of a group of people in Philadelphia who called themselves Move." Nicole told Femi. "And from the gravesite of the young man I told you about, Thaddeus. All the Move people adopted the last name Africa. They wanted to return to Africa, the land of their ancestors."

She opened the jar and poured the contents into the sand. She mixed the dirt and sand together. Femi bent down beside her and dug his hands in the sand to help her. Nicole unclasped a silver cross, that her mother had given her from around her neck as a little girl and buried it in the mixture of sand and dirt.

They each said a silent prayer. Nicole thought about Thaddeus and his dream to come to Africa to work after he graduated from college. She thought about the Move people in Philadelphia, who wanted to claim their African heritage. Today she felt she helped make that dream come true. But most of all, she thought of her mother who encouraged her to follow her dreams. With the dirt and sand mixture still on his hands, Femi took Nicole's hand and they walked silently into the castle.

They heard a tour guide with another group explain that the area they were in was originally a storehouse for goods, but once the castle changed to trading human beings, it was turned into dungeons. Nicole tried to visualize the captive slaves in these dungeons, weighed down with chains, not able to stand up straight.

Nicole entered the area marked for female slaves, leaving Femi outside. Although only five feet two she still had to stoop to fit into the cramped holding space. Inside, she couldn't even stand up. She imagined the slave women, really just girls, huddled together, wearing only their lappa skirts, barefoot and bare breasted. Many captured on their way to fetch water, or to the market. She could almost see them sitting on the floor their eyes glazed from fear, bone weary from being whipped or raped, leaning against each other for support. A few knew each other's language, but most communicated through hand signals, tears and hugs.

Nicole looked out of the porthole. For miles all she could see was the ocean. This is what the slave women saw. No escape. Just miles and miles of ocean. She started to tremble uncontrollably. She felt nauseous and queasy. She felt like she was going to throw up. She felt a hand on her back. It felt comforting and warm. She looked up expecting to see Femi and looked into the eyes of a woman about her age. The woman was bare breasted and barefoot.

"You're not real," Nicole said.

"I am very real Nicole," she said.

"How do you know my name?"

"Let's sit. We do not have much time."

Nicole sat on the ground and the woman sat across from her, holding her hands.

"I know much about you Nicole Jefferson. You are the last born, the baby of Ellafare Crawford Jefferson, and Arselen Jefferson. Two sisters, Barron and Shannon, and your twin brothers who mean the world to you."

I can't believe that after everything I've been through that I pick now to have a nervous breakdown, Nicole thought.

"We trusted our instincts. But we also prayed for divine intervention. Everything is not as it seems. When you need help, look up. Help will come. Close your eyes and pray," the woman said.

When Nicole opened her eyes Femi knelt in front of her.

"You okay?" he asked.

"I want to take part in the ancestral procession tonight," Nicole said without hesitation.

"I thought you said it would be too emotional for you to handle."

"It may be, but I will call on Divine intervention if I need help."

That evening as the sun set leaving a fiery red glow in the sky, hundreds of people from the Africa diaspora gathered. They came from across the United States, from the Islands, Jamaica, St. Thomas, and Cuba, and from London, France, and across Canada. They were dressed all in white and carried lit white candles as they walked in a procession to the slave castle, where their ancestors had been held before being shipped out to America, Cuba or Haiti.

The ancestors of the Africans, who participated in the sale of their fellow humans, walked with them. Nicole and Femi also walked with them. They didn't talk or sing the songs with the other walkers; instead their tears and smiles showed the depth of their emotions. As the procession came to a halt at the entrance to Elmina Castle, the crowd surrounded the castle. A school teacher from Durham, North Carolina wept, but smiled through her tears.

As the Bettencourt Academy group came closer to the slave castle, the significance of the ceremony, and the realization that they were standing on the ground their ancestors last stood on before being crammed into the bottom of boats for the long voyage, overwhelmed them. One of the male students bit down on his lips, so as not to cry out loud. David closed his eyes and stood for a moment to take in the moment, and another student let out a loud "Amen".

Dr. Bettencourt took his first pilgrimage to the slave castle when he turned ten years old. His father brought him, as he had brought all of his other children on their tenth birthdays. Oyami addressed the group.

"At the age of ten, my father brought me here. I can still hear his words. He said, son, remember this place where we stand. Let it be seared in your mind, forever. Look, and take a picture with the lenses of your heart, this place, and other places along the coast of Africa. They used to call it the Gold Coast, where many of your ancestors took their last breath and others saw the last sight of their own land. It was where they cried out. God rescue us. Help us, and I imagine they asked why.'"

Tears streamed down Dr. Bettencourt's face. Femi stepped closer to Nicole. She took his hand. She bowed her head and said a silent prayer for those who weathered the crossing. Many thoughts flooded her mind. She felt awe for her ancestors who survived, hate for those captured who them, and anger at God. Her knees buckled, but she breathed deeply and willed herself to stand tall.

"You okay," Femi asked.

Nicole nodded.

"I've never seen my father cry," Femi whispered to Nicole.

Dr. Bettencourt continued through his tears, "My father said to me, and I say now to my two sons, Femi and David, and to all of you. Remember when you leave this place, take with you, the courage, the dreams, but also the obligation to live your life on purpose. Not to squander the breath that God gave you. Honor the slaves by how you live your life. Much has been sacrificed for you, and me."

Dr. Bettencourt asked his group to join hands in a circle for prayer before the speaker addressed the crowd. Each person went around the circle and gave a prayer, or a word. When it was David's turn, he simply nodded.

When everyone said their piece, Dr. Bettencourt said, "Visiting the slave castles is a tradition for my ancestors. I hope as you all mature, get married and start families of your own, that you bring your families back to visit, to remind you of the sacrifice made by the captives. They chose to survive, they could have jumped ship and drowned themselves or refused to eat and starved themselves. They chose to survive. We don't judge those who killed themselves, or blame them. But our ancestors are the ones who survived the most brutal of circumstance. We honor those who survived the crossing, the hunger and thirst, the beatings, the rapes, the parasites and diseases, and everything else. Because if they hadn't survived we would not be here right now."

As they stood there, Nicole thought about the freedom she took for granted, to eat a big bowl of streaming hot rice when she wanted to, to sleep when she needed to, and to select whom she wanted to love, marry and mate with, and that she had control over her own body. Nicole looked around, committing the moment to memory. She wanted to share the experience with her mother. She wanted to remember each whitewashed stone in the building, and her conversation with the slave woman, who encouraged her to pray for Divine intervention when she needed help-whether or not it was real or imagined.

When she told her mother about the procession of people from the diaspora who returned, she knew she had to make sure she included the stories of the school teacher she shared a plate of plantains with, or the hundreds of students who acted tough in school, but who wept openly there. She wanted to make sure to tell her mother about the cab driver from Cuba, whose mother told him about their ancestors coming from the west coast of Africa, and that someday he must return to honor her, and them.

As Nicole looked at Femi and his father in a deeply private moment, she felt warmth spread across her chest, she felt a connection, not only to the Bettencourts, but to Africa, and she felt like she belonged. She felt the smiles and tears among the crowd. It all came down to love, she thought. The type of love that made a mother give her child away, rather than raise him in slavery. The type of love that made a man sacrifice his life fighting bullets with stones to protect his daughter.

"They lived, so we could live," David said.

Nicole looked up at David standing beside her in his long flowing white boubou. She still had questions about his involvement in the coup attempt. But tonight, at this place, and at this time, she gave everyone the benefit of the doubt. Tonight, she wanted to stay in her moment of love and connection. Peace. In her moment of hope. She wanted to believe the violence had ended. She wanted to believe Jennifer sat somewhere drinking a cold brew, watching the Yankees that Rebecca had no involvement with the coup insurgents, and Femi and David could learn to be real brothers.

She wanted to believe that if her ancestors could survive so much, that certainly the Americo-Liberians, and the indigenous people could find a common ground and learn to live together. She wanted to believe that the pain of her past could be resolved, by her letting go and forgiving. She knew the journey to love required her to run a race unencumbered by the past. As they prayed and cried, Nicole opened her arms and turned her head up to the heaven, smiled and thanked her ancestors for their sacrifice.

She thought about her childhood right there and she let go and forgave Lemuel for his abuse of her grandmother and others in the family. She forgave her father for his abandonment. She forgave Mrs. Goldsmith and all the Mrs. Goldsmiths she had encountered in her life, who tried to make her feel inferior, based on the color of her skin. She forgave them, as the speaker, Dr. Kwesi Gyeke, from Ghana welcomed home the ancestors of the slaves who returned to honor to them.

"What a time is this, what a place is this place," he said. "Over four hundred years ago, your ancestors were snatched from these very shores, and packed in to the bottom of ships to become slaves in a foreign land. The pain they bore; we don't want to imagine. Most of us complain when it is a little too hot, or uncomfortable. To work in the hot weather, from sun up to sun down, with little water or food to produce for someone else, to not have control over your life, or to see a child you gave birth to, given to someone else to nurse so you can work the fields, worse yet, to have that child sold away. Our ancestors endured a lot."

Nicole, Femi, and the others all listened to Dr. Gyeke, each taking in the moment in their own way. He told them to hold their lit candles up in the air and repeat after him.

"On this day we dedicate ourselves," he said.

"On this day we dedicate ourselves," the crowd repeated.

As the call and response continued, Femi and Nicole linked arms. Femi turned to Nicole and whispered in her ear. "I love you Nicole. I know you don't want to hear that, and you believe I'm just a teenage boy whose hormones are talking, and doesn't know what he wants."

Nicole opened her mouth to speak, but he held up his hand and stopped her.

"Please just listen to me. The moment I saw you three months ago at the market, I have thought of you every day. The way I felt then, the way I feel about you now, is the same way I will feel, ten years from now, twenty years from now."

"Femi." Nicole interrupted him. "I know this is a special moment, being here at the slave castle with your father. I know you think you love me. I know I have feelings for you. Our emotions have run high since we met each other, the coup attempt, Jennifer missing, the rebels being caught, You, meeting you and your grandmother and the other Bettencourts, for the first time. It's making us emotional."

"I promise you Nicole, if it takes five years, ten years, however long it takes I will wait until you feel the way I do."

She shook her head. "How do you even know what love is, you're only seventeen. You've never even had a serious girlfriend."

"My parents have that kind of love. My parents show such love and respect for each other. My father still opens doors and pulls out chairs for my mother. He brings her flowers. They've shown me what love is and it's the kind of love I want."

"Femi."

"I will wait for you, no matter how long it takes," he said.

As Dr. Gyeke told the audience to congratulate each other on their journey and reconnection with the land of their ancestors, Femi looked Nicole in her eyes, then he kissed her.

Transformation of the Spirit

NICOLE STILL FELT Femi's lips on hers. She pushed the thought away. He was seventeen. What the hell did she think she was doing? It was 1981. Time had passed since the joint effort between the American and Liberian governments had captured the rebels, and since Femi's return to Atlanta. Every time Nicole went to the Peace Corps headquarters to pick up her mail, she could count on at least three letters from Femi and loads of pictures. He sent pictures of himself throwing the winning touchdown, being tackled. He even sent her his prom picture, and told her not to be jealous. He took Lauren, his best friend. She'd just broken up with her boyfriend and they each needed a date so they went together.

Several colleges recruited him to play football. He told Nicole his father still didn't acknowledge that he played football, but Dr. Bettencourt said he would attend the upcoming dinner for student athletes. He emphasized the student part.

Nicole sat in the coffee shop waiting for Rebecca, reading the latest letter from Femi.

Dear Nikki J,

What's up girl? My father tells me there is a serious issue with malaria in Liberia right now. He said that people on the continent of Africa become sick and some die from malaria each year, but because Americans can't see how this affects them, they don't care. So be sure to spray really good with the mosquito repellant. Dad said there is also a new disease called AIDS that the World Health Organization claims came out of Africa. It is the short name for a long deadly disease. Next time I write you, I'll find out the real name. They say Africans, gay people and junkies get it. Africans and gays supposedly from sex, and junkies from intravenous drug use.

Have you heard of anyone in Liberia or other African countries having this disease AIDS? They say it came from a green rhesus monkey. And that a gay Frenchman, or French-Canadian flight attendant brought it from Africa. Sounds like the Tuskegee experiment to me all over again. I know you're busy in the field and writing your health radio scripts, but let me know if you hear about anyone with this disease. My dad also wants to know. He said to ask you, since you travel so often in the interior. This has piqued my interest so much I'm thinking of majoring in biology for pre-med. Dad is happy, so is mom. She said the Bettencourts need more medical doctors. I'm counting down the days, one more month and I'll see you again.

Love, Femi

"Must be some letter," Rebecca said.

"Girl, don't sneak up on people, you could get karate chopped," Nicole joked.

Rebecca sat down across from Nicole and slung her purse over the back of the chair. Nicole studied her friend. She no longer looked like a fresh-faced country girl from Wyoming. The last year of stress showed on her face. Her spotless skin was sunburned and splotched. She had cut her long blonde hair into a short bob. She had sworn off meat. The fifty pounds she gained from a diet consisting mostly of white rice and peanut butter and jelly sandwiches sat on her hips.

Reading Nicole's look Rebecca said, "I know what I look like."

Nicole didn't answer. Their last conversation ended with one of them storming out. The last time they met Nicole asked her how a girl whose family raised cattle for a living had sworn off meat. Rebecca told Nicole she left home because she didn't want to be like her parents. When Nicole tried to ask her another question, Rebecca grabbed her bag and stalked out. After that fight Nicole sent a message to Rebecca asking, if they could meet in Monrovia the next month to try the new coffee shop that an Ethiopian businessman had opened. She knew Rebecca couldn't resist any offer for coffee. She drank at least seven cups a day. Nicole thought that outrageous, but she wanted to find out why Rebecca had become distant, and in the back of her mind, she still had questions about her possible knowledge of, or involvement in the attempted coup and in Jennifer's disappearance.

"You wear your weight well," Nicole said. "Before you were underweight. I didn't want to say anything."

Rebecca smiled.

"I know you're trying to make me feel better." She reached out and took Nicole's hand.

The waiter came to their table dressed in a long charcoal boubou. He definitely looked Ethiopian, tall and slender with fine curly hair and high cheekbones.

"Ladies, welcome to Buna Daba Naw. In Ethiopian, this means Coffee is Our Bread." He said, handing them two menus.

Nicole watched as Rebecca's eyes registered a glow she hadn't seen in months.

"We have Liberian coffee, as well as other West African coffees, and coffee from Kenya. But I recommend our Ethiopian coffee so you can experience the Ethiopian coffee ceremony." He smiled. "But I warn you, the ceremony can take up to three hours."

Nicole and Rebecca wanted to come there specifically for the Ethiopian coffee ceremony. When they gave their order. The waiter's smiled widened.

"Wonderful. I will return shortly with your coffee."

A few minutes later, he returned and the ceremony began by him placing on their table a handmade coffee pot, called a Jebena and three round coffee bowls that he placed in front of Nicole and Rebecca. He told them the bowls were called Cini. He then lit a fire in an open pit in the middle of the room and a woman entered with a pan of whole coffee beans. She began to roast the beans over an open pit. Nicole and Rebecca watched as the woman jiggled the coffee in the pan as if making popcorn.

Rebecca broke out into a full grin when the woman walked around the room allowing the smell of the freshly roasted coffee beans to waft in the air. She then took the coffee beans and put them into a grinder. The waiter returned to take the finely crushed coffee powder to place in the Jebenas, then he set the pots on the open fire to brew. While the coffee brewed, the waiter brought a bowl of cooked barley and set it between Nicole and Rebecca.

"Ladies, the cooked barley is to be eaten between the coffee servings. There will be three rounds of coffee. If you would like more, it will cost more. Some people go up to twelve rounds. They are small, but strong fare. The basic ceremony entails three servings. We don't use milk in the ceremony. Many Americans request milk, but if you want to have Ethiopian coffee the traditional way, you drink it with lots of sugar or salt, no milk.

"No milk for us. Let's be authentic," Rebecca said.

"Please make sure you bring lots of sugar," Nicole said, hoping her stomach would be able to take it.

The waiter placed the first cup in front of each of them, picked the Jebena up from the open fire and held it high in the air, and poured a long amber ribbon of coffee, into each cup.

"Ladies, this first round, we call Abol. It means transformation of the spirit."

"How do you do that?" Rebecca asked, after the waiter finished pouring the coffee.

"Much practice. I have never missed a cup," he said.

The golden liquid didn't taste bitter as Nicole expected. The taste reminded her more of a light wine. They sat in silence drinking their tiny cups of coffee. Tears welled in Rebecca's eyes.

"Thank you so much Nicole. I needed this today. I see why this is called transformation of the spirit."

Rebecca's tears began to flow, like water from a broken dam. She cried silently. Nicole reached her hand across the table and put it on top of Rebecca's. The waiter discreetly laid several napkins on the table. Rebecca withdrew her hand from Nicole, wiped her face, and took a deep breath.

"So many times I wanted to send you a message and ask you to meet me so we could talk. But I couldn't. I didn't want to involve you, mainly because I didn't want you to think badly of me."

"Rebecca, I know we became friends quickly, but we are friends."

"I know," Rebecca said. "I also know that you think of me as this naïve white girl from the sticks. But I lived like a rebellious wild child in high school. The real reason I joined the Peace Corps was to make amends for some stuff I did in high school."

The waiter noticed their empty cups and refilled them.

"This second serving is Huletegana," he said as he brought the Jebena up high and made a perfect pour into Nicole's cup and then into Rebecca's.

Nicole placed both hands around the cup. She rolled her shoulders backwards feeling the tension ease. The smell of the coffee itself seemed to hypnotize them. Rebecca took small sips of her brew, while Nicole held hers in her hands.

"In high school, I tried to date Anthony, a Black guy to piss off my boyfriend," Rebecca said.

"You already told me this story," Nicole said. "You joined Peace Corps for atonement. You dated someone to hurt someone else. Okay, it isn't cool. In fact, it's pretty lame. But was there really a need to devote the next two years of your life in Africa with the potential of getting bit by a mosquito and getting malaria, or much worse, landing in the middle of a coup attempt to atone."

"Let me finish," Rebecca said. The look on her face was enough to silence Nicole.

"I hung out with a bunch of redneck biker boys after my quarterback boyfriend broke up with me. He used to hang out with them too until they began to worship all things Hitler. What I didn't tell you is that they beat Anthony to death after I told them he tried to force himself on me."

Nicole felt her shoulders and neck tense again. She sat paralyzed. No words came to her mind or mouth. Neither of them spoke. The waiter returned for the third serving.

"The third and final serving, unless you want to keep going is called Bereka. This serving, you must take your time, sip slowly and discuss any palaver you have with each other. Then extend forgiveness to one another. This serving is for your blessing."

He poured the stream of coffee into the cups, stepped back, and bowed. "Many blessings to you both."

They sipped their coffee in silence. The waiter replaced the empty bowl of barley with a new one. The couple beside them finished their ceremony, smiled at Nicole and Rebecca and left. They still sat in silence.

"There's more," Rebecca said.

Nicole looked up from her coffee cup and into Rebecca's eyes. What more could possibly be said she wondered.

"Like I said before another, Emmett Till story-but instead of it being in the fifties in Mississippi, was it the seventies in South Dakota?" Nicole looked down into her coffee cup and said angrily. "I grew up with my mother warning my brothers, be careful. Don't think that because you hang out with white kids and play football, that if you cross the line you won't end up in jail or worse. She told them to be careful who they date not because she was a racist, but because of white girls like you. And to think, I called you my friend. That guy could have easily been one of my brothers."

The waiter returned, laid the bill on the table and picked up the empty cups in one swoop. He didn't say anything this time, or ask any questions.

"Nicole, please, let me explain," Rebecca pleaded.

"You told a group of white supremacists that a Black man tried to force himself on you to get back at him for rejecting you to make your boyfriend jealous and he was beaten to death. Why aren't you in jail?"

"I didn't kill him."

"You may not have pulled the trigger, or tied the noose, or threw the punch, but you killed him."

"I want you to understand. At the time I was a sixteen-year-old kid. Maybe I wanted revenge. I thought I was slumming, that he should be happy to date a white girl, and then he ignored me. He humiliated me."

"He deserved to die for ignoring you." This is as bad as the day Thaddeus was killed, Nicole thought. Rebecca sat in front of her alive, but at that moment she was dead to Nicole. Dead.

Rebecca sat with her eyes closed. She opened her mouth to speak, but no sound came out.

"I fell in with the wrong crowd. I was young stupid, desperate."

"I'd say."

"Sorry. We're not all a perfect martyr like you."

"In this case, I would say that Anthony is the martyr."

"I wish I could go back Nicole. If I could I'd change the role I played in his death. Every day for the last seven years, through my senior year in high school, through all four years of college, and through grad school, I wished, prayed, cried, and worked every day of my life, since the day they killed him, to atone. That's why I joined the Peace Corps, and I studied Africa. I wanted to serve here."

Nicole felt a numbness envelope her. She saw Rebecca's lips moving, but couldn't hear her. Instead she thought of Ari and Aaron. She thought how her mother always told them, that as young Black men, they had to be especially careful. If stopped by a police officer, always be extra polite. Keep your hands where they could see them. Make sure all the lights and everything on the car worked. No broken taillights. Don't give anyone any reason to stop you in the first place. Be early for a practice, class, everything. Work hard. She told them that they could date and ultimately love who they wanted, but in this society, this world, if they married out of their race, there would be consequences. Their Grandma Kaitlan came from a mixed heritage of Irish, and Native American, but once she made the choice to marry a Black man her Irish part of the family disowned her.

Rebecca's voice intruded on Nicole's thoughts.

"In college I volunteered as a Big Sister to a young Black girl. I also worked at the Boys and Girls club helping Black kids. In graduate school, I majored in Africana Studies at Yale."

As Rebecca spoke, goosebumps rose on Nicole's skin. She studied Rebecca's cool blue eyes, and newly cut blonde bob. She tried to make sense of the words coming out of her. She heard her say, "I was only sixteen. A confused mixed-up kid. I wanted to fit in. I didn't believe the things they said about Black people being inferior. I don't think they believed it. But they felt left out. I felt left out."

"It was high school Rebecca. Everyone felt left out, especially those doing the leaving out. Look at me. I was raised in a small town in racist America, in the midst of violence. I never fit in. You're sitting here justifying your actions, trying to tell me that those... those dogs killed that young man, because they felt left out, that *you* felt left out."

Rebecca sat with her hands wrapped around herself.

"I'd hoped you'd hear me out. I wanted you to forgive me. Like you said you forgave Lemuel. All those letters you wrote me about forgiveness and how you forgave those who hurt you. I hoped that you'd understand that I was a stupid rebellious kid. I've tried to make amends. I hoped you would put yourself in my shoes and forgive me. Because there is more, and I want you to hear all of it."

Nicole picked up her backpack. She wanted to hear Rebecca out. She wanted to give her a chance. They had come through so much together, but she couldn't bear to hear another word from her. She never wanted to see Rebecca again.

When the waiter came by, Nicole pulled some Liberian dollars out of her wallet, and slipped them in the server's book. She pushed her chair back, stood up and walked out of the coffee shop.

Things Are Not Always What They Appear to Be

TIME SEEMED TO move slowly in this land of heat and humidity, of palm trees and white star flowers, of kindness and discontent. Nicole rolled the window down in her truck for some fresh air. The gingery smell of the countryside air still amazed her. She'd left Monrovia at the break of day to give herself plenty of time to make it to the Sierra Leonean border before nightfall. She planned to visit with Andrew MacArthur who had taken over Jennifer's teaching post. Nicole smiled, as she thought of her first meeting with Andrew in stateside Peace Corps training. She thought him to be just another smart-ass white boy who thought he knew everything. But he turned out to be a caring teacher and mentor for the Liberian children up country.

He often recruited Nicole to speak to his girl students on female health issues, and abstinence, especially with the new disease AIDS on the horizon. He thought it was important for the girls to see a woman who looked like them in a position of authority. There were the market women who ran their own businesses, but they saw few women in the same positions of authority as men. Nicole shared with them the story of Esi, the female Paramount Chief in their own country. Many said they had heard stories of her but didn't think they were true. When Nicole told them not only had she met her, but Esi thought Nicole to be her long-lost daughter Misu, they lifted their heads higher with pride.

Nicole always checked with the Paramount Chief and the mothers of the village to get their permission and blessing to teach their children. Still many of the young ladies asked her why she did not have a husband, and did she not think at her old age of twenty-three she should be married. Andrew would tell the students, he'd asked her several times, but she said no. The girls would laugh loudly and tell him a beautiful woman like Ms. Nicole couldn't marry him. He would laugh with the students as he nodded his head in agreement, but his eyes seemed sad.

Nicole laughed with the students and Andrew, but lately she had started to feel like an old maid. She received an invitation to her friend Holly's wedding in Philadelphia. Another friend sent pictures of her husband, and their new baby. Even the volunteers in country were getting in on the act, Marvin Taylor and another volunteer he met in country became engaged. They asked Nicole if they could hold their wedding ceremony at her home. They met in Liberia and wanted to get married on African soil. She was the only volunteer who actually had a home close to the city of Monrovia. It was a convenient location for the ceremony.

The main reason for Nicole's trip this time concerned the Bettencourts, and in particular, Femi. She thought about his last letter, which sat inside her bag on the front seat. She wanted to keep it close to her as evidence that he indeed would be landing in Sierra Leone tomorrow morning. Femi wrote her he had graduated with honors, and planned to attend Morehouse, just like this father. He wanted to major in biology, but also thought of architecture. They both dealt with the structure and DNA, one of the human body and one of mortar and cement. He said maybe his mission would be to design and build the schools and hospitals his family built around the world.

He made the football team, but this information he had not shared with his father. His first year he would be redshirted anyway.

In less than 24 hours, Nicole would see Femi. A legally adult Femi. She pulled into the compound where Andrew lived. Before she could even turn off the engine, Gabriel, Andrew's houseboy opened the door with a big smile.

Having a houseboy or a house girl was a new way of life for Nicole. She still wrestled with having child servants. But she knew that she helped to pay for the school fees for the young lady who lived and worked for her. She hadn't gone looking for her. A few weeks after she moved into her home in Logantown, a woman showed up on her doorstep with a little girl about nine years old. The woman just stood back while the little girl spoke broken English.

"My ma say you need hep. I can hep you. I hep you cook, clean, and watch your house when you leave to go up country."

Nicole didn't bother to ask how they knew she traveled up country. She learned secrets didn't exist for long in Liberia. That's why she believed Jennifer Giles where-abouts would be discovered soon, and also why she knew that the coup conspiracy hadn't died with Samuel Kinkeweh. There were too many whispers and hushed conversations among the country people. They told her that Americans and Germans still met in secret up country. Maybe that is why she held on to the tape from Jennifer's house. The little girl came to live with Nicole after Souleymane told her he knew the family and sent the little girl and her mother there to help Nicole.

Andrew's houseboy, Gabriel ran out, and hugged Nicole. He went to the trunk and took out her luggage. Andrew appeared in the door.

"How long do you plan to stay?" he asked, looking at the luggage.

"Can a girl get a hug?"

Andrew walked over to Nicole and they hugged and kissed in the traditional West African way. Andrew seemed to linger a minute longer. Once inside, they sat at the handmade wooden table Andrew had made out of a cotton tree. Nicole rubbed her hand over the shellacked wood.

"This table could probably sell for over a $1000 in America," she said.

"Mr. Traub showed me how to carve," Andrew laughed.

"The old blind man who sits under the tree at the end of the road?"

"Yep. He made the table I gave you for your housewarming present. I started thinking about what our legacy would be in this country-our personal legacy and America's legacy."

Nicole looked up at Andy. His hair seemed blonder and his skin almost matched hers. The dark skin with the white hair made him look like a surfer boy instead of a former football player at Notre Dame.

"I'm glad you like the table. I plan to have Mr. Traub teach some of the boys and girls how to carve, tables, chairs, trays, all kinds of things and then set up a co-op to sell them. They would get the money, not some third party buying the stuff for pennies and then taking it to America to make money hand over fist."

"What a great idea."

After dinner Nicole and Andrew sat outside in two of the chairs he'd carved. They drank Liberian beer and sang songs. In one rowdy rendition of "Shining Star" the coyotes began to howl.

"I think we better call it a night," Andrew said. "We don't want to bring the coyotes out of their hiding places, or worse yet, have them run down here and eat you as revenge for that song."

"Oh, is that what you think of my singing?"

"My dear friend, you're a beautiful, smart, caring, but a singer you are not. Anyway, tomorrow your true love returns."

"We are worlds apart in age and life."

"And so."

"I'm old enough to be his mother. Okay, maybe not his mother, but definitely his older sister."

"I always thought my older sister's friends were hot. But I knew they looked at me as the little brother. But believe me, a guy wouldn't think twice about your age difference, if he really felt a connection with the girl. Okay I understand why you hesitated when he was still seventeen, but eighteen is legal. Plus, here in Liberia, some of these guys get twelve-year-old virgins."

Nicole glared at Andrew. "That makes it right."

"No, I'm just saying it seems okay that a man can have a woman or girl half of his age, but women can't do the same. You're supposed to be a modern woman. If the guy is for you, he's for you. I've felt the atmosphere in the room change when you two are together."

Nicole didn't respond but she thought about his words.

Andrew gave Nicole the bed and he slept outside under the stars. She protested as usual, but she knew he loved sleeping outside in his makeshift sleeping bag. He slept there most nights, at least when rainy season ended.

Directly, across his bed on the wall were pictures of his life. In the center was a picture of Andrew, Rebecca, Marvin and Nicole from their time in stateside training. There was another picture of them at a rally at the Washington Monument to petition for Martin Luther King's birthday to be a federal holiday. Wrapped in scarves with long winter coats, they joined the rest of the people holding placards urging the President to sign the bill. Nicole got out of bed to read the caption. Andrew wrote on the bottom of the picture in script with a black pen, Rebecca, Marvin, Nicole and me on January 15, 1980. Rally on Washington for MLK Day.

Nicole studied the other pictures on the wall. There was one of his family, a posed deal, but not from Sears or some studio in the mall. Herb Ritts, the famed photographer to celebrities and the very rich, had signed the bottom of the photo. Andrew's family picture screamed, "We have money but want to look like everyday folks." Andrew, his four older sisters, and mother and father, all wore white collared shirts with Diesel jeans. Not imported. Somehow Nicole knew they purchased the jeans on a trip to Italy.

They looked like the all-American family. Andrew's mother stayed home and his father brought home the bacon as a broker on Wall Street. When Nicole first met Andrew and heard about his background, she thought he was just another white boy slumming for a minute. Now she knew she'd misjudged him. The pictures he placed on the wall told his story. Yes, he came from privilege, had the best education at Yale, and wore $1000 jeans. But he also traveled 10,000 miles from the comfort of this home to teach Liberia children multiplication, and subtraction. He walked from hut to hut in the village to meet each parent and pleaded with them to encourage their children, even the girls to attend school. He shared with them, the importance of knowing how to count money so they could help their mothers with their transactions at the market, and help their fathers negotiate a good deal on their cattle. After a few minutes Nicole slipped back into bed and fell asleep, while looking at the pictures.

The next morning, she drove through the Bettencourt arches gripping the wheel of the truck. Many letters had passed between Femi and her in the last year, as well as some phone calls; but actually seeing him again made her shoulders tense. Her head throbbed over the temples. She rarely suffered from headaches, so she didn't know what was going on. She'd even recently stopped taking her malaria meds because they made her nauseous.

The arched trees leading up to the front of the academy seemed to welcome her. She reached the gate and buzzed, but before she could say her name, it opened. David stood in front of the house with two students. As soon as she stopped the truck, a student opened the door while another student moved to the back of the truck to get the luggage.

Nicole jumped down from the truck and walked to David, extending her hand for a greeting. David shook her hand and then turned it, brought it to his lips and kissed the inside of her palm. When Nicole jerked her hand away, David smiled.

"Well, my American sister. Welcome," David said.

"David."

"Why so curt? It has been a long time. We have missed you."

Nicole looked up at David, but couldn't see his eyes behind his dark sunglasses.

All of a sudden Nicole felt herself swaying, but she steadied herself. No way would she allow David any opportunity to touch her.

"Is Femi inside?" she asked.

"Grandma Julia asked me to contact you. I am sorry I didn't get around to it with all my other duties. He and his parents will not be here until tomorrow."

"When did this change? Oh, it doesn't matter. It's impolite for me to be here and not greet Grandma Julia."

"She isn't here either. She will return tomorrow. She went to Freetown to do some shopping and will return with Femi and my father."

"Who *is* here?" Nicole asked.

"Well, besides me, the teachers and students."

"No, I meant who is here in the main house?"

"That would be me and you," David said, slipping off his sunglasses and peering into Nicole's eyes.

Looking away from David, she motioned for the student to take her bags into the house and brushed past him.

"I'll have one of the students take me to my room. Don't wake me for dinner. The road wore me down. I'll see you in the morning."

Nicole stayed in the old bedroom of Femi's Aunt Adaisa. The room was now one of the many guest rooms for the numerous visitors. Nicole shut the door and locked it after the student set her luggage on the bed and left. She stood against the door, and started to cry, at first softly and then in choked sobs.

"Are you okay?" David asked from the hallway.

Nicole hoped if she didn't answer he would go away. She slid down to floor and rocked back and forth. Why the heck am I crying, she thought? Why not cry was her second thought. So much had happened. She didn't hear David any longer. Lying on the floor, she fell asleep. Sometime later she heard a knock on the door again. She got up from the floor, flung the door open and faced David who stood there with a tray of hot chocolate and a peanut butter and grape jelly sandwich. She moved aside and let him enter. He sat across from her in the sitting area of the bedroom and watched her eat.

"I always found it quite odd that Liberians, and Sierra Leoneans, well West Africans, entertain people in their bedrooms," she said. "I mean is it the norm to have an entire sitting room in your bedroom and to invite guests in?"

"We Africans like to share. Even our private moments," David answered.

"Well if you share your private moments, how are they private?"

"We don't think like Americans. What do you do with all that privacy? Shut the door and cry to yourself. No. When we cry, we want everyone to cry with us. In some tribes, a woman still shaves her head and wails all night and day for an entire week after a relative dies. The other women in the village join in to wail with her. You all sit in privacy and tell your psychologist your problems. We share our problems, so we don't have to pay anyone to listen to them."

David reached over to wipe a crumb of bread from Nicole's lip. The gesture caught Nicole by surprise and she spilled a bit of her chocolate. David reached for a napkin and wiped the spill.

"Why were you crying?" David asked.

"I don't think you'll understand, because I don't really understand it myself."

"You have no idea?"

"Of course. But it's complicated. Things are not always what they appear to be."

"What is that supposed to mean?"

"Like the story you tell of being Dr. Bettencourt's adopted son."

"What do you know of that?"

"I know what I see. What I sense. You resemble Femi and his father too much not to be a blood relative. I know they are a close family who wouldn't turn their back on even a child born out of wedlock."

"Well, let me leave you to rest," David said abruptly as he stood up.

"David, how did you know I like peanut butter and jelly sandwiches?"

He stopped at the door and turned to look at Nicole.

"You think you know something about me, but it is, what do you say, complicated. More complicated than you think. Sleep well."

The next morning Nicole woke to a bird singing outside of her window. The sun peeped through the white wood shutters beaming rays of light across her face. She showered and dressed in a hurry. Her plan was to be in the parlor when Femi and Dr. Bettencourt arrived from the airport.

She skipped down the steps in her new green and purple lappa outfit and slammed right into Femi. He looked taller and more muscular than she remembered him.

"Hey sleepyhead, are you okay?" he asked as he placed his hands on her shoulders to steady her. "I waited long enough. My dad advised me to let you sleep, but I was on my way to wake you the heck up. I'll only be here for a few weeks. We have to make our time count."

"A few weeks, I thought school didn't start until August. That's three months from now."

Femi put his finger to her lips and nodded his head to the side for Nicole to be quiet and follow him to the gardens.

"It seems like so long ago we stood here under the acacia trees. It *all* seems so long ago," Femi said, looking around the lush countryside.

"Look at you. All grown up, and a Morehouse man, like your daddy."

"Can you believe it?"

They sat in the garden, below the same tree they'd sat under over a year ago, holding hands.

"Nicole, you look the same. Beautiful."

She looked down at their hands laced together.

"That day at the slave castles, I changed," Femi said. "Knowing what they went through, the pain, the confusion, gave me a greater respect for my dad. For the work he does, and his commitment to the people here, that they're not just numbers. Like old man Traub, the blind wood carver. He went blind because of diabetes. My father makes sure he doesn't end up with other complications, by providing the medicine he needs. I keep thinking about that little girl who was killed by a simple infection because she couldn't get the medicine. I wanted all my father's attention. But now, I understand the great work he is doing."

"Fem, it's good you realize the sacrifice your father made, but don't feel bad about wanting to spend time with him. That's natural," Nicole said.

"We're a lot closer now."

"Good."

"But the reason I'm leaving in a few weeks, is if I plan to play football I have to arrive early at school to start practice. Even red shirts have to attend practice." Femi pulled out his acceptance letter to Morehouse and read it out loud. "Welcome to Morehouse and to the Maroon Tigers, the Morehouse football team."

Nicole leaned over and hugged him.

"Fem, congrats. What do your parents have to say?"

"Yes, what *do* your parents have to say?" David asked.

Nicole turned to see David standing behind her.

"It's none of your business," Femi answered.

"Wrong little brother, I am your elder. We all know in this culture, maybe not in America, but here in Africa, the big brother's say goes a long way."

Femi stood up and the brothers faced off.

"I told you when I first met you, I'm an only child," Femi said.

"I suggest you step back," David countered.

Before Nicole could speak, they started fighting. Femi with his muscular upper body strength seemed to have the upper hand. He pushed David back and then landed an uppercut to his jaw. David fell back, but with his strong legs from soccer he quickly jumped up and landed a blow to Femi's stomach. The two men became a jumble of elbows, fists and legs. Blood dripped from Femi's nose, but he kept fighting.

"Stop it! Stop it, right now!" Nicole yelled. You're both acting like grade school boys."

David pushed Femi off and the two men stood facing each other panting.

"Well, then you should be happy Nicole, since you like young boys," David said angrily and then walked away.

Femi grabbed David from behind, bringing them both to the ground. At that moment Dr. Bettencourt came running up the hill with a woman Nicole recognized from the family photos as Esther, Femi's mother. Grandma Julia followed behind them.

"David. Femi. Stop it now!" Dr. Bettencourt ordered.

The sound of his voice cut through the anger and bitterness between them and they separated, each taking deep gulps of air. Grandma Julia stood with her arms folded, looking at her grandsons.

"You two go clean yourselves up," she said. "We run a respectful place around here. Everybody meet in the parlor in twenty minutes. This will be settled before dinner today. Bettencourts don't air their dirty laundry in public."

She strode down the hill leaving everyone looking at her. Halfway down the hill, she turned around and said, "That goes for you too Ms. Jefferson. By the way, good to see you and welcome back."

Esther looked at Nicole from her head to her toes. She didn't speak. Nicole didn't blame her. She thought to herself, what if Femi was her son. She wouldn't speak to the older woman who didn't seem to know, that although he looked like a man, he was still a boy. He had Morehouse to attend, football to play, dances to go to, girls to date. What was he doing getting mixed up with a woman, who, in Liberia at her age, was thought to be an old maid?

In the parlor, Dr. Bettencourt stood in front of the fireplace, David sat on one side of the room and Femi on the other side with Nicole. Esther wasn't there. Nicole thought Esther's absence spoke volumes. She sat close to Femi, but didn't touch him. All this was her fault. She blamed herself for the fight between David and Femi. Grandma Julia bustled in the room.

"Esther doesn't feel well. If she can join us, she will. Let's get down to business."

"I think we should start with a prayer," Dr. Bettencourt said.

"Please lead Oyami," Grandma Julia said.

"Gracious father we come before you, humbly asking your presence as we request your guidance to resolve this palaver. May we do your will and not our will. Amen."

Grandma Julia didn't immediately speak. She seemed to be studying her hands. The winds battled outside, making drumming noises against the house. When she finally spoke, her voice competed with the wind.

"One time when I was helping my grandmother in the kitchen, I cut my finger. Blood flowed from the cut. My grandmother kept pinching the blood out of my finger. I was sure that all the blood in my body had concentrated in my one finger and my grandmother was going to squeeze the life out of me. I started to cry, not from any pain, but from fear."

She looked slowly around the room at each of them.

"My grandmother explained to me that, before she could clean the wound, she needed to get rid of all the contaminated blood and pus. That if she let the blood and pus sit there, the wound would become infected."

She looked at Femi and David, then continued.

"Your anger and emotional pain, are like the cut on my finger. We must acknowledge them, feel them, and let the blood and pus run out of them before we become bitter angry people. The cornerstone of this family has always been and will always be, love. We did and will have our moments of doubt, fear and division, but love prevails."

Like the long-standing fight between Dr. Bettencourt and his father, that didn't get resolved until the elder Dr. Bettencourt lay on his death bed. And the discord between Femi and Dr. Bettencourt, about his desire to play football, Nicole thought.

"In this family, we fight and have our disagreements, like any other family. But in the end we lick our wound clean, and patch up our differences."

"How does trespassing on to someone's property make you a member of this family?" Femi asked. "I have yet to figure that out."

David jumped up and walked to the door.

"David, sit back down." Grandma Julia ordered. "Families form in many ways, through blood, through love, through commitment to each other. Whether you like it or not Femi, David has become part of this family. He is a Bettencourt. Our hearts expanded and let him in."

Dr. Bettencourt looked at Femi, and then David. Nicole wondered what he felt. A man of little words, he seemed to always be observing, and making mental notes. He was protective of his family. Although he made a deal with Nicole to leave Femi alone, in an odd way he seemed to support their relationship. He brought Femi to her Peace Corps graduation ceremony in Liberia, and invited her to Ghana to visit the slave castles with them. Maybe in his struggles with his deceased father over his marriage to Esther at such a young age, and his choice to be a medical doctor made him more understanding of Nicole's and Femi's relationship. She felt Dr. Bettencourt to be an honorable man, a man with a legacy that he carried well. She could see that having Esther with him made a difference in him. The way he looked at his wife wide eyed in awe.

On the hill after Femi and David stopped fighting. Dr. Bettencourt took Esther's hand and coaxed her down the hill back to the house. He made tea and took it up to their room. Nicole thought his concerned look was less about his sons and more about his wife. While Dr. Bettencourt seemed to like Nicole, Esther was another matter entirely. From the moment she saw Nicole, she looked like she smelled rotten boney fish.

"This tension and anger, between the two of you, is my doing. When my father fell ill, and I came back to Sierra Leone, so often when Femi was still in elementary school, it created a wedge between us. Before I Grandpa Anderson's death, he and I were each other's shadows. As the old folks would say, I was peat, and Femi was repeat."

Was David really Dr. Bettencourt's son? Nicole wondered. She knew the pain David's relationship caused Femi, and witnessed David's manipulation of that sore spot. Nicole heard her mother's words in her head. "Pick your mate and friends carefully, because you can't choose your family."

She did not know what David's real relationship with the Bettencourts was, and didn't care. Grandma Julia's words rang true; there were all kinds of families. If their ancestors could weather slavery, and a white man from England could forgo his family inheritance to marry his black slave wife, buy their children's freedom, cross back over the Atlantic Ocean, settle and built Bettencourt Academy, an educational institution that after four hundred years still ranked as one of the most prestigious universities in the world, surely Femi and David could make amends. She thought about her own family.

Nicole received a letter from one of her cousins, while in Liberia, that Lemuel had been arrested for using his big rig to traffic drugs from Pennsylvania to Ohio. She hadn't seen him in years. The summer when she advanced to ninth grade she came home to find Lemuel gone. He'd moved across the river with his mistress, Belle. Grandma Kaitlan simply tossed all his clothes in the BBQ pit outside-threw some kerosene on them and set them on fire. When he called three months later to get his things, she told him she'd burned them, and would do the same to him if he ever set foot on her property again. Since his departure Kaitlan repainted the house purple, the door turquoise and planted yellow sun flowers all over the place. When Nicole remembered Grandma Julia's words, she found her own words. She whispered to Femi, so only he could hear her.

"Femi, do you think, for your grandmother's sake, you could give David a chance?"

He looked at her, but before she could say another word, she felt a sharp pain in her temple.

What You Give, You Get to Keep

NICOLE SLOWLY OPENED her eyes.

"Hey sleepyhead." Femi greeted her as she struggled to sit up.

"The last thing I remember is being in the parlor. Now here I am flat on my back in the bed," Nicole said.

"At first I thought it was your way of getting us out of there, but then I realized you really had fainted. You've been doing that a lot."

"I bet your family thinks I'm the biggest hypochondriac. Every time I come here, I either faint, or I'm nauseous and queasy. I read that when a person is under stress their immune system comes under attack, and they begin to manifest their stress physically."

"Son, do you mind if I examine my patient in private?" Dr. Bettencourt said from the doorway.

Femi winked at Nicole and said, "Okay, Dad. But I'll be right outside if you need me"

"Am I sick enough to be a patient?"

"Ms. Jefferson."

"I thought we settled on Nicole."

"Not when you are my patient. As a friend, you are Nicole; as my patient, you are Ms. Jefferson."

"Am I a friend?"

"Yes, I believe you are, Nicole," he smiled, then turned serious. "My wife checked your bag. I hope you don't mind. We had to ascertain what medications you were taking. But we didn't find any, not even your Aralen. The Peace Corps requires all volunteers to take it to prevent malaria."

"Malaria. That's what's wrong with me?"

"I am afraid so."

Nicole felt beads of sweat dripping down her forehead. The moisture on her body made her nightgown stick to her.

"You will need to rest. Dr. Brandt and your PO know you are here with us."

"Thank you, Dr. Bettencourt."

⊶⊷ ⊷⊶

Nicole woke several times during her sickness. Every time she woke she saw one of the Bettencourts sitting beside her bed, but never Esther. One time in a haze, she even thought she saw David and Femi at her side. Then one day, Esther was at her bed.

"Sip slowly," she said. "My husband tells me your fever broke. In a couple of days, you will be up and walking."

She held Nicole's head up with one hand and a cup to her lips with the other hand. Nicole took a small sip of the homemade chicken broth. Esther stood with the cup feeding her the soup until it was finished.

"How long have I been sick?" Nicole asked.

"Nine days. It could have been much worse. The average time according to my husband, is ten to fourteen days. So you have come through like a champ."

Two days later, Dr. Bettencourt allowed Nicole to join the others in the parlor for afternoon tea. He kept her on a diet of tea, chicken broth, crackers, and water. She learned Esther made the chicken broth fresh every morning. She'd also washed and dressed her every day.

Nicole remembered the last time they were in the parlor and the fight between Femi and David before that. But when she entered the parlor on Esther's arm, she saw them sitting at a table across from each other playing chess, while Dr. Bettencourt sat nearby reading. They all stood, when she entered the room.

"Look who I found wandering around," Esther said.

"Come sit here. The sun will warm you." Grandma Julia said offering her a seat.

Femi helped her into the chair.

Nicole wondered if she was still sick and hallucinating. She couldn't believe Femi and David were playing chess. She'd been on bedrest for eleven days and a lot had changed.

"Glad you are feeling better," David said. He then turned to Femi. "We will finish the game later. I need to check the irrigation system before the sun goes down."

One by one, each Bettencourt found a reason to leave the parlor.

"Kind of obvious huh?" Femi said sitting down on the stool in front of Nicole. He tucked a twist that had fallen in her face behind her ear. His hand felt cool against her warm skin.

"I honored your wishes, and I am giving David a chance. I still don't trust him and don't think I know the full story of how he became a part of this family. But for you and my family, I made amends."

Nicole cupped Femi's face in her hands. She placed her forehead against his, and they sat like that in silence for a while.

"What a courageous and loving thing to do," Nicole said.

"My grandmother always said what you give, you get to keep." I gave up being jealous of David. But I still don't trust him."

"What is that saying again?"

"What you give, you get to keep. Give jealously, keep jealously, give understanding, keep understanding."

That night Nicole woke with a start. She felt a presence in her room. The moon shone through the open shades. She sat up and looked around. Esther sat across from her in a white silk bathrobe, with her hair flowing down her back.

"You look like an angel," Nicole whispered.

She picked up the glass of water on the nightstand and put it to Nicole's lips.

"Sometimes, you scream in your sleep. At first I thought your fever was causing you to be fretful. But you still had them after your fever broke. I sat in here with you at night, to give my son a break. If it was up to him he would sit here all day, watching over you."

"You disapprove of our relationship."

"My first two sons, died. One miscarried, and the other lived for only three days."

"Femi, never told me."

"Femi does not know."

"I feel safe with him."

"I know he looks like a man, and in many ways, he is a man, but he is still my boy."

"He is legally an adult now," Nicole said.

"Think about yourself at eighteen. I want what every mother wants for her child, a good life, an honest life, a Godly life. My son has his own mind. He knows I disapprove of your relationship. I have been very clear about it. I can't forbid him to see you. First, I don't have that power, plus it will make him want to see you more. It doesn't mean I don't like you. On the contrary, you are a delight."

"Everything you're saying, I already told myself. Well, not about me being a delight. I mean that Femi is too young for me. What do you want me to do Mrs. Bettencourt? I mean Dr. Bettencourt.?"

"Call me Esther. I want you to let Femi live his life."

"What you give, you get to keep," Nicole said.

The deep bond that formed between Nicole and Esther that night became apparent to the entire household. Femi fought his mother for Nicole's attention. As Nicole recovered and regained her strength, she spent time with Esther. They would roll out the dough for the Sunday morning cinnamon rolls. They took long walks in the gardens talking. When Femi wanted to extend his stay a few weeks to make sure Nicole was okay, she knew it was time to go or he would miss football practice. And she knew it was time for her to return to Liberia, and her work. Esther made her promise to come back before she and Femi left for the states in two weeks.

"I knew I married a smart woman. Good thing I saved you from that lonely life you led, studying on Friday nights in the Morehouse library," Dr. Bettencourt said as he helped Esther pack the new hand dyed lappa cloth, leather sandals, and other gifts she had bought for Nicole.

"Why do you say, I'm smart?" Esther asked.

"You have made a friend of Ms. Jefferson."

"Of course, I like her. And it was not the Morehouse Library, it was the library at Spelman."

"We both know the two schools shared the library. But as I was saying, you made a friend of Ms. Jefferson to diffuse her relationship with Femi. I can learn a thing or two from you."

"No, I would say I learned from you on this one," Esther replied hugging her husband.

The morning Nicole left, Grandma Julia and Esther prepared a brunch of fried plantains, rice, chicken and gravy, turkey sausage, eggs and sliced mangos from the tree outside the kitchen. Femi and David planned to escort her into Monrovia. Femi would ride with Nicole with David following. They all lingered over breakfast for one more cup of coffee. Grandma Julia finally rose from her chair, and brought everyone to attention by clinking her fork to the Wexford water glass.

"We Bettencourts, do not say goodbye," she said. "We know life is a circle."

With that, all the Bettencourts stood and with raised glasses, looked at Nicole and said. "Faith. Family. Friends. Forever.

May God watch over you as you travel."

Half an hour later with the car loaded up, the only thing left was for Nicole to leave. Grandma Julia told Nicole she didn't like long drawn-out goodbyes, so she wouldn't walk her outside. But she took her to the side.

"I am an old lady now. I fell in love with Femi's grandfather when I was a little older than you. I am still in love with my husband, although he is gone. I know Femi's mother thinks you two do not match. Take it from an old lady. Give each other time. Don't let other people, not Esther, not my son, not your family, not anyone make the decision for you both. He is eighteen now. Don't let the difference in your age deter you. Determine if he is the one for you and you are the one for him."

She then hugged Nicole so tight that they both gasped.

Part of a Real Family

NICOLE RAN UP the stairs to the Peace Corps offices. It was 1982. In three months, her assignment would end. The Peace Corps Director, Dr. Brandt conducted exit interviews three months prior to the end of every volunteer's tour of duty. Director Brandt wanted to make sure those leaving knew the support systems that were available for their re-entry into America and to discuss the extension of their assignments with those who elected to stay for another tour of duty. Nicole didn't want to make another two-year commitment. But she wasn't ready to leave Africa.

She opened the door to the cool air. It blasted her, causing goosebumps on her arms. How Liberian she had become. She even wore sweaters in eighty-degree weather. Brandt's office door was closed, signaling she hadn't finished her interview with Marvin Taylor.

Resting her head against the chair Nicole closed her eyes and tried to imagine herself back in the US working in Corporate America. She knew they wouldn't like her twists or her African clothes. She rarely wore American clothes now. She couldn't go back. She thought she would need to buy a whole new corporate wardrobe, and straighten her hair. What did she have to go back to anyway-a PhD program at Harvard?

Everyone else talked about getting engaged, or married. Some even talked about starting a family. Nicole wanted to be part of their conversations, but more than that she wanted to get married. Or did she want to be married to fit in, to belong? She knew she wanted to experience life, to be a part of something bigger than her.

Femi was nowhere ready for a serious relationship. He's just a kid, she thought. A kid who still had undergraduate, and since he was a Bettencourt, post graduate school to attend. Could she wait for him? Would he wait for her? Did he even really consider them being together, or was it just a schoolboy's crush on an older woman?

When she thought of Femi or spent time with him, she felt a sensation she couldn't quite articulate. It felt like a river flowing in her soul, or the warmth of the sun on her face. She felt like her mother finally showed up in the navy-blue station wagon to bring fresh baked oatmeal cookies like the rest of the mothers, (not store-bought ones) to Nicole to share with her elementary school classmates. Being with Femi made up for the feelings she had of being alienated or left out. The two of them could sit for hours without speaking, just enjoying each other's company. She felt whole around Femi.

But was it Femi she desired or did she want to be a Bettencourt, to be part of a real family? Femi told her he fell in love with her the moment he saw her. Maybe it was the hypnotic heat of Africa, or just Africa itself. But maybe, just maybe, they belonged together despite, their age difference.

Nicole hadn't spoken to Souleymane since the induction ceremony. She thought many times of sending a note to him through her driver, but then thought better of it. If he wanted to see her, he knew where she lived. Maybe it was time for her to go home to America, or maybe she should just find a job with the United Nations. Despite everything, America was home. Could she continue to live away from her family? At one time she thought she loved Souleymane, and she knew her feelings ran deep for Femi, but was she really in love with either of them or was she really in love with Africa? Many thoughts crowded her mind. She wondered why she over-thought and over-felt everything.

The door opened and Marvin walked out.

"Hey girl," Marvin said.

"What's up Marvin?"

"Dr. Brandt said, give her about fifteen minutes. She'll come out and get you. I told her not to worry, you and I had some catching up to do."

He sat down in the chair across from Nicole.

"I know you can't wait to get home to see your bride," Nicole said.

"Yeah, it has been a long six months. Her mother wants us to do the wedding over again. She wants the whole church thing, with family."

"That's understandable."

"I don't mind. I'd marry Marlene a hundred times."

Nicole smiled at Marvin and looked down at her ring less hand.

"How did you know she was the one?" Nicole asked.

She'd heard people say they found 'the one,' or their soulmate. But what did that really mean? Did everyone have a soulmate, and if so, was there only one? Was love just chemistry? Or something man made up to quench his lonely soul?

"We clicked." Marvin said after a few moments. "I know a lot of people hooked up because they were thrown together in a foreign country. Not us. First we just hung out together as friends and co-workers. You know we taught at the same school. I always looked forward to school every day. I realized it was not just school, I was also looking forward to seeing Marlene."

"How did you go from friends to a couple?"

"One day during rainy season, we arrived at school to find it flooded. Mud had seeped in and covered the floor. Tears welled up in Marlene's eyes. She started digging out the mud with her bare hands. To lighten things up, I threw mud at her. She threw it back on me. By the time it was over we were both covered with mud. We ended up laughing, and then I just grabbed her and kissed her. That's when we both knew."

Marvin leaned forward and lowered his voice.

"What about you Nicole? I thought you and Andrew would end up together. At first it pissed me off. I was like that white boy better leave my girl alone. You know you're my homegirl, like a sister. But then as I got to know Andrew I saw him not as a white boy, but just as Andrew. I started to root for him."

"Our relationship is not romantic. We never had those kinds of feelings for each other."

"Speak for yourself. It's written all over Andy's face. Everyone knows how he feels about you." Marvin saw the surprised look on Nicole's face and said. "Don't tell me you didn't know he digs you."

Dr. Brandt opened the door before Nicole could answer. She waved Nicole into her office and said goodbye to Marvin.

Nicole sat through the interview with Dr. Brandt, but her mind wandered.

"I'm sorry, what did you say Dr. Brandt?"

"Do you want to stay?" she repeated.

Dr. Brandt clicked her pen several times, waiting for Nicole's response.

"Sorry," Nicole said.

"Well, I don't know where you were just now, but not here. I have another proposition I want you to think about. Would you consider staying on as a Peace Corps staff member? The contract goes from year to year. If you decide after the first year it's not a good fit, you can leave."

Ten minutes later, Nicole left the Peace Corps office as she arrived, undecided, but she had an opportunity to work on staff. She jumped into her truck and sped off. Halfway to her house, she made a U-turn and headed to Souleymane's. She'd only visited his home once. He took her there to show her where he lived, in case she needed to contact him and didn't want to send someone with a note. Guards stood outside his compound 24/7. As she pulled up to the gate, a guard approached her.

The guard told her that the general was not at home. As she pulled off, Souleymane appeared at the gate and buzzed it open. Nicole saw him but continued to back up. Souleymane ran to the truck.

"Nicole, what is it?" said Souleymane. "Are you okay?"

"I thought you weren't home."

"That is what they are trained to say if someone arrives without an appointment. What is going on? You never come out here."

"Nothing. I shouldn't have come."

"But you did. There must be a reason."

"Souleymane, why haven't you contacted me? You know my assignment is up in three months," she shouted.

"Okay," he stammered.

"Is that all you have to say?"

"Nicole, get down from the truck so we can talk."

A woman, with her hair in braids down to her waist wearing a fitted yellow lappa outfit, came to the gate.

"Oh, I see now why I haven't heard from you," Nicole said.

Nicole hit the gas, backed out, turned and zoomed away, leaving Souleymane in a cloud of gravel and dust. She drove for hours, past her house up country. Tears slid down her face. When the sun started to set she turned the car around and headed for home. When she pulled into her driveway Souleymane sat on her porch. He heard her before she saw him. She turned the ignition back on but before she could put the car in reverse Souleymane reached through the window and grabbed the keys.

"Nicole, what is going on with you, baby?"

"Me, what is going on with me? And don't call me baby."

"That woman is a family friend. She is Liberian, but she lives in America now. She is married."

He pulled the door open and lifted Nicole out of the car, and into his arms.

"This can't be about that woman. You didn't even know she was there when you came," he said as he looked into her eyes.

"I told you when we first met you that you are a serious woman who needed a serious man. I am that man. I have been waiting on you to get over your crush on the Bettencourts, including that young man."

"Do you want me to stay Souley?"

"I have wanted you to stay since I saw you that day at the embassy."

"I won't sneak around anymore. I don't care what the American officials have to say."

"Normally, married people do not sneak around."

He then put her down and kissed her.

That Type of History, That Type of Love

NICOLE SAT ON her bed still in her nightgown. She held the latest letter from Femi to her nose. He must have sprayed the letter with Old Spice cologne. Pictures of him littered her bed. One with him and his father in Soweto for Youth Day. He wrote that June 16 of every year since 1976, South Africans celebrated the uprisings of the Black youths who protested apartheid. Dr. Bettencourt had been invited several times by the organizers to speak, but always declined the invitation saying he was too busy. Everyone knew the real reason was the Bettencourts reluctance to become involved in politics. Nicole opened the letter and read it.

> Dear Nikki J,
>
> David came to Atlanta to visit us. He may apply to one of the colleges here, either Morehouse with me, or at Clark. I see your hand in this. Did you talk to him about completing his education? He and I teamed up on Dad, and persuaded him to attend the Youth Day rallies in South Africa. I told Dad that you said what good does your education do you or anyone else, if you don't take a stand on anything?

Nicole smiled, and continued to read.

> It crushes me that I didn't make it to Liberia this summer, but since your assignment will end in a few months, I'll see you stateside. The

Crescent line on Amtrak takes about thirteen hours from ATL to Pittsburgh, but David said he would drive down with me and pick you up.

I still have my doubts about David. My parents are happy that we're spending time together. I stay in the dorms, but come home for Sunday dinner. Dad doesn't acknowledge that I'm on the football team. I guess because I'm redshirted.

I want to tell you all about South Africa. We left Soweto and went on Safari in Kruger National Park. We saw the big five—lions, leopards, rhinos, elephants, and buffalo. We also spied crocodiles, hippos, and when I saw the giraffes I thought of you. We went to a town called Knysna, which is in the heart of the Garden Route. We met my mom there and went to the beach. David and I went diving in the lagoon while my mom and dad fished. Can you believe they have the most beautiful white sand beaches you have ever seen? There is also one of the largest Rastafarian communities there. David and I also went mountain biking in the forest. There is a cycle route that ends in a place called the Garden of Eden. Imagine that. I would like to tell more about Joberg, and the rest of South Africa, but my biology test will not let me. I will write you again tomorrow.

Love, Femi

Nicole looked away from Femi's letter to the long white dress hanging on the armoire in front of her. The dress, handmade by a local seamstress, combined traditional western designs with African ones. It was made of white silk, with long lace sleeves. It had a strip of handmade kente cloth from Souleymane's mother's wedding dress on the bodice in the back. His mother left him the dress after her death, requesting he give it to his bride. It was Nicole's idea to cut a piece of the fabric to attach it to her dress and use a piece of the material on the crown of her veil as well. She felt old. She knew part of it was due to living in a country that the culture taught any woman past twenty, and educated needed to hurry up and jump the broom before all her chances for matrimony got swept away.

When she thought about marriages with backbone, she thought of the Bettencourts. Not one divorce had been recorded in their family since the shipbuilder married the slave woman and crossed the ocean back to Africa. She wanted what the Bettencourts had, that type of history, that type of love.

The knock on the door brought her back to reality. It was her wedding day. She gathered the pictures of Femi and the letters, put them back in the shoebox she kept them in and shoved them under her bed.

"Can I come in?" Andrew asked. "You okay in there?"

"Come in."

Andrew sat down on the bed beside Nicole. She leaned her head against his shoulder. He pulled her close to him and wrapped his arms around her.

"I wish my mother was here. Or anyone in my family," Nicole said.

"You can always wait."

Nicole shook her head. Their assignment with the Peace Corps ended last week. At the end of the assignment, out of the twenty-five volunteers who stayed after the attempted coup, sixteen finished their assignment. Rebecca was the only one to sign up for two more years. Both Andrew and Nicole decided to leave the Peace Corps, but not Africa. Andrew planned to return to the states to raise money for his cooperative with the African artists, but he would return, and often. The people from the village where he taught would make hand-carved stools, chairs and even the armoires like the one Nicole's wedding dress hung from. Andrew would find the markets to sell the goods. The split would be eighty percent for the villagers, and twenty percent for him.

"I'm here," he said.

"Thank you, Andrew. Who knew at the end of two years of our assignment, we would still be standing?"

"The three of us made it. Rebecca signed up for two more."

"I wrote her. I asked her to come. I should have never walked out of that coffee shop without letting her finish."

Andrew picked up the picture of Nicole and Souleymane on the table beside her bed.

"He loves you Nicole. He's a good man."

"I know."

"Can I ask you something?"

"You know you can."

"Anything?"

"Anything."

"Do you love him?"

"Yes." Nicole said and then took a deep breath.

"Then put that wedding dress on and let me walk you down the aisle. The two of you will figure out the rest."

Nicole looked in the mirror. She couldn't believe she was a bride. She heard all brides had the jitters, but she felt like she was having a full-blown breakdown. She looked out the window.

She fingered the white lace on her sleeves, the material felt cool in her hand. If only her mother was there to advise her. Why was she marrying Souleymane, and not waiting for Femi? She'd thought about that question over and over again since Souleymane had asked her. The answers varied, the heat, baby fever, living in a country where not being married by twenty made you an old maid. Souleymane loved her. He was a man with responsibilities. He needed a wife, but her final answer was always that she loved Souleymane.

The wedding ceremony took place at the Moore Center. Nicole and Souleymane requested Bai T. Moore perform the ceremony. They planned a small event, since Nicole's family couldn't come, and Souleymane's parents had passed. He was an only child of only children, but many people from his mother's birth village made the trek for the wedding, and many of the elders from his father's village, where Esi had been the chief, also came. Souleymane wanted his childhood friend David Kumah, now Bettencourt to be his best man, but he'd moved to the states with his adopted parents. Their meeting in Liberia didn't happen. After the coup, Souleymane stayed busy with his military work, hunting down the insurgents, and keeping President Tanner safe. EXO Dubose was his best man. Vera Whittaker was Nicole's maid of honor.

To signal the beginning of the ceremony drummers dressed in purple boubou marched down the center aisle. Carrying the straps of the drums around their necks, they lifted their right hand with the drumstick and beat the drum, and followed up by their left hand. They didn't miss a beat. Female dancers sauntered down the aisle in purple and orange flowing ankle length dresses. Dubose walked behind them down the aisle in full military attire.

Souleymane entered and applause rose up from the guests. He strode in with a purple boubou with matching pants and hand dyed purple sandals, a gift from Andrew made by one of the artists in his co-op. He walked like a man on a mission. His coffee skin against the deep purple fabric made him look even more regal than usual.

Vera came down the aisle next wearing a fitted purple and white lappa outfit with her hair flowing past her shoulders. An usher pulled the white silk runner down the aisle, followed by Nicole's house girl and other little girls dressed all in orange with baskets of white, gold and purple orchids that they tossed on the runner.

All twenty-four drummers hit a drum roll. Then total silence. Nicole entered, on top an oversized drum carried by four men. Her twists cascaded down past her shoulders. Her western wedding dress, an ivory lace, hugged her waist and flared out to a fitted long skirt with a train. Kente cloth trimmed her see-through veil. She was barefoot. Andrew walked up to the drum and he lifted her off. Nicole and Andrew then walked down the aisle with their arms hooked together. Halfway down the aisle, Souleymane met his bride. He smiled at Andrew who released Nicole's arm.

Nicole and Souleymane made their way down the aisle together and stood in front of Bai T. Moore. Nicole felt the blood rushing through her veins. She envisioned herself ripping off the dress and running away. She knew she loved Souleymane, but could she love two men? What about Femi?

"Do you take this man to be your lawfully wedded husband?" Dr. Moore intoned.

Nicole looked around the room, at the guests, the other Peace Corps Volunteers, and Souleymane's aunties from the village, and did a double take. She hadn't invited her, but sitting beside them was Grandma Julia. She smiled at Nicole and nodded. Nicole felt lightheaded. No way on her wedding day would she faint. People already thought her to be a little odd. How fair would that be to Souleymane? A wife, how could she be someone's wife, when she found it difficult to take care of herself? A hundred and one thoughts felt like they were trying to get out of Nicole's head.

Out of some place deep in her, she heard herself say, "I do." With those two words she married Souleymane Guindo and became one that day Nicole Jefferson Guindo. Mrs. Guindo. The reception went by in a blur. She rarely drank and neither did Souleymane, but later when she called her sisters and they asked her to describe the reception all she could remember was biting the kola nut and drinking palm wine with Souleymane at the reception. She remembered changing from her wedding dress into a lavender lappa outfit with a matching headdress to complement Souleymane's outfit.

The wedding feast consisted of a combination of African, American and Native American foods. White rice, the staple of the African diet, with Nicole's favorite, Jolloff rice. There was a roasted pig, a tradition; but, because either Nicole or Souleymane ate pork, platters of local mangos, watermelon, papaya and pineapple sat on each table. Collard greens cooked in champagne with parsley, along with stewed chicken, and sliced beef and tomatoes. A large platter of homemade sausages with handmade pasta called Dorsey was made to honor Nicole's grandmother's Native American culture. They decided to postpone an official honeymoon until the following year.

->==◎ ◎==<-

Nicole immediately went to work with the Peace Corps as the Cross-Cultural Director. Her former Peace Corps coordinator, Ed Hawk, called a meeting with, Dr. Brandt. He attempted to block Nicole from obtaining the position. He said that she posed a threat to American security because she was married to a Liberian national. And not just any Liberian national, the Minister of Defense. Vera intervened to make sure Nicole received the position. Souleymane and Nicole made a pact not to discuss any sensitive information from their work, but in the end they rarely discussed their work at all.

The married couple fell into a routine. Nicole's childhood pain of isolation, and feeling unconnected after the twins left, didn't cross over to her marriage. With the exception of not talking about their work, they talked about, and shared everything else. Nicole moved from her small cottage with the turquoise door into Souleymane's home. They made plans to build their own home. She learned

Liberians didn't buy already built cookie cutter homes like in America. There was no real estate agent who took you around to look at pre-existing homes, or builders to ask you what kind of wood you wanted for your kitchen cabinets. People in Liberia saved their money to purchase land, bartered something for the land, or their family gave them a gift of land, as part of the marriage dowry. An architect drew up plans for the home, or usually there was a group of family homes within a compound.

President Tanner, who attended the wedding ceremony for a few minutes with his wife, gave Souleymane and Nicole a large parcel of land on the beach, as his wedding gift to them.

Ari and Aaron planned to come for a visit with their fiancés soon. Who could have imagined the twins would be engaged to twins? Shannon said it was too weird for her.

In their third month of marriage, Nicole and Souleymane pulled out the wedding china Vera gave them. It was from Limoges and had a blue willow pattern. The exact pattern Grandma Kaitlan had. She polished the silver, a gift from Andrew's family and set the table for five people. They pulled out their handmade teak wooden salad bowl, with the matching salad spoon and fork with camel bone handles, and decorated the table with tiny blue and yellow gourds. The perfect match of American and African.

Vera, and Dubose agreed to grace their table as the newlyweds' first guests. The fifth person, yet to be identified, was the EXO's surprise guest. Nicole assumed the guest was to be his daughter since Dubose had recently reconnected with her, and he said she would visit soon. That morning Nicole drove to the local outdoor market for fresh produce.

Nicole selected plantains, potato greens, and boney fish, a dried fish in palm oil. She felt a lightness in herself when she walked through open-air markets in Africa. The colors of the fruit, the orange sherbet color of the fresh-cut papayas, and the market women's pineapple so yellow and juicy that its smell couldn't be contained within the uncut fruit made her mouth water. She eyed avocados the size of small melons, heart red tomatoes were still attached to their stems waiting for someone to bite into them or slice a huge chunk to eat like one would eat a peach or plum in the states.

Lost in the world of vivid colors and smells, Nicole paid no attention to the other early morning shoppers. She reached for a bunch of monkey bananas and she felt a hand on her waist. She was then pulled back into a tight embrace and spun around. The next thing she felt was someone's lips on hers.

She dropped her basket of produce. She kneed the man in the groin and when he released her, she fell on the ground. The man held his hand out to her to help her up. Nicole looked up into David's eyes.

"I couldn't wait until this evening's dinner to congratulate you on your marriage," he said.

Nicole slapped his hand away and one of the market women came to her rescue wielding a broom.

"Mommy, you okay?" she asked stepping between Nicole and David.

She held the broom and swept it toward him, but didn't touch him. He backed up, but he didn't take his eyes off Nicole. Nicole heard the market woman's voice, as though through a fog that had settled in the middle of her head.

"What go on here, leave her, look you spoil her produce. You leave, before I call the police."

David pulled out a wad of money from his wallet and handed it to the market woman. She reached for the money, but then moved her hand away. The money fluttered to the ground.

"Go on you goat. Get out of here, and take your filthy money with you," she said.

David turned to Nicole, "See you tonight at dinner."

The market woman pulled Nicole off the ground. She brushed the dust off her clothes, and looked in her eyes to make sure she was okay. She then swept up the bills into a pile, shook the dust off and handed them to Nicole. Nicole shook her head no.

"He spoiled your market," she said.

Nicole shook her head again.

"Money is money," the market woman said. "We all need to eat."

"You keep it," Nicole said. The market woman picked up her basket and replenished it with fresh fruit. When Nicole opened her purse, she shook her head.

"You go home now," she said "You stay away from that man. He is no good. He and your husband used to be like brothers. You be careful."

"How do you know that?" Nicole asked.

"Mommy, this is Liberia. All is known. Be careful of that man. Tell your husband."

As Nicole drove home she kept her eyes on the rearview mirror to make sure David wasn't following her. In one of Femi's letters, he told her David had extended his visit to Atlanta for several months and might even stay indefinitely to apply for college. She tried to remember the date of the letter. In his most recent letters he hadn't mentioned David. She had to get to Souleymane.

She drove directly to the Presidential Palace. Nicole never visited, or bothered Souleymane at work. He sometimes called her on the phone from work or on their secure walkie-talkies issued by the Liberian government.

Everyone claimed the lines were secure, but she knew everyone monitored the airways-the Liberians, the Americans, probably the Germans and Russians, who knew who else. Souleymane told her he had their personal walkie-talkies programmed on a secure line; in case she had an emergency she would have direct contact with him. She wanted to talk to him, face to face, before David showed up at their home that evening with Dubose. No matter how David tried to cover up his true self, his deception showed through his actions.

The way he seemed to show up out of nowhere, when least expected. Even from the beginning, she thought that story about him showing up at the Bettencourt Academy looking for shelter and food over twelve years ago, didn't ring true, and the rumors about him consorting with rebels.

Then there were the stories Slopadoe, told her years ago, but made her swear never to repeat, that David was actually working with the rebels. But no one could prove it, and since his childhood friend was her husband, the Minister of Defense, no one would touch him, unless they had irrefutable proof. Even Femi told her he still sensed evil intentions in David.

She needed to talk to Souleymane immediately. She sped to the Presidential palace. The guards at the front gate recognized her, but still didn't open the gate. They walked up to the car. Nicole rolled down the window.

"You just missed your husband ma'am. He left to do some inspections at one of the bases."

Nicole sighed.

"Do you want me to have someone radio him?"

"No, that's okay. I don't want to alarm him. It isn't an emergency. I'll see him tonight."

"Yes, ma'am. I heard him tell his friend who was with him that tonight his wife will make a big big meal. His friend said he needed a big big meal after being in America so long. He needed some Liberian food."

Hearing that, Nicole knew the person with Souleymane was David. She decided to speak to EXO Dubose. Nicole drove to the embassy and parked. On her way to the lobby, she hoped she didn't run into Vera or the ambassador. She paced up and down in front of the receptionist waiting for Dubose. Nicole sat down in the new red suede chairs in the lobby. She'd heard that the Ambassador flew a professional designer in from New York to redecorate the entire embassy, every office, every lobby. After the decorator finished, a team of professional landscapers would arrive. All this would be paid for by the American taxpayers, but would go under the heading of foreign aid to Liberia.

"Mrs. Guindo, EXO Dubose will see you now," the receptionist said.

A Black marine stood at the reception desk waiting to escort her to the elevator. He waved her in and pushed the button but didn't accompany her. The elevator descended a couple floors. When it opened Dubose stood waiting for her.

"I expected you some time ago," he said.

They stood smiling at each other. When the elevator started to close Nicole ran out and found herself in Dubose's arms. It reminded her of the first day she arrived in the country and he'd helped her to her feet. He hugged her as a father hugs a daughter and gently kissed her forehead. Tears started to pour down her cheeks. He pulled a handkerchief out of his pocket.

She smiled and nodded her thanks, thinking of the first day when he'd given her his handkerchief. It smelled the same, like ginger.

He led her to a conference table.

"What did you mean by you expected me some time ago?" Nicole asked.

"I've known for some time that you wanted to ask me about Souleymane and David. I think the time has come for you to know their story. David told me he saw you in the market this morning, and that you were upset that he was back in town. He said you felt he was going to somehow be a threat to your marriage."

"That is a lie," Nicole stammered.

"Hold on Nicole. Hear me out. As a young graduate right out of The Citadel, I was assigned to Sierra Leone, where I met two little boys in a village not too far from my post in the neighboring country of Liberia. The boys were best friends, more like brothers to each other. Through my relationship with Chief Esi, I became a mentor to the boys. They became like sons to me."

Dubose came from around the table and sat in front of Nicole.

"They both loved to read and learn. I stayed in touch with the young men over the years"

"Souleymane and David," Nicole said.

Dubose nodded, then continued.

"Souleymane's mother died. His father was still alive; but heartbroken over the loss of his wife he went into a deep depression. Souleymane was an only child of only children. At that time, no child could be an orphan in Africa. Before the coups, diamond wars and little boys with guns, someone always took in a parentless child. Chief Esi took care of Souleymane, but she knew he needed a male figure in his life. I went back to America, married and had a child of my own."

"Your daughter who wears her hair like mine," Nicole smiled.

"My wife followed me to Africa, but the heat made her straightened hair brittle. The mosquitoes caused her flawless skin to become pocked and she wrinkled from the constant sun. She returned to America. I followed her, but Africa's magic wooed me back. I dreamed of the wide blue skies in the day, and millions of stars at night. I smelled the ginger sunshine smell of the continent and longed to return."

Dubose closed his eyes and seemed to transport himself back in time.

"Chief Esi's daughter Misu had gone to America with her father and never returned. I tried to find her, but the chief advised me that it would help ease her pain of losing her daughter if I were to make sure Souleymane and David continued their education in America. But she insisted they return home to their country as well. I couldn't afford to send for both of them at the same time, so I sent for Souleymane first, since he had no family with his mother dead and his father despondent. Souleymane went to America and attended, The Citadel. Souleymane's father died a few years after his mother and left him the farm and his wealth, which he could not touch, according to their custom, until he turned twenty-five. He joined the Liberian military and in his twenties became the highest ranking military man in the country."

He rubbed his mustache three times and continued.

"David on the other hand was a different story. I lost touch with him for years. I heard David's entire family had been killed by rebels. I didn't even know David was alive, until I saw him at the embassy with Dr. Bettencourt one day."

Nicole sat listening to the story of Dubose, Souleymane and David. She wanted to tell Dubose that David had assaulted her. He pulled her close to him and kissed her, knowing she was married to his childhood friend.

"So for years, you didn't hear from David?" Nicole asked.

Dubose nodded. "I contacted the Paramount Chief. When my wife and I separated I returned to head the US forces in Liberia. On several occasions I even traveled into Sierra Leone to look for him. Everyone assumed he was killed by the rebels along with his family."

"So for ten years, he lived in Sierra Leone with the Bettencourts and no one knew he still was alive," Nicole said. "Don't you think that's bizarre?"

"When the massacre happened, he was just a boy. We don't even know what he saw. We still haven't really talked about it. He probably blanked out much of what happened. To see your parents and siblings killed in front of you has to be a harrowing experience."

"Unless he killed his parents himself," Nicole mumbled.

"What did you say?" Dubose asked.

"Nothing." She didn't realize she'd spoken out loud.

"Are you concerned about David and Souleymane being in contact again? Souleymane and I are the closet thing David has to a family. Well, besides the Bettencourts, but I sense there is tension there. He hasn't gone into details. But I know that David would never hurt Souleymane."

"David followed me to the market this morning and assaulted me."

Dubose sat without saying a word. He looked down and away from Nicole. She couldn't see his eyes.

"I don't know if your heard me."

Dubose looked into Nicole's eyes. He did not seem surprised.

"I'll handle it. David will never bother you again. I take the blame for all of this. I should have sent for both boys back then. David wouldn't have been there when the rebels came. He always did want everything Souleymane had."

"That's your explanation?"

"Nicole. Don't mention this to Souleymane. I'll handle him."

"I can't keep this from Souleymane. I don't want David in my house."

"I said I will handle it. If we don't come tonight, it will cause more problems. After tonight David will be out of your life. I will make sure of it."

That evening, Nicole heard Souleymane as soon as he arrived home. She continued to cut up the pineapple and mango for the fruit salad. Her back to the door, she felt his eyes on her neck, and then his arms around her waist. He turned her to face him. He put his hand underneath her chin and pulled it up so he could look in her eyes.

"Are you okay?"

"Just tired," Nicole said. "You're home early."

"The guards radioed me as soon as you left the Presidential Palace. I came as quickly as the jeep could get me here."

He hugged her to his chest. Nicole stepped back out of his arms.

"Souley. I need to tell you something."

"I should know better than to interrupt newlyweds," David said from the doorway. "I tried to follow closely behind Souleymane, but he left me in the dust."

Nicole looked over Souleymane's shoulders into David's eyes. Souleymane turned around.

"Welcome bro. I didn't mean to run off and leave you."

"I understand. You thought your woman needed you. Hi Nicole. Good to see you again." David said reaching past Souleymane to hug her.

Nicole stepped behind Souleymane blocking David's touch.

"David, I'm a mess," she said. "Let me leave the two of you. Souleymane came home early. I didn't expect you at all. It's not nice to catch a girl off guard."

At dinner an hour later, Vera talked about the redesign of the embassy. She tried to keep the conversation going, but decided, since she seemed to be the only one talking, to shut up. David clanking his fork and knife against the china made the silence even more deafening. David appeared to deliberately scrape his utensils across his plate while Dubose moved the food around on his plate with his fork. He sipped his wine, and asked for several refills. In between sips, he kept his gaze fixed on David as if to warn him to stay quiet. Nicole broke the silence.

"What brings you back to Africa David, specifically Liberia? The last I heard you planned in stay in America for some time, maybe even attend school."

Souleymane raised his eyebrows and looked at Nicole.

"I hadn't heard that you were going to school over there," he said. "That is great."

"This is delicious Nicole. Did you purchase the food at the local market?" David said, instead of answering Nicole.

Nicole reached for the bottle of wine that sat in front of David and knocked it over. Before anyone could stop catch the bottle the red wine spilled across the table and on to David's white pants. He jumped up.

"What the hell!" He took his napkin and wiped at the wine, but that only made the stain bigger.

Everyone looked at him.

"Excuse me. Let me get some white vinegar for that stain," Nicole said in a high pitch voice. She then disappeared into the kitchen.

"Nicole hates cursing, man," Souleymane said. "I am sorry she spilled the wine on you. But I think you owe my wife an apology."

Souleymane followed Nicole into the kitchen.

She took the white vinegar and poured some into a bowl, then grabbed a dishtowel. Souleymane stood next to her.

"Something is bothering you. I know you. You started to tell me something, when David arrived. What is bothering you baby? I can't help you if you don't let me in. We are a team now right?"

The words stuck in Nicole's throat. She wanted to tell him. He was her husband. But David knew about her and Femi. Nothing happened between them. David could twist things. But he had a right to know that his so-called best friend disrespected his wife. But more importantly word on the street was that David was involved in the coup attempt. She had promised herself not to say anything to anyone, since she didn't have any solid evidence. What proof did she have of his involvement? It was one thing to tell him what she actually knew, and another to share what her gut told her. And what if she was wrong? While her intentions were to tell Souleymane, at least what she knew, when she opened her mouth, out popped, "I'm pregnant."

"What? How? When?" He picked her up and held her close to his chest. "I mean I know, how, but we were not intimate before we married. Did you go the doctor's? How do you know?"

"I knew the moment I became pregnant. It was our first night together. I haven't had my period for months. I went to the palace to tell you, then decided to wait until I confirmed it with the doctor."

Vera stood in the doorway smiling at the newlyweds.

"Well, you two. David already took off and Dubose, well I believe we will go as well. It's been a long week."

Nicole turned to Vera. "I feel terrible. Please stay. I made a fresh coconut cake for dessert."

"Well, in that case I must stay. Souleymane, go visit with the EXO. Let me help Nicole," she said.

When Souleymane left the room, Vera got busy grinding the coffee beans, and measuring the water to make coffee. Nicole wanted to ask her what she knew about David, and also about EXO Dubose. As if she'd read her mind Vera said, "Be careful of David Kinkeweh. He claims to forget so much of his life before his parents, his entire family was killed."

"Kinkeweh. That is the same last name of the man who led the coup attempt, Samuel Kinkeweh. I thought David's name was Kumah before he changed it to Bettencourt," Nicole said.

"One in the same. Samuel was David's older brother by twenty years, from another mother. 'Same pa, different ma,' as they say here. Samuel left Liberia many years ago to attend school in Germany. Kumah is David's mother's maiden name. Their father's last name was a Kinkeweh. Not many people know they're related. I'm not sure if your husband even knows. Our intelligence picks up lots of useful information."

Nicole couldn't believe what she was hearing. David was Samuel Kinkeweh's brother, the man who led the coup. If that was the truth, then she had to tell Souleymane, and Dubose. But maybe they already knew.

Nicole remembered seeing Dubose and David with the German couple in the hotel. Vera pulled a pen out of her purse, scribbled some numbers on a piece of paper and placed it in Nicole's hand.

"Memorize this number and call it on your walkie-talkie, if you ever need help."

Nicole looked at the numbers and committed them to memory. Now close your eyes. Can you still see them?"

Nicole closed her eyes and saw the digits in front of her.

"Are you sure you have the numbers?"

Nicole nodded to Vera, then ripped the scrap of paper into small pieces and put the coffee grinds over it.

A Safe Harbor

DAVID DIDN'T SHOW up again at Nicole's and Souleymane's house. She knew from Femi's letters, that David was still in Liberia. She learned from Femi that David was applying to colleges in the US. David told his parents he had to return to Africa immediately because he had some projects to complete at the academy, but he hadn't contacted any of the Bettencourts, since he'd returned to Africa.

Nicole had received a message at the Peace Corps office that Femi was only hours away in Sierra Leone. He arrived with his father the night before. He wanted to surprise her. He would be in Monrovia in two days to meet with David. Nicole didn't like surprises. She thought she had time. At three months pregnant she wasn't showing. What would she say to him, what could she say to him? "By the way young blood, I forgot to tell you I got married three months ago and I'm pregnant."

She left a note on the bed for Souleymane, then threw a few lappas in her bag, along with the makeup bag from Vera and a pair of jeans. Now on the road, she felt conflicted. What would she say to Femi when she saw him? If she drove all night she could make it to Sierra Leone before they arrived in Monrovia. She ran several scenarios through her head.

"I got pregnant, so I had to marry him."

Besides being a lie, he would hate her even more, since she encouraged him to stay a virgin until he married.

"I wanted to get pregnant so bad. I wanted a baby."

She could tell him how difficult living in Liberia was for her when most women her age were married with children. At least that played a part in her saying yes to Souleymane, or she could just tell him the truth.

"I made a pact with your father to leave you alone, but even more important I promised your mother, as one woman to another, that I would leave you alone. I wanted you to have the opportunity to live your life. To make the winning touchdown, kiss the girl, backpack through Africa, all the things as a young man who is unencumbered can do. And more importantly, I love Souleymane."

She kept her eyes moving from the road in front of her, to the rearview mirror. Every once in a while, a car on the other side passed her. The stars above seemed to light a path directly to Femi. On the road she saw what looked like a boy crossing, she veered off to avoid hitting him. The truck rolled over, off the road, landing back on all four wheels. When Nicole came to, she was dazed. It took her a few minutes to focus. She looked around, trying to figure out what happened. The doors and roof of the truck were dented, the windshield was cracked and the drivers' window was completely smashed.

Nicole felt her body for bruises and cuts. Although covered in glass she was, somehow, alive. Her seatbelt had kept her in her seat. The road was empty and there was the key still in the ignition. She turned the key, but the car wouldn't start. She pumped the gas pedal. The engine wouldn't turn over. She pushed her smashed driver's door open with her full weight, and jumped down out of the truck. She landed heavily and felt a pain in her leg from where it was bruised. She couldn't tell if she was near the border of Sierra Leone, or not.

She could wait with the truck or start walking. She opted to walk. Someone would pass soon. She stayed to the side near the bush, so she would be able to see the lights either way. She slipped on her backpack and limped off the main road into the bush to the back trail the market women used for safety. Hugging the side of the road, but in far enough that she could dart out to wave someone down from behind a bush or tree if headlights appeared on the road. The moon, three quarters full, gave enough light for her to find her way to the academy. Nicole and Femi had cut through the bush many times during their walks. When the rubber trees turned to the silk trees, she knew she had crossed the border from Liberia into Sierra Leone.

Nicole was careful to not crunch a fallen branch or startle a raccoon, or worse a coyote, or wild dog. When she had traveled a good hour into the dark she saw a fire glow several feet away. She tiptoed close to the fire, but stayed hidden behind a tree. She heard muted conversation. Several men were talking at once. There was English and another language being spoken. In her travels up country she heard many different languages spoken. She picked out a few words. It sounded like Krauhn, the language of the killed coup leader, Samuel Kinkeweh, David's brother.

Nicole peeked from behind the tree to get a better look. Around the fire sat several rebels from the Liberia Freedom Fighters (LFF). She could tell they were LFF by the signature green bandanas around their necks.

She watched as one soldier downed an entire twenty-ounce bottle of Liberian beer without taking a breath. When he finished, the other soldiers patted him on the back congratulating him as if he had just thrown the winning touchdown pass.

Another man, not dressed like the soldiers, but in a gray suit looked in her direction, it seemed straight at her, but she knew he couldn't see her. Nicole started to perspire in the cool night. It was David. She hadn't seen him since that night several weeks ago at her dinner table. The academy was still a good hour away. But she needed proof that David was involved with the rebels.

She searched her backpack for her camera. Even if David denied his presence with the rebel leaders in the bush, the picture would show the truth. Under her journal, miscellaneous papers and her food supply of turkey jerky, water safety pills, and vacuumed packed tuna fish, she found her camera. She couldn't use the flash, because as soon as she snapped the picture she would give away her location. Long ago in a photography class at Temple, she learned how to capture more light by opening the aperture. She focused the camera, opened the aperture as far as she could and clicked the button.

David stopped talking and held up his hand for silence. She knew he couldn't have heard the camera's almost inaudible click. But she also knew that part of living in the country made you more sensitive to sounds. David started to walk toward her. He pointed for another man to circle around the opposite way.

She strapped on her backpack. Placing one foot on the trunk of the tree and another on a branch she slowly climbed up. The big shiny distinctive leaves of the rubber tree helped hide her. She found a sturdy branch and held her breath. David signaled for the men to circle the area. She didn't know if he could see her footprints or not. He looked up into the tree. The other man joined him, shaking his head.

"No one bossman," the soldier said. "No one here. You too jumpy."

"All this has to stop," David said. "Samuel's dead for what? I want this to end."

"Too late bossman. Too many other folks running the show now."

"Souleymane Guindo must not get hurt," David said.

He looked up into the tree and then at the soldiers again.

"His wife either. Neither one of them must be hurt. If anything happens to either one..."

"It will not bossman."

Long after they extinguished the fire and the rebels and David departed, Nicole lay in the inner branches of the rubber tree. She pulled her backpack off and used it as a pillow. The kick on her right side at first felt gentle and then a series of little kicks came. The sun began to break through the night sky. Nicole lifted her head and registered that she had slept in the tree. She put her hand to her stomach. The baby kicked again. Nicole shook her head, and smiled. Her baby, she and Souleymane's baby kicked. Until then, the pregnancy hadn't felt real. She looked down at the ground.

"Unbelievable," she said. "I'm pregnant and I slept in a tree. That is a story your momma will tell you much later. That the first time you kicked, I was up in a tree."

She scanned the area again to make sure no one was around. She dropped the backpack to the ground. It was one thing going up a tree with it, but quite another coming down. She thanked Barron for all those years the two of them climbed trees and even lived most of the summer in their tree house. Who knew it would come in so handy, it may have saved her life. She jumped down from the lowest branch landing softly on both feet

"Don't worry little Araba. Momma isn't going to let anyone hurt you," she said rubbing her stomach. She then slipped on her backpack. She and Souleymane had already selected the name for a girl. They didn't have any boys' names. With the early morning light, she could see the silk trees. She was closer than she thought. It would take her ten minutes to get to Andrew's place. Knowing he might be outside sleeping, she didn't want to alarm him. As she approached his compound, she saw a lump covered with a gray blanket on a mat. She knelt beside Andrew who slept curled up in a ball.

"Hey, Andrew. Do not trip."

He lifted his head and smiled a lopsided grin.

"This is a nice surprise. You look like a real jungle girl." He yawned and sat up. "Are you okay?"

"That could be a racist statement, and Yeah. I need a bath and something to eat."

"I agree, about the bath, and I meant no harm." he smirked.

After a shower and a bowl of oatmeal, Nicole told Andrew she wanted him to drive over the border to Bettencourt Academy and bring Femi back. She needed to speak to him. She told Andrew about David and the rebels.

"I have a number for Vera Whittaker. I need to contact her, but my walkie-talkie is dead. Can we get to a phone? And I also need to talk to Femi before David gets to him, and tells him I'm married."

Andrew sat across from her and stirred his oatmeal over and over again, making swirly designs.

"I thought you told him."

"I wanted to… I tried."

"Nicole, this is messed up. On this one, I can't support you. You're just plain wrong."

"I know."

"When did you become a liar?"

"Wow." She knew Andrew was right. There was nothing she could say to defend herself.

"You're the one always talking about being honest, and standing for the truth."

"I already told myself everything you're saying to me."

They sat across from each other in silence until Andrew left.

Nicole waited at Andrew's, while he drove to Bettencourt Academy. As much as Nicole wanted to see Dr. Bettencourt and Grandma Julia, she knew she couldn't risk running into David. She knew Femi's grandmother hadn't told him she was married. He never mentioned it in his letters. At the reception, she told Nicole that it wasn't her place to tell him.

She heard the car door slam and before she could move from the chair Femi stood in the doorway. He looked taller. Broader. His presence filled the space and she felt as if the walls of the hut were closing in on her. He walked across the floor and picked her up. She hugged him around the neck. When he put her down he bent to kiss her and Nicole turned her head, and pushed away from him.

"What's up, Andy coming to get me. And you're acting weird. Are you okay? You look really, well worried. I thought you wanted to surprise me."

"Femi. I need to tell you something. Can you please sit down?"

"Whatever you need to tell me I want to hear on my feet. People always tell you to sit down when there is bad news. Like sitting down will help. Whatever you got, give it to me while I'm standing."

Nicole closed her eyes and then said in one long sentence, "I married Souleymane Guindo, and I'm pregnant. I didn't mean to lie to you, or lead you on. Hurting you is the last thing I wanted. I knew our lives wouldn't work together. I wanted to tell you in person."

Femi closed his eyes and rocked back on his heels. He stood like a statue for what seemed like hours clenching his fists, but was just a few moments. Then he pulled Nicole close to him and kissed the top of her head. He released her and looked into her eyes. A singular tear escaped his left eye.

"Aren't you going to say anything?" she asked.

"Congratulations. Souleymane is a blessed man. Contact me Nicole, if you ever, and I mean ever, need anything."

He turned and left. Andrew sat waiting in the jeep. Femi opened the door and climbed in. Nicole stood outside, watching them pull out.

As the jeep turned the corner she prayed, let him turn around and look at me. Just let him look. Femi turned his head, and placed his palm flat on the window. Nicole raised her palm. She then turned around, putting one foot in front of the other until she was back inside. Pulling out the chair at the kitchen table, she rested her head on the table and cried herself to sleep.

She woke to a buzzing sound. The sun was setting and only a few rays of light shone through the window. Her purse sat next to her. She realized the buzzing was from her walkie-talkie which she thought was dead. Reaching into her purse, she saw the code for Souleymane. He had called her several times. Did he know she went to see Femi? Was he calling her to tell her not to come home? The walkie-talkie buzzed again, right in her hand. She dropped it on the table. If he didn't want to be with her anymore, she deserved it. She should have come clean with both of them.

She pressed the button.

"Souleymane."

"Nicole. Thank God you are all right."

"Souleymane, I'll be home as soon as I can."

"They found your truck on the road, not too far from where there has been reports of rebel activity. We thought they captured you."

"I'm American. Why would they capture me?"

"You are my wife. Look David is here with me. I don't have much time. Listen to me."

"David, is standing right beside you! Souleymane, I need to tell you something."

"Hey Nicole, it's David. Please listen to Souleymane."

"David, put my husband back on. I have nothing to say to you."

Souleymane came back on.

"Souley listen to me. Don't ask me how I know this, but I do. David is one of them. He meets with the rebels. His half-brother was Samuel Kinkeweh."

"I grew up with David. Yes, I know Samuel was his half-brother, but David was trying to get the rebels to turn themselves in. Please listen to what I am trying to tell you. There has been another coup. President Tanner is dead. David saved my life. He warned me. We don't have much time. When someone reported your truck on the road, and you were nowhere to be found, we thought the rebels had kidnapped you."

Nicole gripped the walkie-talkie. She was shaking. She couldn't believe what Souleymane was saying. There had been another coup. President Tanner was dead.

"Nicole, are you there."

She nodded her head.

"Nicole?"

"I'm here."

"Listen to me. If they find you, they'll try to take you. Because of who I am. I am a target. That makes you a target. Dubose is on his way to you. Do whatever he says."

"But he doesn't know where I am."

"There is a tracking device in your walkie-talkie."

"You put a tracking device on me."

"For your own safety Nicole."

Another Coup, 1983

"FOR YOUR OWN safety." Those were the last words Nicole heard Souleymane say. She played those words over and over again in her head. "For your own safety." For. Your. Own. Safety.

"Another coup," she said out loud. Would it ever stop? But she knew the makings of the recent coup in Liberia and coups all over the world started in the hearts of people who wanted power, or change, or both. Some wanted power over the gold mines, or diamonds. Some wanted change to be able to take their baby boy to the clinic to get medication, when he wouldn't stop vomiting, or the fever wouldn't break. Some wanted what they saw others had, the big cars and fancy houses. Some wanted clean water and food to eat on a daily basis. Some didn't know what they wanted. Nicole knew what she wanted. Souleymane. Her husband. Her husband she had betrayed.

Dubose picked her up from Andrew's and drove her over the border to the Bettencourt Academy. Maybe they were reluctant to get involved in politics before, but now it concerned one of their own. Grandma Bettencourt said that she thought of Nicole as one of her own. The Bettencourts took her in over Oyami's protests. Even Esther sided with Grandma Julia that they should protect Nicole and use Bettencourt Academy as a safe harbor for her.

Nicole spent her days in front of the fireplace in the parlor waiting to hear from Souleymane. She waited for a word from across the border. She waited to hear when she could return to Liberia and her husband, to her life. The United Nations Peace Keeping Troops had arrived to secure the border between Liberia and Sierra Leone, to stop the gunrunners. But the rebels seemed to have a steady supply of guns and beer. They made beer in Liberia, so she knew where that came from.

Nicole sat for hours watching the flames in the fireplace burn. Even in the heat of the day, she wanted a fire. Days passed into nights, and nights passed one over the other. Weeks went by. When they brought her breakfast tray to her, it came back with a pinch of the biscuit gone, a bite of the apple, a sip of the orange juice. The lunch tray sat untouched. The dinner tray became peanuts, fruit, and tea sandwiches. Sometimes she ate one or two items on the tray, mainly for Araba. She had to think of more than herself now.

Dr. Bettencourt left for Freetown. He said the new hospital in Freetown kept him busy, too many meetings with government officials, planning committees, and the banks. He had set the meetings up months ago and if he didn't show up, people would think something was odd. But he contacted the local midwife, a Sierra Leonean, to see after Nicole. She was well trained. She'd done her undergraduate work at the Bettencourt Academy and her graduate work in England, he had every confidence she could look after Nicole.

Someone needed to look after her. The news kept coming from people who came to visit. The rebels took over the main road from, Monrovia, but government soldiers still controlled the airport. Nicole knew that "government soldiers" meant Souleymane and his men. Dubose brought in more troops from America to help the Liberian government soldiers, or what people began to refer to as SS, Souleymane's soldiers.

The Liberian Congress called an emergency session. No one was in charge in Liberia. The Vice President had fled the country. Many government officials were executed. The rebels even broadcasted the executions on Liberian TV. The country needed an interim president. Someone had to take charge, or there would be chaos. They swore Souleymane in. President Souleymane Guindo. Her husband. Nicole thought. My husband is the President of Liberia, which means I am the First Lady. It meant nothing to her without Souleymane.

Nicole sat, day after day, with her shoulders slumped forward, and her red and blonde twists dry and brittle, eating little and speaking less. On the sixth Sunday after the coup, when Grandma Bettencourt returned from church, she went into the parlor with yarn balls of pink and green and sat in the side chair near the fireplace, so Nicole could see her. She took out a pair of knitting needles and looped the thread through the needles. The next day she returned, but this time she sat right in front of the fireplace blocking Nicole's view. Nicole watched her, but didn't say a word. For days, Grandma Bettencourt sat in front of Nicole looping thread over and under, in and out, knitting a baby blanket. One day she brought an extra pair of needles and left them on the leather lounger Nicole sat on. Days later, she entered the parlor to find Nicole looping the needles to create her own square. One day, Grandma Bettencourt showed up with some olive oil and beeswax in a little silver bucket.

"I tell you," she said. "The way one's hair grows while pregnant makes up for all the morning sickness, even the swollen feet. Your hair has grown, so I just want to massage your scalp for you, like my momma used to do when I was pregnant. Since your momma isn't here, allow me to stand in."

She took the warm oil olive and rubbed it in her hands, then she pulled the twists apart. Nicole's twists, now matted from lack of moisture and care sprang back to life under Julia's hands. Sometimes, as she massaged her scalp, Nicole would fall asleep. Once the entire scalp glistened with the olive oil, Grandma Julia dipped her fingers into the beeswax and ran the substance down each twist strand. Nicole's blonde and red twists once again framed her face like a halo. The two ladies sat in front of the fireplace, now daily, knitting squares for Araba's receiving blanket.

Grandma Bettencourt barred anyone from discussing anything to do with the coup, or the war across the border. If Nicole asked, they could answer. But she didn't ask. She waited only for a word from Souleymane, mainly that he still walked and breathed. The rebels put a $100,000 bounty on his head. There were many rumors of where they received their money and guns. Little by little, the fog started to lift from Nicole's eyes, and their sunbursts started to sparkle again. She started reading every baby book she could get her hands on.

"Raising children is common sense," Grandma Bettencourt said.

"Well, I'd better make sure I read everything because we know I am lacking in that department."

On another day, Grandma Julia showed up in the parlor with a bucket of hot water in the foot bath and pedicure instruments. She placed Nicole's feet in the tub to soak, and then removed one to a pink towel on her lap. She pulled out the cuticle remover and commenced to removing the dead skin. While she gave Nicole a pedicure one of the house workers massaged her shoulders.

Now when the breakfast tray showed up Nicole ate all the eggs with vegetables, but no bacon. The next day no bacon appeared on her tray, but a side of oatmeal. She ate it all. On her lunch tray, she didn't touch the pita bread, or soup, but she devoured the chicken salad. The next day she had a double helping of chicken salad. By the time Malaika, the midwife, a little wisp of a woman with a voice that sounded like a bell chiming arrived, Nicole had gained five much needed pounds.

"Everything looks good," Malaika said. "Your pressure reads fine. Grandma Bettencourt tells me your appetite recently picked up. That is good. You could stand to gain a little weight."

"How's Araba?" Nicole asked.

Malaika raised her eyebrows and looked at Nicole.

"My baby."

"Well, I don't know your child's gender, but the baby is fine."

"I do. It is a little girl. My husband wants a little girl. He said he will take her hunting for bush meat, but also make sure she wears pigtails with pink ribbons. I thought he would want a little boy, like a lot of men. But he said he wanted a little girl, who looked just like me."

"President Guindo is a great man. He and his troops will defeat the rebels. The people of Liberia love him. Tanner was another story. I believe you will return home to your husband with your baby girl and live happily ever after. You heard it here first," Malaika said.

She then hugged Nicole and told her if she had any problems, call; but Dr. Bettencourt planned to return to the Academy before he left Sierra Leone. He would do her next checkup.

Nicole continued to knit, blankets, booties, sweaters. After she'd made piles of attire for Araba, she started to make shawls, hats and sweaters for the village women's children. When they recounted how the coup actually took place, the stories varied, but in the end Nicole thought, what does it matter how it happened? It happened. Some say Tanner slept the sleep of a small child in his mother's arms, well fed, warm and wanting for nothing. But in the wee hours of the night, an army of young men, some as young as nine scaled the walls of the mansion, walked into the palace and slit the throat of long standing President William Tanner, while his wife watched. They say she told him that was for all the years he cheated on her. Some say, after the soldiers slit his throat, his wife cut his penis off and put it in a jar to make witchcraft medicine.

So it was not so much a coup for power, but an angry wife who suffered years of neglect and abandonment. The days after the coup, rebel soldiers (LFF) and government soldiers-Souley's men-battled each other for territory. They fought over the airport, and the government soldiers won. They fought over the palace, the government soldiers won. They fought over the road leading out of Monrovia, the LFF won.

Ambassador Watkins didn't evacuate Americans. He didn't call them in from their posts. He did put word out on the street, that if any American was hurt, the rebels would pay dearly. A curfew was established, no one was allowed outdoors after 6 PM. Safe at the Bettencourts' in neighboring Sierra Leone, Nicole spent her time preparing for baby Araba. Days passed into weeks, weeks into months.

Femi requested a delayed admission for the winter semester at Morehouse, due to a family emergency and it was granted. The Bettencourts just donated ten million dollars to the school. Grandma Bettencourt bustled around taking care of Nicole. Femi and Nicole rarely ended up in the same room with each other. He often looked in on Nicole to make sure she had a glass of milk, or had her feet elevated as the midwife recommended. He never sat down in the same room with her alone.

News came that the rebels' last stronghold right outside of Monrovia, had been taken over by Souleymane's men. The new President sent word to his first lady that she may be able to return to Liberia in a few weeks, but he wanted to wait and see.

A few days later Grandma Bettencourt came into the parlor to find Nicole knitting a baby blanket for one of the teachers at Andrew's school. Femi came into the room, greeted his grandmother and Nicole and said he was going to go work in the garden.

"Nicole, why don't you join him?" Grandma Julia said. "I am sure you miss your garden in Liberia."

Nicole and Femi looked at each other.

"I believe it is time for you two to reconcile. We are family here. At some point, and I think better sooner than later, you should talk."

Nicole and Femi walked the hill to the garden. Some students from the eighth-grade class had already started pulling weeds, and preparing the soil for planting. Students studying agriculture worked in the gardens as part of their curriculum, but all the students spent some time there. On the academy grounds, gardens sprang up everywhere. There were flower gardens and vegetable gardens, and gardens for the students to experiment with hybrid plants and flowers. Then there was Grandma Bettencourt's own personal garden that she spent hours in. She grew tons of roses in the soil everyone said wouldn't bloom a thing. But who doubted her. Here was the woman who had bred giraffes in West Africa.

Femi and Nicole headed for her garden. Nicole found herself huffing to make it up the small incline. Femi took her hand and helped her up the hill. At the top of the hill she released his hands, bent over and panted.

"This pregnancy thing is no joke," she said. The familiarity of Femi's hand made her smile.

"You okay?"

He plopped down on the hill and patted the ground beside him.

Nicole put her hands on her hips, then patted her protruding belly.

"You must be joking, if I sit down there I don't think I can get up."

"Girl, you aren't that big. Besides I'll help you." He held out his hand. She took it and sat beside him.

"How does it feel?" he asked her.

"To be pregnant?"

"No, to fly," he joked.

"You know there are flying Africans. Some flew out of slavery."

Femi looked down at her belly. "You're avoiding the subject."

"Femi. I don't know what to say to you. I lied to you, betrayed you. How can you even look at me? Don't you hate me?"

"Nicole, I told you I fell for you the moment I saw you in that market in Sierra Leone. I could never hate you. No doubt you hurt me. But you have a life in you. You need all of our love and support. Your husband is a President of a country under siege. Now is not the time for me to think about myself."

How such a young man became so wise, Nicole wondered.

"Did Grandma Bettencourt tell you to say all of that?"

"Yes, but I had already felt most of these things. She gave my feelings words."

"How did you grow up to be this caring, unselfish young man?"

"It's in the genes. I come from a long line of remarkable people; men who envisioned a better life for their families, and women who worked and prayed right alongside those men. And partly because of you. I met you, a woman who left her own country, because she believed she could make a difference in the lives of others."

"Femi. You and I, we can't be together."

"Nicole, I wouldn't even think about that. You're married. I honor your marriage."

"We need to get back," Nicole said. "Your dad is supposed to come back today and do my examination before he heads to the clinic to do vaccinations."

Femi stood up, held out his hand to Nicole. She took it and he helped her back down the hill, as he promised he would.

Dr. Bettencourt returned to the academy carrying the weight of his son's betrayal. In Freetown, he'd heard the rumors of David's involvement in the coup. His face showed his weariness, with permanent furrowed lines creased across his forehead.

"Ms. Jefferson, I mean Madam First Lady. Everything looks great with little Araba. I understand from the chart notes that Malaika made that your appetite has picked up. That is good. Please continue to eat well. What about moving around a little more? I remember you used to take long walks over the hill to the gardens."

"So we're back to formalities."

"You know, I call all my patients by their last names."

The nurse looked at Dr. Bettencourt and then at Nicole.

"I didn't set out to harm your family. Since your return from the city, I haven't had a chance to talk with you."

"You can get dressed, Nicole. We can talk in my office."

Dr. Bettencourt scribbled some notes on Nicole's chart. He handed the clipboard to the nurse, who left the room. His office, half the size of the three examination rooms at the clinic, could only fit his desk, chair, and a chair for the patients. Oyami sat behind his desk in his white coat, writing on another chart. Nicole stood in the doorway until he acknowledged her.

"I understand Femi and you have straightened things out."

"We have."

"That is what counts with me."

"May I sit down?"

He closed the file, and motioned for Nicole to sit. She continued to stand, she was staring at the pictures on his desk. There was one of their wedding, Esther was wearing a long white dress and he was in a white tuxedo with a kente bow tie. Beside that was another picture of Femi as a baby in Esther's arms, and then a recent picture of Esther, Femi, David and Oyami at Femi's high school graduation. Dr. Bettencourt waved his hand again, motioning her to sit down. She sat across the desk waiting for him to speak.

"What do you know about David?"

Nicole shifted her weight in the seat. She bit her lower lip, trying to process the unexpected question.

"Souleymane told me they were more like brothers than friends. They grew up together, played soccer in the field behind their small village. Both of their fathers farmed, in an area where most worked on the rubber plantations. They met EXO Dubose as boys. He sort of adopted them, sponsored them in school. Souley and David even came across the border from Liberia to take some summer college prep course here at the academy."

Dr. Bettencourt took his glasses off and laid them on his desk. "Then you know the EXO sent for your husband, and David stayed behind. The rebels killed his family and David came looking for me at Bettencourt Academy."

"I know you must feel a great burden," Nicole said.

"Esther knows. It was years before we were married. I didn't know that I'd impregnated his mother. I was home on school break. His mother attended school here at the academy. One day she just didn't come back to school, and I went back to Morehouse. I found out later that my father paid them to move back across the border to Liberia. He knew I wanted to finish college in the US. If I had known David's mother was pregnant, I would never have left. I guess in his own way my father supported me being a doctor. But it was wrong. He should have told me."

"She didn't tell you she was pregnant with David?"

"I didn't know anything about David until he showed up at the academy already a teenager. While pregnant with my child his mother married another man in Liberia. She died in childbirth with her fifth child."

"But I thought David came from a large family, with several brothers and sisters."

"David's family lived the traditional way. His father married four times. Folasade, David's mother was his third wife. His older brother and sisters belonged to the first and second wives. They all knew David was not his child, when his mother died, the entire family shunned him. His stepdad tried to protect him because he promised David's mother he would, but when his stepdad was killed by the rebels for resisting, David fled in fear for his life. David is my son just as much as Femi is my son. His stepdad left him instructions in case of his death he needed to go to Bettencourt Academy and look for my father, and mother."

Nicole knew the rest of the story, Dr. Bettencourt visiting from the United States came to the school to find David sleeping on one of the children's cots.

"I knew as soon as I saw him that he was my child. I knew he was a Bettencourt. He looked just like an older version of Femi."

Oyami handed her the photo of the four of them together.

"Does Femi know?" Nicole asked.

"We told him the night of the fight, but he does not talk about it."

-->==o o==<--

Weeks passed and Nicole's belly grew larger. Femi and Nicole continued their daily walk in the garden. Femi pulled weeds while Nicole clipped roses. Since Dr. Bettencourt's return to Freetown to meet with the United Nations Funding committee, Nicole pushed any thought of David's role in the coup out of her mind, but she knew she needed to show Souleymane the picture she had taken.

One of the teachers at the academy planned to take Femi to Freetown in a few days to meet his father so they could fly back to Atlanta. Classes at Morehouse started in a few weeks. No one knew where Nicole was. Not even her family in America, but they knew she was safe. Dubose told her the fewer people who knew her location, the safer she and Souleymane would be, especially since she was pregnant. If the rebels captured her they could use her to get to Souleymane, or worse kill her. But David knew she was at the Academy. Maybe he was trying to protect them after all.

Nicole clipped each rose stem and placed it in a basket. The first sharp pain started in her pelvis, then shot up her spine. She bent over. A wet substance dripped down her legs. Only six months. She knew it was too soon for her water to break. She wiped her hand on her leg and it came away red with blood. Her mind raced recalling all the baby books she read. Miscarriage. No stillbirth, she thought. A miscarriage can only happen in the first twenty weeks. She calculated the months. When she left Liberia, Araba was twelve weeks, about thirteen weeks had passed since she arrived at the academy. It didn't seem that long, because for the first six weeks she sat in front of the fireplace in a fog. Now the labor pains seemed to be splitting her in two. She breathed through her nose and out of her mouth. There wouldn't be any stillbirth here. She rubbed her belly. Araba just wants out. Araba wanted to see mom's face now.

"Femi," she called breathing from her diaphragm. She remembered one book saying that if premature labor occurred and you couldn't get to the hospital, lie still and get help right away. Femi heard her and ran to where she lay in a pool of blood. He pulled his gloves off, wiped his hands on his pants and knelt down beside her.

"I need to leave you for just a minute to get the midwife and Grandma Bettencourt. Keep breathing like we practiced. Just keep breathing and don't move."

Nicole lay on her back with the basket of roses beside her. She called on the strength and knowledge of her grandmother, the midwife and her mother, the nurse. Lying on her left side she prayed. Femi came running up the hill followed by Malaika, and shortly afterward Grandma Julia, several teachers, staff and even students. They placed Nicole on a gurney and carried her down the hill back to the house. A few hours later Araba Kaitlan Julia Guindo screamed her way into the world. Fair-skinned, like her great grandmother, she weighed a little over three pounds with a thick full head of straight black hair slicked down on her head. She looked into her mother's eyes and smiled.

Dr. Bettencourt arrived in time to check the vital signs of mother and daughter. Araba checked out fine. Nicole needed bed-rest for the next month or two. He postponed his return trip to Atlanta.

Every night when the clock struck midnight, Araba opened her dark black eyes with specks of gold, looked into her mother's identical eyes and wailed. She started out with a whimper, but soon a roar rose out of her little body. Nicole's breasts couldn't produce the milk Araba needed. Grandma Julia hired a local woman to care for mother and baby in the night, but in the day time she fed, and bathed both Araba and Nicole.

Every day Nicole insisted she hold Araba, even if just for a few moments. Grandma Bettencourt took lots of pictures with Nicole feeding Araba, with Araba curled up in Nicole's arms asleep, and even pictures of her crying at the top of her lungs, while Nicole rocked her. Still not able to speak to Souleymane, Nicole wrote in her diary to share with him later, every yawn, tear shed, and smile. Araba looked like both Souleymane and Nicole. She had Souleymane's high forehead, and Nicole's distinctive eyes, her lips and nose.

Femi came every day to hold Araba, while Grandma Julia took care of Nicole; and every night when Araba screamed he walked her around the room, made silly faces, or took her outside for a stroll. Araba would stop crying for a few minutes, sometimes even ten or twenty minutes, but most nights she cried on and off until the clock struck 6 AM. When she finally slept, Nicole slept. Their days ran into nights that ran into weeks.

After six weeks, Dr. Bettencourt announced that he needed to return home. He said Nicole was recovering well, and little Araba, despite her low birth weight ate well, pooped even better and had the lungs of a trumpet player. Traditionally, the naming ceremony in West Africa can take place anywhere from eight days up to a year after the baby's birth, depending on the ethnic group or tribe. Nicole didn't wish to have the ceremony without Souleymane. Grandma Julia suggested they have two ceremonies, one before

Dr. Bettencourt and Femi returned to the states, and one when Nicole reunited with Souleymane. Nicole agreed.

The Bettencourt household began preparations for the naming ceremony of their new addition. Esther called, during the planning stages and said that although school started in a few days she wouldn't miss the ceremony. The household staff pulled down all the blinds, curtains and other window coverings to clean. They opened the windows to allow the cool breezes to refresh the house.

What started out as an intimate naming ceremony, soon blossomed into a family reunion. Many of the Bettencourts returned home to meet Femi and the new baby. Some mistakenly thought the baby was a blood Bettencourt. When Grandma Julia sent out the invitation, she worded it, "Please join us for a new addition to the Bettencourt family. The naming ceremony will take place at the end of next month."

Aunt Adaisa and her husband, and all of Femi's other uncles and aunts arrived with their children, and grandchildren. All came pouring into the Bettencourt household to welcome little Araba into the world. Aunt Adaisa, the only childless Bettencourt, fought Femi for Araba's attention. Aunts and uncles, first cousins, second cousins, all flew in from France, the United States, Germany, South Africa, Mali, Spain, and other places. Over two hundred Bettencourts arrived.

When the sun rose, the ceremony began. Grandma Julia knocked on Nicole's door, and entered the room with the women. Nicole, still asleep, lay in the bed with Araba tucked in her arms. The gold and white linens on the bed draped around them cocooning them from the morning cold. Little by little, Nicole opened her eyes and looked up into Grandma Kaitlan's eyes.

"She looks just like you, those black eyes with gold specks."

Nicole opened her mouth, but no words came out. She wrapped her arms around her grandmother's neck. Over her shoulder she saw her mother and her sisters.

"When...? She tried to form sentences, but only tears came. One by one, her mother, then Barron, then Shannon hugged her and kissed Araba. Nicole looked around her. Then she saw Ari and Aaron and lost it. Tears flowed.

"You did good girl," the twins said at the same time.

"May I hold her?" Ari asked.

She was so happy to have her biological family and her adopted family all together. If only Dubose, Vera and of course Souleymane were there it would be perfect.

While all the hustle and bustle took place around her, Nicole said a silent prayer. "Dear Lord, I am grateful for all you have given to me. I am joyful now, with my family here, with the love that surrounds me, for Araba. My heart overflows with love for her. I never knew I could feel this type of love for anyone."

The naming ceremony took place on the veranda under twinkling stars. For the ceremony they wore gold and black lappas with headdresses. The women entered the parlor dancing to the drums. They moved their hips to the rhythm, dancing the tradition dance of harmony and well-being for baby Araba. The men followed. They marched in two by two, wearing their free-flowing boubous. Ari and Aaron led the way, Dr. Bettencourt and Femi followed, Andrew was paired with one of Femi's uncles. Nicole walked in with Araba swaddled in her receiving blanket. The elders, Grandma Julia, and Grandma Kaitlan took the center of the room.

"Who names this child born from love?" they said together.

Everyone answered, "We do."

"Who will stand for this child in this world to protect her, care for her, rear her?"

Everyone answered, "We do."

Nicole handed Araba to Dr. Bettencourt. Femi opened the door to the patio. Dr. Bettencourt walked outside. Everyone followed him. He lifted Araba up to the sky. The moon shone full and the stars competed with it with their brilliance. As Dr. Bettencourt stood with Araba raised in the sky, with all heads bowed and eyes closed, he began to pray.

"Gracious father we give this child to you today. We know she came into this world for a purpose, and we are blessed to be able to play a part in her life. Will the mother and father step forward?"

Up until that moment, the ceremony was going well, Nicole thought. She couldn't understand why he didn't just say would the mother step forward. She could hear his voice again calling for the parents to step forward. Ellafare stood beside Nicole and nudged her forward.

She tried to move her feet, but they wouldn't take the command. He meant to say mother, she thought. That is what he was used to saying, parents; but the occasion no longer seemed appropriate. She turned to go back in the house when she saw Souleymane step from behind her twin brothers. Dr. Bettencourt handed Araba to Femi who handed her to Souleymane who lifted Araba up to the sky. Nicole froze. Months had passed since she had seen Souleymane. He now sported a beard and his hair was no longer cut short to the scalp. He had a small Afro. She smiled, then laughed, and then began to cry, but still did not move.

In the moment that passed while she stood there like a statue, she thought right now, with her husband, Souleymane, her daughter Araba, Grandma Kaitlan, her mother Ellafare, sisters, her brothers, Femi and all the Bettencourts, Nicole's heart soared above the moon and the stars. She knew this moment is what she had waited for all of her life, to feel this cocoon of love and belonging. She walked to Souleymane who wrapped his arms around her and Araba. Everyone formed a circle around the three of them while he held their Araba up to the sky for the blessing.

Mr. President, 1986

ARABA SAT UNDER her daddy's desk playing jacks. Nicole straightened Souleymane's tie. She looked into her husband's eyes and held his gaze. After years of fighting, the rebels finally agreed to allow the people their say. Elections were held. Souleymane became the first democratically elected President of Liberia. Anyone eighteen and above who wanted to vote simply needed to register with a government issued identification. It took over six months to reach the people in the interior. Few had any identification. Some didn't even know their birthdates, but with the help of the United Nations Peace Keeping Commission and the International Free Election Council, they were able to register Liberians in the interior.

The opposing party nominated Griffen Mobabo, one of the original rebels from the Liberian Freedom Fighters, to run against Souleymane. No one could link him directly to any of the atrocities of the war, so he was put on the ballot. Souleymane won by a landslide. The country people voted for him because he came from the village and was an indigenous man. The exit surveys reported the main reason people voted for him was due to his accomplishments as the interim president. In his interim administration he completed the Clean Water Initiative, which brought clean water to the villages. He created jobs for the villagers by hiring them to help dig the wells, instead of using outside contractors. He hired consultants and scientists who captured the enormous amount of rainwater, which through reverse osmosis was made into clean drinking water.

He also courted private organizations and people to make loans to the indigenous people to start businesses. Reliable and longtime friends of Africa, Harry Belafonte and Muhammad Ali, donated money. A group of anonymous

African-American businessmen sent generators to bring electricity to the villages. Also windmill and solar panel energies were being explored. Education became his number one priority, and not only for boys. Government campaigns encouraged girls to go to school, and explained to their parents the benefit to the entire family.

"Well, Mr. President let's go get sworn in," Nicole said proudly.

Souleymane smiled at his First Lady, slipped his hand into hers and his other hand into Araba's and walked to his destiny.

An outdoor stage was erected for the event. Journalists and camera crews from all over the world came to witness the culmination of a successful election in an African country, where coups and takeovers had become the norm. Dubose was one of the first there for security reasons, but also because this day was one he told Nicole he had waited for over twenty years, a free Liberia, where the peoples' votes counted. In the hallway of the Presidential Palace, Nicole spotted Dubose. She walked over to him and hugged him. Tears welled in his eyes, but didn't spill down. She looked at him as he fought not to show his emotions; but a man who could stop his tears from flowing scared her.

"What a day. Do you believe it?"

"I do, Nicole. I believe it. I worked for it, prayed for it, hoped for it. I held this dream of real elections in Africa."

"EXO, thank you for everything. For being a father to both Souleymane and me. The father neither of us had. For standing in the gap for us. I don't know how we will ever repay you."

I Will Find You, 1989

NICOLE AND SOULEYMANE opened their eyes at the same time.

"Is it happening Souley?"

He put his finger to her lips to quiet her.

"I am going to get Araba," Souleymane whispered.

Nicole slipped quietly out of bed behind him. He signaled for her to get dressed and get her evacuation bag. She dressed quickly in what looked like a schoolgirl's uniform, plaid skirt, white shirt and blue sweater. Because her blonde and amber twists would stick out, she wrapped her hair in a white scarf. To cover her distinctive eyes, she slipped in dark brown contact lenses.

They had trained for this for months. Nicole did not understand. This election was supposed to stop another coup. Hadn't the people spoken with their votes? EXO Dubose made them train for a coup attempt. "Trust no one, not even me. If you think something is not right, then it is not," he told them. What an odd thing to say about not trusting him, Nicole had thought.

Souleymane returned from the adjacent room with Araba in his arms. She woke and smiled at Nicole.

"Mommy, why are you dressed like a school girl, from the academy?"

"Go back to sleep sweetie. Remember, I told you sometimes Mommy still plays dress up like she is a teenager, like you will be one day, it's just a game."

Souleymane opened the door to find his main intelligence officer Geoff George and his personal guard Ian Pola standing outside.

"The word is they have infiltrated the Presidential Palace. I think we might have less than fifteen minutes. We opened the underground tunnels for your evacuation," Ian said.

"I'm not going. My wife, and daughter will go."

"Sir, your brother David is on his way."

"Souleymane, I'm not going without you," Nicole said as she dressed Araba in a matching schoolgirl uniform. Souleymane placed his hands-on Nicole's shoulders and looked into her eyes.

"We knew this day may come. You will follow the drill."

He kissed her and, pulled her close to him.

"Take them now," he said as he released her.

One of the soldiers picked up Araba from the bed and Nicole grabbed Araba's little teddy bear, shoved it into her backpack and slipped it on her shoulders. She looked back at Souleymane as she walked out the door.

"I will find you and Araba."

They hurried down the stairs into the underground tunnels below the palace. Several soldiers loyal to Souleymane surrounded them. Araba slept, as the soldier carried her through the water-filled tunnels. Nicole kept her eyes on the soldier carrying Araba. When they reached the end of the tunnel an American truck sat waiting for them. Nicole looked over her shoulder. Out of the corner of her eye, she saw David standing at the end of the tunnel.

"What are you doing here? They told Souleymane you were on the way to help him."

"Change in plans. I need to get you and Araba over the border to the Bettencourts."

"I don't want to bring any trouble to them," Nicole said.

"They know you are coming. It will be okay."

A soldier Nicole knew as Tede was driving the truck. David sat in front with him. Nicole sat in the back with Araba in her lap and soldiers on either side. They all carried weapons. They drove for hours. Finally, they stopped and changed trucks to a little four-door Peugeot with Acme Construction Company written on the side. The two soldiers drove away in the truck leaving Nicole and Araba with David, and the driver.

About two hours out from the Sierra Leone border a dark blue jeep started following them. Before the driver could react another truck skidded in front of them. The driver turned off the main paved road onto a graveled side path. The truck bumped over rocks and uneven pavement. Araba looked up at Nicole, who held her tight and whispered into her ear to remember their game they played where Araba was to say nothing at all and stay perfectly still until Nicole gave her the signal. They reached a boulder in the road and David directed everyone out of the truck.

Another truck sat waiting for them. David opened the door and motioned for Nicole to get in the waiting truck, the driver's side. She shook her head and looked up at him.

"Nicole get in. You have to get out of here. You know how to drive that truck. They will be looking for all of us. No one will think that you would be on the road by yourself. After all you are the President's wife."

Nicole got in, belted Araba in and started the engine.

"Stay crouched down, baby so no one can see you," she told Araba.

She heard gunfire behind them. After she was sure she was out of David's sight she pulled over to the side of the road, and turned to Araba.

"Araba, you know how you like to run. How you always race your daddy. We are going to run and not stop. I want you to hold my hand and not let go. Do you understand?"

Araba nodded. Nicole got out of the truck and unfastened Araba's seat belt. They then ran off the main road through the bush. Sweat poured off of them like rain, but they kept running. They ran until they came to a cabin Nicole had never been in, but she knew who lived there.

"Why are we stopping Mommy?"

"I need you to be a brave girl. See that cabin over there, down the hill. My friend lives there. She doesn't know I'm coming. I'll be back in a few minutes. Count to a hundred, I'll come back for you in a few minutes. Stay down."

Nicole crawled on her belly closer to the cottage. She could see Rebecca inside. She stood in front of a small hotplate stirring something. Nicole pulled the pistol Dubose had given her from her back waistband. She approached the door from the side and tapped lightly. There was no answer. She tapped again. Rebecca flung open the door. The two women faced each other with guns drawn. Neither said anything. Rebecca cocked the gun.

"Duck Nicole. Now!"

When Nicole hit the ground, Rebecca pulled the trigger. When she looked up Rebecca was bleeding. She collapsed next to Nicole on the floor. Nicole looked behind her. Outside the cabin was Tede, the driver. He was lying dead on the ground in a pool of blood, a gun still in his hand. Nicole knelt over Rebecca.

"You were trying to kill him, not me."

Rebecca blinked her eyes. Blood gushed from her neck.

"Hold on Rebecca."

Nicole found a scarf and pulled it tight around Rebecca's neck to slow the bleeding. She dragged her to the wall and sat her up.

"I'll send help for you. My daughter is out there. I need to get her."

Rebecca smiled.

"I told them I wouldn't harm you or your family."

Nicole looked into Rebecca's eyes, her friend who she started her journey with, and thought of their dreams. Their African dreams, to serve, to bless, to make a difference.

"Thank you, Rebecca."

"Nicole."

"Shh. Save your strength."

"No. Please. Look in there." Rebecca pointed to a chest.

Nicole knew she needed to get back to Araba, but Rebecca's breathing was faint. She went to the chest and opened it. On top sat the blue material that was stolen from her at the market in Sierra Leone when she first met Femi. There was a letter on top.

"That day when you went to go meet Jennifer at the market, those men mugged you trying to find the tape but all they found was your blue material. The people I work for had you followed. I knew one day I would give it back to you and explain all of this."

Nicole hugged the fabric to her chest. She knelt beside Rebecca as she took her last breath. She died with a smile on her face. After grabbing a canteen of water, Nicole stuffed the blue cloth along with the letter in her backpack. She ran back up the hill, forgetting that Rebecca's blood was on her face and clothes.

"Mommy, you have red spots all over you."

Nicole looked down at her clothes, put the canteen of water to Araba's mouth and made her drink. She took some military packed sardines and crackers out of her backpack.

"Eat. We need to get back on the road."

Nicole looked at Araba. She came to Africa to help children. Now she needed to help her own child. They walked through the bush staying off the main road. The sunset found them near the village where Andrew lived. She decided not to risk going to his house in case he was being watched. She was close to Chief Esi's village, she could get help to make it to the academy from there.

They stopped at the stream, so Nicole could wash the blood off her face and hands. She cupped water in her hands to pat Araba's curly hair down. But the water only made it spring up more. She took the blue material Rebecca had given her, wrapped it around her waist and tied it. They would be looking for two people disguised as students. She placed the other piece of material on her head and made a head wrap.

She then changed Araba into a pair of shorts and a T-shirt. Looking at Araba, she pulled out a pair of scissors.

"Honey. I need to cut your hair."

Araba looked at the scissors, then she took off in a run. Nicole stood for a moment frozen, then she took off after her. She chased her through the high grasses until she reached a clearing. In the distance she could see a man holding Araba's arm. He had his back to Nicole. Fearing the worst Nicole ran as fast as she could. As she ran, she prayed for God to protect her daughter. As she got closer he looked familiar.

"David, let her go!"

The man let her go and Araba ran to her mother. He turned around and Nicole looked at him. It wasn't David at all.

"When you were born, after the midwife, I was the first one to hold you. Even before your mother," Femi said to Araba.

She hadn't seen him in years. He was no longer a teenager. He looked more like David than ever. He stood in the clearing, very straight and tall, like the silk wood trees surrounding the clearing.

"Nicole, your clothes, what happened"

Araba slipped down out of Nicole's arms, and ran back to Femi.

"Momma, he knew my name. He said I looked just like you."

"The eyes," Femi said.

Nicole walked to him and touched his cheek. She forgot about the rebels chasing her. She took a deep breath to steady herself. It was so good to see Femi.

"I didn't know you were even in Africa. What are you doing across the border in Liberia? David said we were going to meet your father and he would help us get out of the country."

Femi knelt down and put a rock in Araba's hand. She played with it, rolling it back and forth from hand to hand. He looked up at Nicole lifting his right eyebrow, and held her gaze.

"You don't even know what I am talking about do you?" Nicole said.

He stood up and took both of her hands into his.

"My dad lands later tonight. He traveled to France for an AIDS conference. The others are on their way. Aunt Adaisa, you remember her, she's taking care of Grandma Julia? She's really sick. I was on my way back from Chief Esi's village where I bought some traditional medicine for her and I heard gunshots."

"Grandma Julia is sick. Oh Femi, I'm so sorry. No, I hadn't heard. I would've come."

"We hope the medicine will help her. Are you okay? Is that blood on your clothes?"

"It's a volunteer's. I have so much to tell you. Do you know what happened in Monrovia?"

Femi looked down at Araba and then at Nicole. "Another coup?"

Nicole nodded. Femi pulled Nicole into his arms and kissed the top of her head.

"Nikki. I'm so sorry. Is Souleymane all right? Let's get to the house. You'll be safe there."

They walked through the bush where Femi's truck was parked and made their way over the border to the Bettencourt house. At the border crossing, the guards saw Bettencourt Academy on the side of the truck and waved them through. A few minutes later, they were at the academy. They entered through the back gate into the courtyard. They passed through the kitchen without notice, and took the back stairs up to Grandma Julia's suite.

Grandma Julia lay in bed propped up with several pillows. She smiled when she saw Nicole and Araba.

"Come," she said.

Araba wrapped her arms around Nicole's leg, when they stood at her bedside.

Nicole kissed Grandma Julia cheek to cheek.

"I wished to see you and you came."

Nicole nodded.

"Let me see our big girl now."

Nicole turned to Araba. "Come, you remember your Grandma Julia? She sends you all the teddy bears you love so much."

Araba put two fingers in her mouth and smiled. "Thank you. My favorite teddy is in my momma's backpack. Can you let her see it Momma?"

"Not right now."

"Femi, will you take little Miss Araba to the parlor for something to eat while I talk to her mother," Grandma Julia said.

Femi left with Araba waving at Grandma Julia. Nicole sat on the edge of the bed, and held Julia's hand.

"I may be an old lady, on my way out, but I still hear things."

"You know about the coup?"

"I heard it on the radio. Adaisa tried to turn it off before I could hear. I told her to leave it on."

"When will they end?" Nicole asked. "I don't even know where Souley is." She felt close to tears.

"I don't know baby. I do know that despite the coups, Africa will survive. Our dream of an Africa with a stable government, clean water, health care and education will not be seen by me, I know that, but Araba will experience such a day."

"I have to go Grandma Julia. They know I was heading here with Araba."

"Then they must not find you. Adaisa will help you. She is a Bettencourt, and you are family."

Grandma Julia called in a favor or two to obtain fake passports for Nicole and Araba. They planned for Araba to travel with Adaisa and her husband back to Mali, and Nicole would travel on her own and pick her up in Mali. The rebels would be looking for a mother and daughter, not a single woman, or a couple with a child.

"I don't know if I can leave her. I was going to cut her hair and put a cap on it to make her look like a boy, to take her with me."

"Still cut her hair. In Mali, go straight to the American Embassy, and have them contact Senator Giles in Washington D.C. He will help you."

Nicole took Araba into the bathroom and locked the door. She sat Araba on the closed toilet seat, and knelt down in front of her.

"Araba, I need you to go with Aunt Adaisa and her husband for a little while. You'll get to fly. All of you are going on a plane like you did when we went to visit Grandma Ellafare in America. When you land I'll meet you. Do you understand?"

"Why can't you go with us?"

"I'm going to come later. I will bring a surprise for you, won't that be nice." It broke her heart to send Araba away. But it was for their safety.

"A surprise, yippee. A puppy maybe?"

"Well, I do not know about a puppy, but it will be a good surprise sweetie. But I need to cut your hair first so you can hide it under your hat. For right now we don't want anyone to know that you are a little girl."

"Why Mommy, you said girls rock."

"I know honey, but this is just a game. Close your eyes."

Nicole snipped Araba's curls and a piece of her heart seemed to scatter with the locks to the floor. Nicole cut two pieces from the bottom of the blue lappa material she wore and wrapped a few of the locks in the material. She placed one in her backpack. She took the hair and her wedding ring from Souleymane and wrapped them in the other cloth. Her heart was breaking but she had to protect Araba. There was no sacrifice she wouldn't make for her daughter.

Nicole pulled out Araba's little teddy bear, unzipped the back, and placed the fabric with the ring and the locks of hair inside the bear. She then handed the bear to Araba.

"Don't let anyone take teddy from you. Scream as loud as you can if they try."

When Araba nodded Nicole hugged her then stood up. She unlocked the door, took her daughter by the hand and walked back into the bedroom. Femi and Adaisa were standing at Grandma Bettencourt's bed. She handed Araba to Adaisa, and walked out the room with Femi. Halfway down the steps she ran back up and hugged Araba again. She looked into her daughter's face, now half way covered with her cap. She kissed her left cheek first, then her right cheek, then her forehead. She hugged her one last time, then let her go.

Too Much to Hope For, 1991

NICOLE CUT THROUGH the back alley to reach the green line of the LA Metro system. She ducked under the stairwell to get a look at the man who had been following her all day. Few people took the Metro Rail system in LA after 7 PM. Those who did knew each other's faces and some knew each other's names. Almost no one was on the rail today because of the rain. Nicole always kept to herself. It was almost two years since she'd fled Liberia and she was still in hiding. She smelled his scent before she saw him-the familiar scent of ginger and lemons-the smell of Africa. Nicole turned around and stood face to face with him. She looked up into his eyes.

"You." She said leaning against the railing. The rain had slacked up, but water had soaked her clothes, making them cling to her body. She thought about running, but even with more than twenty years on her, he could still out run her any day.

He looked the same, like a Fula man. The high cheekbones, the copper-colored skin, but now gray peppered his hair. She remembered his words when he stepped on the plane all those years ago, "I will protect you."

He had protected her for years. Through two coup attempts and he helped her flee Liberia. But the whole time he worked with the rogue CIA, and the rebels. He helped to orchestrate the coups. She wondered back then who could smuggle guns into the country when the US military helped to secure the borders. Of course now she knew, someone in the US military. Dubose was the highest ranked military person in Liberia. He had placed clues right in front of her, but she still refused to believe the man she considered her father, who had been the best man at her wedding, had deceived her. Much worse he betrayed Souleymane, and the continent he claimed to love.

During the Senate hearings in the US, on the coup attempts, several people testified against him, implicating him as the ring leader who led the coup on the American's side. He was never charged with any crime because Ms. Blue Shoes refused to collaborate their stories.

Nicole now saw blood on this temple.

"I never meant to hurt you. If anything, I tried to protect you. I think of you as my daughter," Dubose said.

"What happened to your head?" Nicole asked. "Not that I should really care."

A lifetime had passed since her days in Liberia. Just when she'd finally accepted her husband's death, Dubose showed up to rip open barely healed wounds. The last time she saw her husband was at the Presidential Palace when she and Araba fled. The last time she'd seen Araba was when she handed her baby to Aunt Adaisa. She didn't even need to close her eyes to remember. Her face was permanently etched in her mind. She vowed she would dedicate her life to finding her daughter.

Femi took Nicole to a money bus driver who took her to the train station. Once at the train station, she took the three-day trip to Upper Volta, and then another train to Mali. When she reached the safe house in the Dogon Village in Mali she heard wailing. The household members greeted her in white, and the women with shaved heads. They handed her a secure walkie-talkie and Dubose told her the rebels had reached the palace in Liberia. Souleymane was killed and his headless body displayed on the steps of the Presidential Palace.

Many said it wasn't him, but droves came to mourn him. Some said they knew he still was alive, but now after two years, Nicole no longer held on to that dream. She still looked for her daughter. Adaisa said, at the airport, a man recognized Araba and detained Adaisa's husband and Araba. No one has heard from either of them, since that day at the airport. She could still be alive. No bodies were ever found. Her family had been destroyed by the man standing in front of her. The family she yearned for as a little girl.

The rain started again, just as quickly as it had stopped. Dubose pulled out a handkerchief to wipe her face. She thought about the one he'd given her on the first day she arrived. After all these years she still kept it wrapped around the tape recorder, now in a safe deposit box.

When she didn't take the handkerchief, he stepped back to get a better look at her. "You look the same. I see you have straightened your hair and dyed it brown. And you're wearing contacts to hide your distinctive eyes. But your essence is still there. You and Souleymane were the hope for Africa. I would never have hurt you."

"What do you want? Why are you following me? I changed my name, changed my appearance. I tried to forget what happened in Africa. What I will never forget is my daughter and husband. I will continue to look for my daughter. Words can't express the pain you caused in my life."

"If I found you, others can as well. I'm not the only one following you. This blood on my face is from a man who broke into your house to find the tape. You can't go back there. He's dead, on your living room floor. You're a loose end. I need that tape. I suspect you have the original one. The one you sent to Senator Giles was a copy. It was edited. The original tape implicates me, and many others. It still puzzles me how you were able to even get the tape out of the country."

Dubose pressed the handkerchief to his head to stop the bleeding. "I need you to lead me to Souleymane. If we have you, he'll come out of hiding. He is still the legal President. The people elected him. That crook in office put himself in charge. The only way this war will end is if Souleymane comes out of hiding and sits down at the table with the rebels. I don't want to hurt him. I want to help put him back in power, and for this civil war to end."

Nicole could hardly breathe. What was he saying? Souleymane was in hiding. She felt faint. She breathed deeply trying to calm herself. She breathed from her diaphragm, and counted. Ten seconds in, twenty seconds out. Moving from the rail she stood up, straightening her shoulders and pulling her stomach in.

"He believed in you." Nicole said.

Dubose held the handkerchief to his temple but the blood soaked through. "We don't have much time."

"The last time I heard those words from you, we were under attack from the rebels. You forgot to tell me they were under your command."

"Nicole, listen to me. I know it will be hard to believe anything I say. It looks like I'm guilty, but the only thing I am guilty of is loving Africa. Things got out of control. I orchestrated strings to get Tanner out of power. The rebels took matters in their own hands. A coup attempt on Souleymane was not supposed to happen. He won that election fairly. If you and others want to indict me for something, let it be for my dreams of an Africa where they hold true democratic elections; and the diamonds, gold, rubber and other natural resources benefit Africans, not just America, Britain, or all the other countries that suck the life out of Africa."

"I don't want to hear your speeches. I'm not that starry-eyed girl any more. You can't fool me."

"I'm trying to make things right in Africa. To nullify the deals made hundreds of years of ago that siphoned the natural resources out of the country; the one-dollar deals made by American rubber companies for the rubber, or the diamonds purchased for pennies but sold for thousands, will be null and void and new deals will be made to benefit all. Don't you see it makes no sense that Africans are starving when they hold the key to our survival on this planet."

"You're a child killer. You recruited children. You stole little boys from their families and gave them guns. Gave them liquor, poured hatred into their hearts. This was your solution?"

"I never thought those guns would end up in their hands. Never! I made the mistake of dealing with people who cared more about money than lives."

She lunged forward pushing her full body weight on Dubose. They fell on the ground, she landed on top of him. She thrust her knee into his groin, but he pushed back with his knee. He easily flipped her over on her back and straddled her, holding her hands over her head. She lay motionless with her eyes closed.

"Nicole," he said loosening his grip to check her breathing. She saw her chance, and kneed him again. This time he wasn't fast enough and he rolled off her in pain. She scrambled and ran out of the alley. She ran through the wet streets. Her lungs felt like they might burst. She finally reached the entrance to the metro. She ran passed the cashier and jumped over the turnstile. The cashier slammed the door and blew his whistle. Before she could move another foot, the subway police handcuffed her.

At the transit police station, they asked for her ID. She explained that she lost it when a man attacked her. One cop with a short blonde buzz cut looked like he wanted to stomp her. She had interrupted them from watching Monday Night Football.

"Okay sister, you jumped over the turnstile because a man attacked you and you were running away from him."

"Exactly. You asked the same question two hours ago. My answer is the same."

"Okay sister, where's the man?" The cop, with the buzz cut, asked.

The other two cops let him do all the talking. They sat on the other side watching TV.

"Sister. Tell me one more time. I'm a little slow.

"Sir, no disrespect. But please stop calling me sister. I'm not related to you."

"Oh, so now you want to tell me what to do."

"No, I want to watch the football game. Just like you. Let me watch the game and I'll tell you everything. Of course there isn't any man. No one chased me. I just didn't feel like paying. Who knew you guys would act so quickly or be so smart."

Buzz Cut put his hands on his utility belt and turned to the other cops. "Do you guys hear what Ms. Thing here is saying?"

"Man, stop with the ethnic bull," one of the other cops said. First you call her sister, now Ms. Thing. That's racist." He looked at Nicole.

"Well if she would tell us her name I'd know what to call her."

"You look familiar." The second cop said still looking at her.

"Maybe she's a movie star. Maybe you saw her on TV, Ian. Maybe she's from Africa like you, and hangs out in the jungle eating bananas."

"Shut up Dempsey. You're getting out of hand." The third cop said. "Why don't you take your behind outside and cool off. You know, as well as I do, that this five feet two woman can only cause so much trouble. Unless you're looking for a lot of paperwork, I'd apologize for your racist comments, and hope she doesn't press charges. Take a walk. In fact, I'll go with you. The game's playing in the bar across the street. I think Ian has this under control."

Dempsey picked up his keys mumbling something that sounded like "apologies my ass", then he walked out of the room.

"Madame First lady," Officer Ian Pola said.

"You know who I am?"

"Of course. You don't remember me? I served in the Liberian military guarding your husband when he became President. I came here after the coup. Since I already had military training I attended police academy here and got hired on as a transit cop."

"I'm sorry, so much has happened. I remember you, Ian."

"Madam, we all thought you were dead."

"Long story. I need to get out of here. Part of what I said is true. I jumped over the turnstile to get away from a man who helped plan the coups in Liberia. He said something strange about needing to find Souleymane. It didn't make sense. Souleymane is dead."

"Many believe he is not dead ma'am."

"But if he's alive he would've found a way to contact me.

"Some say he still leads the troops behind the scenes. That he will not surface until the rebels, as well as the foreigners helping them are caught. Maybe he believes you are dead, as well."

"But they displayed his dead body in front of the Presidential Palace."

"They displayed the body of a headless man. It could have been anyone.

Souleymane might still be alive, she thought. It was almost too much to hope for, but it meant that Araba could also still be alive.

"I need your help Officer Pola."

The Africa of Their Dreams

Nicole arrived at Atlanta International Airport around midnight. She traveled under her assumed name of Julia King. The last time she saw Femi was when he put her on the bus to Mali.

Now he was a published research doctor, a graduate from Harvard Medical School, who had joined his father at the CDC in Atlanta, sourcing and tracking diseases from all over the world. She followed his career through the medical journals and newspaper articles. He was the lead expert on the HIV disease and was working with pharmaceutical companies to develop an inexpensive cocktail drug to prolong the lives of people living with the disease.

She walked through the terminal to baggage claim. Would he recognize her? Thinner now, she barely weighed a hundred pounds, and her red and amber twists had been straightened into long dyed brown strands, which reached down the middle of her back. She wore brown contacts to hide her sunburst eyes.

Femi stood by the baggage carousel. In his late twenties, he still had boyish good looks. He wore his hair in dreadlocks and he had a dark mustache and goatee. He ran to her and picked her up off the ground and swung her around.

"Hello, Nicole Jefferson," he whispered in her ear.

"You recognized me."

"I'll always recognize you. When you're 102, without any teeth, and your Tina Turner wig on. I'll still recognize you," he said laughing.

"Do you have the tickets?" she asked nervously. Her hands were shaking. Breathe, she commanded herself. Breathe.

"I do. We'll fly into Accra, Ghana, and travel the rest of the way by land."

Suddenly, she felt the cool metal of a gun shoved against her back. His smell always gave him away, the ginger sunshine man. Femi outweighed him by thirty pounds of solid muscle, but Dubose had a gun. Dubose indicated that they follow him out of the airport, into a waiting car where David sat.

"Hi bro," David said.

Dubose motioned Nicole to the back seat.

"We need your help. We know Souleymane is still alive and commanding the troops from Sierra Leone. We need you to contact him," Dubose said.

Nicole shut her eyes and tried to take in what Dubose was saying.

"Even if he's alive, which I don't believe. He would've contacted me. Anyway, why should I help you?"

Dubose pulled a picture from the inside of his jacket; it was a girl about eight years old with dark black eyes with golden flecks. Nicole snatched the picture from his hands and studied it. She held it to her chest.

"We will give you Araba for Souleymane."

Femi looked at Nicole through the rearview mirror and raised an eyebrow. He quickly jumped into the back seat on top of Dubose. The gun fell to the floor. Dubose kicked the gun with his foot toward him and pinned Femi on top of Nicole. He cocked the gun. David hit the EXO on his head with the butt of his pistol. Dubose fell back on to the seat and dropped his gun on the floor. Nicole scrambled for the gun, grabbed it and flung open the car door. She and Femi scrambled out and ran into the terminal. David jumped out the driver's side and ran after them. Inside the airport, Nicole pulled the gun out from under her coat. She wrapped it in her scarf and threw it in the trash can before they entered security. David grabbed her arm and she pulled away and joined Femi in the security line.

"Wait, take this," he said, handing Femi an envelope.

"What is it? Why are you giving it to us?" Nicole asked.

"Inside are documents you'll need. Passports, money and names of people who will help you. Friends of Souleymane."

"Is Araba really alive?"

David nodded yes.

"What about Souley?"

He shrugged. "No one knows. I don't think so."

"Why are you helping us?" Femi asked David.

"Because we are family, and I am sick of the violence," David answered. Then he turned and walked out of the airport.

"Femi, you asked David why he helped us. Now I ask you, why do you continue to risk your life helping me?"

"Remember the giraffes from Bettencourt Academy. Remember how surprised you were to see giraffes in West Africa. You and I are like those giraffes. Just when people count us out, and say we will not make it, God's grace restores us. But this is bigger than us. We need to find Araba and to find out for sure if Souleymane is still alive. The continent needs leaders like Souleymane."

Femi and Nicole walked through the terminal and boarded the flight to Africa. The Africa of their ancestors, the cradle of civilization, the place of secrets, civil wars, long necked giraffes and gracious people. The Africa of their dreams.

About The Author

Mimi Washington raised in a small town outside of Pittsburgh, Pennsylvania excelled in writing in high school, and won a scholarship to attend Point Park College in Pittsburgh. She transferred to Temple University where she graduated with a degree in Journalism. After college, she served as a Peace Corps Volunteer and Peace Corps staff member for three years in Liberia after a coup.

After Peace Corps, she lived and worked in Northern California where she raised her daughter Kiah. She has traveled extensively through Europe, China, Israel, and Africa.

The resiliency of the people on the continent of Africa to keep going despite the civil wars, coups, drought, and depletion of their resources inspired her to write her first novel.

Mimi presently lives in Southern California, and is a member of the National Writers Association and the Academy of American Poets.

www.ingramcontent.com/pod-product-compliance
Lightning Source LLC
Chambersburg PA
CBHW071141170626
46809CB00002B/724